WAXING THE MOON OF LEWEI

TALES OF A FORMER SPACE JANITOR

JULIA HUNI

IPH MEDIA

Cover designed by German Creative
Editing by Paula Lester at Polaris Editing

Julia Huni
Visit my website at juliahuni.com

First Printing: February 2022
IPH Media

CHAPTER ONE

MY FISTS THUD rhythmically against the bedroom window, like an anemic drum circle. I'm not pounding very hard, so the lack of crashing glass and the resultant sucking vacuum of space isn't surprising. Plus, SK2 is a well-built station—punching the windows is only going to hurt the puncher's hands. It's a gentle act of rebellion rather than actual anger.

My door chimes, and I flick the unlock key. "What?"

Hy-Mi, my mother's ancient and ageless major domo, stands in the doorway. "Sera Annabelle, Dame Morgan requests you not pound on the windows."

I give Hy-Mi the stink eye. "Don't call me that. My name is Triana. And it's not a real window—wait a minute, how did she know I was doing it?" My eyes dart to the corners of the room. "Has she installed surveillance in my bedroom?" I make a mental note—increase the frequency of my scans.

A slight shake of Hy-Mi's head does not reassure me. "It was an educated guess. She's not at home right now." Hy-Mi speaks on my mother's behalf so often, I think it's his default setting. "But if she were..."

I heave a dramatic sigh, like a petulant teen. "Fine."

He bows. "May I inquire as to why you are pounding?"

"You know exactly why. Because the Ice Dame is demanding a huge wedding. Despite all our arguments against it. You backed me up, right?"

"I explained your position and offered a corporate reception, planned and funded by her. She declined."

I cross my arms and drop onto my bed. "She knows I'm an adult, right? I could run away and elope right now."

He pulls out the desk chair but waits for my nod to sit. Part of our evolving relationship. He's trying to remind me of my role as the officially recognized heir to the Morgan dynasty.

"Well?"

"Between you and me, she's got you in a bind. She knows you won't elope—Ser O'Neill's family would be devastated."

I play with the thick brocade draped across the bed, folding and creasing the heavy fabric. "Maybe I'll let *them* plan the wedding on Grissom. We can have it at their house, like Lili and Jie did. They can refuse to let Mother's CEO buddies in."

"You could do that—if you don't mind burning your bridges. She will not forgive you—at least not for many years. Look how long it took her to reconcile with your father."

"That wasn't a grudge—that was… I don't know what that was." About a year ago, my mother admitted my father wasn't a faceless number from a paternity catalog, as I'd always been allowed to believe. My birth was the result of a wild fling during an interstellar cruise. She'd cut contact with my father when the ship docked and had never told him about me. A few months after we met, R'ger Chaturvedi told me he'd known about me since I was a little girl but that he'd respected my mother's desire to raise me on her own.

Growing up, I'd always thought my life was normal. Ha!

"Incidentally, I'd be okay with a break."

"Ser O'Neill might not." Hy-Mi drums his fingers against the table. For him, this is an uncharacteristic display of disquiet.

"What's bothering you?" I ask.

He shakes his head. "Nothing you can repair." He squares his shoulders and nods, as if to remind himself why he's here. "What, specifically, has you upset today? The wedding issue is nothing new."

I pull up a file on my holo-ring and flick it at him. "This. I've been summoned to a meeting with her and Lilia, the 'Nuptial Architect,' tomorrow afternoon." I make air quotes around the title.

"You knew Dame Morgan had hired her to plan the wedding."

I heave another huge sigh. "Yeah, I knew. But I'd hoped—"

"How long have you been your mother's daughter?"

I force a chuckle. "I'm glad you're getting some entertainment from this mess."

"I'm not. I don't like to see you at loggerheads with your mother, but I also don't want you to be unhappy. I can make another attempt to reason with her. So should you." He holds up a hand as I open my mouth. "Be reasonable—see if you can find some financially compelling arguments."

"I doubt saving money by firing Lilia will convince her."

"You aren't thinking big enough. Your mother is all about marketing and business. What could you package for her to sell that would be more valuable than a wedding?" He pushes himself out of his chair, moving more slowly than usual.

Something is clearly weighing on him, but just as obviously, he has no intention of sharing it with me. I stand and walk him to the door. "I'll talk to her. I don't want to get between you and your boss."

His eyes light up, as if this is what he's been waiting to hear. "I will leave it to you. Let me know if you need my help."

Impulsively, I hug him. "Thanks, Hy-Mi. I love you."

His arms tighten around me, and his voice chokes up. "I love you, too, Sera."

THE NEXT MORNING, I follow the scent of cinnamon and chocolate to the breakfast room to find my mother waiting. She usually has tea and dry toast in her office in the mornings, so something is up. "Good morning, Mother."

"Annabelle, please have a seat." She sits at one end of a two-meter-long table. Her long blonde hair is loose today, flowing over her shoulders and down her back. Her ice-blue eyes glitter in a face that looks at least thirty years younger than it should. Anyone who didn't know us would think she was my younger sister.

I grab a plate of croissants from the sideboard and pour myself some coffee with lots of cream and sugar before sitting. "To what do I owe the honor of your company?" I lean heavily on the word honor.

The tiniest of smiles makes a passing acquaintance with her lips. "Nicely done. I see you've been practicing your social skills."

"I knew all those hours of watching brutish shows on *Ancient TēVē* would pay off."

"I believe it's British, not brutish, and yes, they're excellent training for polite society." She re-drapes her napkin across her lap and toys with a spoon. "Before our meeting with Lilia, we have another matter to discuss."

I sip my coffee, then add a generous dollop of chocolate syrup. "What matter might that be?"

She picks up her teacup, with one pinkie sticking out, just like the *Ancient TēVē* characters. "I'm sending you to Lewei."

"You're—what? Lewei is a dictatorship. A police state. Why would you send me there? Is this because I argued about Lilia?"

"Don't be ridiculous. This has nothing to do with the wedding. I have business interests in Lewei, and I need a representative to meet with someone."

"You can't do it virtually?"

"This is a new venture, and they want to meet with us in person. It's part of their culture—they won't do business without it." She sips her tea, then replaces the cup with the faintest of clinks. "This will be your first chance to represent the family and SK'Corp solo."

"I'm going by myself?" I put the chocolate croissant back on my plate—the flakey pastry suddenly tastes like dust. "Is that safe?"

"You'll have a security team, of course. I meant I won't be there to hold your hand."

I'm pretty sure the last time my mother held my hand was—actually, I can't remember her ever holding my hand. "You won't be with us virtually—like you did for the Families Meeting on S'Ride?" I had been physically present as the family representative, but she'd joined all the important discussions long-distance. My presence had been one hundred percent window dressing.

She eyes me for a minute, then gives her head a tiny shake. "I will not. They expect to meet with someone authorized to negotiate." She holds up a finger. "Not that you will be negotiating anything. We will do all of that remotely, once you've made the initial connections. You will be present for those sessions, of course—you'll be the face of Morgan Enterprises and SK'Corp, as far as the Leweians are concerned."

"If I do this, I want something in return." I grip my hands together in my lap, hidden beneath the starched white tablecloth. "I want my wedding to be private. You can have your corporate reception, but the real wedding—that's for family and friends, not your marketing machine."

"No."

"No? This is a negotiation. You can't just say no."

"This is not a negotiation. I don't need any concessions from you. You'll go to Lewei because it's your duty as the Morgan heir. And you'll do the wedding because it's good for the family." She leans forward, pinning me with her icy blue eyes. "You *are* Morgan now. *Everything* you do is for the family. That's what being the official heir means."

"Maybe I don't want to be the official heir." I shove back my chair and jump to my feet.

She raises an eyebrow at me. "I thought you and Tiberius agreed that was the best way forward for your relationship."

Frappe. She's got me. Ty and I did decide that—I would take up my role as Mother's heir and he would stay on Board Security. For some reason, he loves his job with SK'Corp. Maybe I can use this trip to Lewei to find a new job for him—something that will allow us to get away from my mother and her control issues.

"Fine. I'll go to Lewei. But no promises on the wedding." I toss my napkin on the table and turn away.

"We have a meeting with Lilia at two," Mother reminds me.

"You have a meeting with Lilia at two. I will be studying Leweian culture and business practices." I turn slowly and raise my nose. "If this wedding is going to be a marketing bonanza, you can plan it without me. Unless you think it's more important than the trip."

Mother smirks. "I knew you could be reasonable. I'll have Lilia send you a transcript of the relevant decisions after the meeting."

CHAPTER TWO

MY FIANCÉ, Tiberius O'Neill y Mendoza bin Tariq e Reynolds, shoves a hand through his thick, wavy hair. It stands on end for an instant, then falls back into place. Every time. Shiny as always. He slides an arm around me. "Don't let her get to you. My family doesn't care what she does with this wedding—as long as they're present for the big event."

"She already tried to put them on the overflow list." I lean my head against his shoulder and close my eyes. "I don't know why she cares so much. Most of these top-levs don't even know what a wedding is."

"There's your answer." He shakes me a little. "They're looking for a unique experience."

"I knew we should have done a ten-year contract like normal people."

He laughs and jostles me again. "Normal for you. And I don't want a ten-year contract. I want forever. Don't let it bother you. As long as the people we love are there, who cares where it is, or what they do with it? We can always have another party later—Mom and Dad would host something at the house."

"I don't want to think about it anymore." I open my eyes and sit up, looking around his office. It's on Level 82 of Station Kelly-Kornienko, right below the board members' penthouses on 83. It's beautifully appointed—as you'd expect for the deputy director of board security—real wood furniture, a comfortable couch, and a cozy eating space with AutoKich'n.

The large view screen on the wall behind his desk shows our favorite sandy beach scene with gently swaying trees. The immersive tech includes a hint of salty tang and the impression of sea-flung mist. "Where is that, anyway?" I point at the screen.

He glances at the floor-to-ceiling panorama. "I'm not sure. Might not be real at all."

I flick my holo-ring and run a visual search. The results pop up as we watch. "It's Casadia beach on Tereshkova." My shoulders slump. "Not much chance of visiting then."

He grins and points at me. "There's your silver lining. If we're going to Lewei, maybe we can get a side-excursion to Tereshkova."

"But Tereshkova belongs to Gagarin, not Lewei." I scroll through the hits on my search and pull up a tourist site. "This says you have to get a visa months in advance to visit."

He gets up from the couch and crosses to the desk. "This is one advantage of being the Morgan heir. We have ways to leap-frog over the bureaucracy. Leave it to me. We'll go for our honeymoon."

I follow him across the room and wrap my arms around his waist. "You're amazing." I lean in for a kiss.

Just before our lips touch, the door chimes.

"That'll be Vanti." He kisses me quickly, then releases me and flicks the door control.

"I'm surprised she didn't just appear in the room. What's a locked office door to Vanti?"

The door slides open, revealing Lindsay Fioravanti. As always, she's wearing form-fitting black, and her copper hair hangs in a sleek curtain to her shoulders. "I try to be polite when I can."

I laugh. "You've never bothered knocking on my door. You just come in through the window, or find a secret passageway, or rappel through the skylight."

A thoughtful look crosses her pale face. "I don't think I've ever rappelled from a skylight—not to see you. That would require a vacuum suit and portable airlock here on the station." She turns to O'Neill. "I've got the paperwork for the Lewei trip. You aren't on the list."

"What?" He snaps his fingers and holds out a hand.

Vanti flicks a file to him, and it pops open on his holo-ring.

"How can he not be on the list?" I demand. "He's my primary security asset."

"No, he's not." Vanti raises one eyebrow. "You fired him ages ago, remember? Because you never listened to him anyway, and you didn't want to ruin his career. I'm your personal chief security operative, and I've decided having him along would be a distraction."

O'Neill takes a step forward. "You can't take me off the list—I'm your boss!"

I stand next to him. "And I'm his boss, and I want him to come."

"No, Don Said is his boss. Griz doesn't work for Morgan Enterprises, he works for SK'Corp. And while those two entities might be indistinguishable in your mind, they're very different organizations in reality. Sure, Morgan owns part of SK'Corp, but not all of it. Don Said would have to release Griz to you—or he'd have to take vacation time, which he's saving for the wedding."

"Griz" is Vanti's private nickname for O'Neill. They still haven't told me the story behind the name, and Vanti loves to use it to drive me crazy. At least I think that's why she does it. Or maybe my reaction doesn't figure in at all. I never know with Vanti.

"I'll ask Don Said for a temporary reassignment." I flick my holo-ring to bring up my message app.

"No, you won't, because it won't do any good. I won't have him on my team." Vanti points at O'Neill. "He's not objective where you're concerned. If you want him to come along as a guest, or in some other capacity, then we can talk. But I'm in charge of security for this mission, and he's not welcome on my team."

I swing around to look at O'Neill. "Are you going to let her decide that?"

"She's right." He lifts both hands. "I'm one hundred percent subjective when it comes to you. I let you talk me into all kinds of stupid things."

"Are you saying I'm stupid?"

He reaches for me. "Of course not, but you can't deny we get into some pretty dangerous situations when I'm supposed to be protecting you. I wouldn't want me on your protection team, either."

I take a step back. "But Vanti takes me into dangerous situations all the time. How's that any better?"

He shoves his hand through his hair again. "Vanti usually knows what she's getting into. When you're in the lead…"

"What?" I put my hands on my hips and give him the evil eye. "Do go on."

His eyes flicker. "You're getting that Ice Dame stare down." He turns away, then swings back. "You're too impulsive. You wander into dangerous situations without any understanding of how bad they are and no backup plan. Then I follow you in and—"

"Save me? I've saved you on more than one occasion!"

"I wasn't going to say that." He steps closer and runs his hands up my arms. I try to ignore the frizzle of bliss that zings through me in response. "We get out of danger through a lot of improvisation. But I'm terrified for you the whole time. I don't like being that out of control."

I give up and lean in, letting his arms fold around me. "And you think it will be better if you stay here while I run off to a dictatorship with Vanti?"

He goes very still. After a long moment, he takes a deep breath. "Good point. I'll be stressed out the entire time. Vanti..." He looks at the agent. I'd almost forgotten she was here. "I need to come along. If SK'Corp is going to do business in Lewei, I need to evaluate the security of the situation for, uh, future visits and stuff."

Vanti's lips twitch at the lame ending. "I was wondering when you'd come up with a good reason. Fine. But you're attending as a deputy director, not an agent. An executive position. All security will be my responsibility. I'll assign a two-man team to you."

He releases me. "I don't need security."

Vanti's lips stretch into one of her rare smiles. "You do if I say so."

CHAPTER THREE

WHEN I RETURN to the penthouse level, I meet Lilia, the wedding planner, in the Level 83 lobby. She pauses in the doorway to my mother's compartment and looks me over, her eyes flicking from my neatly pinned hair to my understated tunic and skirt and down to my matching flats. "Sera Morgan, I almost didn't recognize you."

She annoys me, so I raise my eyebrows in a look borrowed from my mother. "And you are?"

She flicks her virtual ID to me, but I don't bother looking at it. "I'm Lilia. Your Nuptial Architect? We met a few weeks ago? Dame Morgan and I just finished planning the wedding."

A little spark of anger runs down my spine, but I squash it. "You don't say." I push past her into the foyer. "Don't let me keep you." The door swooshes shut behind me.

Hy-Mi stands in the entrance to the living room, his head shaking slightly side-to-side. "I never thought I'd see…"

"Me acting like the Ice Dame?" I roll my eyes and kick off my shoes. "Get used to it, I guess. It's my destiny." I pick up the flats. "It is kind of fun to use it on someone like Lilia, though. She's so superior." I lift my nose and drop my chin in what I think of as my "posh face" and imitate my mother's voice. "Really, Hy-Mi, some people are so much more worthy of our disdain."

"Well done." Mother steps out of her office and crosses the foyer. She flicks her blonde hair back, and her voluminous purple skirt swirls around her ankles as she walks. A dark pink sash drapes from one shoulder, the fine gold embroidery catching the light. "But save that for situations where it's useful. Upsetting the wedding planner can backfire."

My face heats, and I duck my head, so I don't have to meet her eyes.

"Speaking of the wedding, she'll send the details to your account. If you have any questions, take them up with her when you get back." She smiles faintly and turns away.

I take a step toward her, tucking my shoes behind my back, hoping she won't notice them and comment. "Wait. I thought the trip to Lewei wasn't until next week?"

"Correct. I assumed you were going to Kaku this week."

"Kaku? Why?"

She swirls around to face me again, her huge skirt undoubtedly creating eddies in the space-time continuum. "Isn't your friend due this week?"

How could I have forgotten? Kara's baby is supposed to arrive tomorrow! "I didn't realize you were keeping up on that." Or that she'd change my schedule to allow me to be there.

"I keep up on everything." Her eyes flick to Hy-Mi, then back to me. "I'll expect you back on Friday. We'll spend the weekend reviewing the details of the Leweian meeting, and you'll leave on Monday." She starts to turn away again, then pauses. "Good idea taking Ser O'Neill along for a security consultation."

Before I can respond, she's gone. I turn to Hy-Mi. "What was that about? Was she being sarcastic?"

"Believe it or not, I think she was impressed. Having the deputy director review the local security situation is an excellent plan. We'll need a full evaluation to develop policies and procedures."

I flush. My instinctive pleasure at the idea I'd impressed my mother disappears. "I didn't think of it—Ty did."

Hy-Mi nods, as if he understands. "Surrounding yourself with smart people is an excellent strategy for success. And as the boss, you get the credit."

I TAKE the regular shuttle to Kaku under my Triana Moore identity. I shoot a message to Vanti after the ship has launched, so she can't follow me—at least not right away. She may think I need security, but I don't. I lived on Kaku for four years without a protection detail, so I know how to stay safe.

We land at Pacifica City, and I take the HyperLoop to Paradise Alley. Kara, her partner, and her mother are staying at the Morgan estate while she waits for the baby. Medical care in Pacifica City is good, but it's excellent in the wealthy enclave of Ebony Beach.

I find the Rent-a-Bubble stand and, ignoring the cheerful employee in a bright yellow tunic, connect my holo-ring to the auto-kiosk. I scroll down the agreement, wave my hand through the accept icon, and wait until my ring vibrates, alerting me to the unlock code delivery. Then I pick up my bag and turn toward the door.

"The garage is clear," Vanti says.

I jerk to a halt in surprise. "What? How are you here?"

She nudges me toward the garage. "I'm tracking you, of course. You've proven you're a flight risk time and again."

"I'm not a flight risk." I cross the cool, dim garage, following the pull on my holo-ring toward a mid-level bubble hanging from its charging cord like a pumpkin. "I just like to be on my own sometimes."

"That's going to have to stop." Vanti follows me as I walk around the bubble, checking for damage. "You are a public figure now, and you need to let me do my job. I can't believe Griz put up with your shenanigans for so long."

I flick the accept button on the Rent-a-Bubble app and climb inside. "My shenanigans? Half the time, those shenanigans were your fault! Who took me to Shikumen Palace when the place was infiltrated by terrorists? And the cupcake truck on S'Ride? And the time we went around the west wall to the Lewei estate? Those were all you!"

Vanti pulls the door shut and buckles the seat belt over her lap. "Like Griz said, those were calculated risks. I was aware of the dangers and watching your back the whole time. When you run off alone, you've got no safety net."

"You're right, I need a security detail to watch me as I drive to Sierra Hotel." I flick open the bubble's map, tap the Sierra Hotel front gate, and click "Go." Then I make a big show of looking around the garage as we travel through. "There might be terrorists out there!"

The bubble stops at the garage entrance, and a man with a *CelebVid* logo on his shirt jumps in front of us. "Sera Morgan! What are you doing on Kaku?"

I scrabble at the controls, turning the opaque feature to full.

Vanti throws me a sardonic look, then activates the external speakers. "Step away from the bubble, or we will prosecute you under statute 4528.3 of the Kakuvian Privacy code."

The man's jaw drops, and he leaps away from the vehicle. "Sorry!"

Vanti swipes her hand toward the front of the bubble in a "proceed" gesture. "You're welcome."

WHEN WE ARRIVE at Sierra Hotel, the security gate slides smoothly open, allowing us entrance. It snaps shut before the bubble behind us—another *CelebVid* reporter—can gain access.

I glare at Vanti as the bubble stops in front of the long, low building. "Thank goodness you were here to protect me from the paparazzi."

She doesn't respond. She knows me well enough by now to realize I'll try really hard not to make her job more difficult—when I think about it. But I still want to be cranky about the need for it.

Her understanding makes me even crankier.

I stalk to the front door, which swings open at my approach. We stride across the enormous entry hall and down the wide steps to the second-floor landing. I wave my hand at the single door, and it pops open. A faint hint of lemons and jasmine wafts out as we step into the family room.

"Triana! You made it!" Kara lounges on the comfortable couch in front of the fireplace. Her partner, Erco, sits beside her, his eyes sleepy. He jumps up when he sees us—but probably in response to Vanti's glare rather than respect for me.

"Don't you dare get up." I hurry across the room and throw myself down beside Kara, wrapping my arms around her. "How are you?"

"I couldn't get up if I wanted to. This sofa is the black hole of luxury. I'm sucked in for eternity." She giggles. "And I'm good. After all those false alarms, Baby Freya is being stubborn."

"She knew she'd better wait for Auntie Triana before she made her appearance." I pat Kara's belly, then stand to give Erco a quick hug. "How's dad?"

"I'm fine. Good to see you, Sera."

"Erco, I've told you before. Call me Triana." I look around the room. "Is Elodie still here?"

"She went back to Pacifica City—had to get back for some presentation at school. But she'll be back tonight. Dame Morgan loaned her a private Hyper-Loop pod!"

I blink. I wasn't sure my mother even knew Elodie existed. "That was nice."

"Triana!" Leonidas, the Sierra Hotel caretaker, dressed in his signature caftan and turban, swoops out of the kitchen. His real name is Ervin, and he was the heir to the Lewei Premier—before he ran away and his dad got deposed—but we still call him Leo.

We have a lot in common.

I jump up for a hug, then step back, sniffing. Chocolate. "Did you make something special for me?"

"Of course. But you can't see it until dinner." When I make sad eyes at him, he grins. "That won't work on me. Impervious Leweian, remember?"

"That reminds me—I need to pick your brain about Lewei. I'm going there next week." I turn back to Kara, but Leo grabs my shoulder and swings me around.

"Why would you go to Lewei? That's not safe."

I shrug. "Mother has something going on there, and she needs me to glad-hand a few high-end muckety-mucks. Don't worry, Vanti will be with me. And Ty."

Leo's hand falls from my shoulder, and he smiles. "That's okay, then. Vanti will keep you out of trouble."

I look from him to Vanti to Kara. "Why does everyone say that? Vanti gets me into trouble all the time!"

"But she always gets you out." Kara points at Vanti. "I may not be Lindsay's biggest fan, but I have to admit she's kept you safe."

Vanti flourishes her hands and bows deeply toward Kara. "Thank you for that vote of confidence. But please don't call me Lindsay."

CHAPTER FOUR

THE SECURITY SYSTEM announces "Elodie Ortega Okilo has returned," just before Kara's mom whirls through the door. She's wearing pink, orange, and purple leggings that look like a neon cat vomited all over them and a baggy, bright orange sweater that goes almost to her knees. She carries a backpack over one shoulder, and a dark, scruffy-looking fur wrap hangs over her other arm.

"*Larin!*" Kara starts to rise from the sofa but gives up, stuck between the gravity well of the plush cushions and the weight of her enormous stomach.

Her mother surges forward to kiss Kara's cheek, then Erco's. She drops her things in an empty armchair and hurries to me. "Triana! I'm so glad you came back. She's due to pop any minute."

"I'm not going to 'pop,' *Larin*." Kara glares ineffectively at her mother as she rubs a hand over her belly. "But I'm definitely ready for this baby to be on the outside instead of in here kicking me."

The pile of black fur shivers, then stretches. Two legs poke out, with huge paws that knead the couch cushion. A fluffy tail springs upright.

I point. "What is that?"

"That's Apawllo. Isn't he adorable?" Elodie scoops him up and holds him toward me. "Look at that face."

The face is wide and flat, with a long scar running from the right ear to the jaw. The left ear has a huge chunk missing, and golden eyes squint at me as if measuring my soul and finding it wanting.

"Adorable is not the word I would have used." I put my hands behind my back, so she won't expect me to take it.

"Aww, how can you say that? He's the cutest thing!" She turns the cat and rubs his nose against hers. The cat purrs and pushes the top of its head against Elodie's cheek. "He's so sweet."

"Where did you get a cat, *Larin?*" Kara waves her hands at Erco, and he takes them, leaning back to extract her from the black hole of tranquility.

"One of my classmates is moving off world, and she can't take Apawllo with her. So, I said I'd take him. I know you aren't supposed to have cats around pregnant women, but you're almost done being pregnant, so I thought it would be okay." Her eyes grow wide as she turns to me. "You don't mind, do you?"

"I'm not sure how the Ice Dame would feel about a feline guest, but she's not here to argue. Do you have everything you need for him?" I glance at the backpack—it doesn't look like it holds a lot of cat paraphernalia.

Her face scrunches in thought. "I got him a cat toy and some catnip. And the cutest little pink collar. I thought Leo could feed him. Or maybe we could sneak next door and find some *terkfiske.*" She giggles.

Terkfiske is a Leweian dried fish delicacy that smells as bad as it sounds while its drying. I have no idea what it tastes like—I haven't been brave enough to try it.

I flick my holo-ring and do a quick search on cat food. I choose one at random and place the order. "Where does he, er, do his business?"

Elodie cradles the cat in her arms, stroking the black fur. "I'm not sure. I guess I should have asked LeBrana." Apawllo purrs and wraps his tail around her arm.

Okay, that's kind of adorable.

"Is he an outdoor cat? We'll need to set up some way for him to get outside." I look doubtfully at Vanti who has ignored the entire conversation. She's sitting in a corner, swiping through her holo-ring screens, her eyebrows drawn down in concentration.

"No, he lives inside. That I do know. The apartment where LeBrana lived didn't allow outside animals." She sets Apawllo on the floor, and he winds between her legs, rubbing against the shins of her eyewatering leggings.

I pull up a page about cat care, muttering under my breath about needing a Hy-Mi of my own to do this kind of stuff.

I can't believe I just thought that. My mother's complete reliance on Hy-Mi has always seemed like a crutch—and a way to get out of doing the dirty work. I don't want to be like that. I can handle my own garbage, thank you very much.

The kitchen door slides open, and a cloud of savory deliciousness wafts into the room. "Dinner in ten minutes!" Leo calls out. He and Elodie exchange air kisses, and she follows him into the kitchen to help. While she and Erco set the table, I order everything a cat could possibly need on a rush delivery. I don't know which items are essential and which are required, but this cat will lack for nothing.

That's how you take care of business, Ice Dame!

When Leo returns bearing a tray, Vanti closes her holo-screens and joins the rest of us at the table. I cast an uncertain look at Apawllo, but he's curled up on the couch with his tail over his face. With a shrug, I flick my napkin into my lap.

Dinner does not disappoint. Although my suite at Sierra Hotel is equipped with a state-of-the-art AutoKich'n with a complete set of food maps—and when I say complete, I mean every map ever made—there's nothing like a meal cooked by a master chef. Leo studied at the Child-Hooper Institute, and he is one of the best.

We start with a selection of appetizers—crunchy bread slices topped with grilled tomatoes, fried yellow balls of something that taste salty and creamy, and a cold, chopped seafood mix with tiny crackers. Then he serves beef roast wrapped in a layer of crispy, puffed pastry, greens sautéed with garlic and caramelized onions, and a baked pureed potato dish covered in melted white cheese. The salted caramel and chocolate torte tastes even better than it looks.

I moan as I eat the last bite of chocolate. "I'm so full. But I want another piece."

Leo shakes his head. "No, you don't. Not really. Besides, there will be more tomorrow."

I glare at my reasonable friend. "How are you not five thousand kilos?"

"All the surfing helps." He glances at Vanti, then back to me. "You two want to join me tomorrow?"

Vanti nods enthusiastically. "I've already double checked the virtual perimeter, so it's safe enough. And I haven't been on the water in a long time."

"Great. Breakfast smoothies at five." Leo toasts Vanti with his water glass. Out of solidarity with Kara, none of us are drinking anything stronger than lemonade.

"Five sounds terrible but for surfing... I'll be there." I have only surfed once—when Leo taught me the last time we were on Kaku—and I wasn't very good at it. But I definitely want to try again.

"Anyone else?" Leo looks around the table. "Erco? Elodie?"

"Tempting, but I will stay with Kara." Erco pats his partner's hand.

Elodie pouts. "I have class at nine, so I won't have time. Maybe on Saturday."

As we clean up the dishes, Elodie tells us about her marketing classes and the other students. Her stories have us howling with laughter until the security system announces, "Package for Elodie Ortega Okilo."

She looks up in surprise and almost drops the platter she's washing. "I didn't order anything!"

"It's the cat stuff." I bound out of the room and down the hallway to the service stairs. Packages are delivered to the garage. I trot down the steps, with Vanti on my heels. "Where are you going?"

"I need to check the package before you open it." She pushes past me and out the door into the dim garage.

I swipe the controls on my holo-ring, and the big room lights up. The lights of the delivery drone glint as it swoops out the rear access. A big pile of boxes lies in the middle of the wide garage.

"That's a lot of stuff for one small cat." Vanti pulls a long, slim device out of nowhere and runs it over the boxes. She has to stretch to her full height to wand the tallest one. "What *is* this?"

"A cat tree. The article I read said cats like high things to perch on. Like a bird." I grab the tall box and wrestle it through the door. It's big but not heavy. "Bring that small one—I think it has food inside. He must be hungry."

We get the first of the boxes to the family room. Elodie squats beside the kitchen door, a grin on her face as Apawllo demolishes something on a small plate. "He likes the cioppino."

"You're spoiling that cat." Leo crosses his arms. "I was going to save the leftovers for lunch tomorrow."

"I only gave him a little." Elodie strokes the cat. He ignores her, focused on bolting down the seafood.

"Vanti's got the cat food." I pull the big box into a clear space near the door, retrieve a knife from the kitchen, and cut through the tape.

"Are you using my good fillet knife to open boxes?" Leo demands. He grabs my hand and uncurls my fingers from the knife handle. "Bad Triana."

"Sorry, Leo. I'll buy you a new one." I close my eyes for a second. Another Ice Dame thing to do. Ugh. I'm becoming my mother.

CHAPTER FIVE

AFTER A FRUSTRATING EVENING trying to put together the cat tree—*easy sweedish instructions*, the box claimed—I give up on the half-built thing and go to bed. The others disappeared long ago, Elodie taking Apawllo with her. The cat turned up his nose at the crate with the plush blanket as well as the felted green, wool sphere that was supposed to be a cat haven, preferring to curl up in the box the food came in. After being served cioppino on fine china, he also refused to sample the KittyDeLites I poured into his new plastek bowl.

I've just changed into my pajama shorts and tank top when a screech echoes through the house. "She's in labor!"

I have no idea how Elodie managed to trigger the house-wide announcement, but I don't really care. I yank on a pair of leggings and a big sweater, shove my feet into the closest pair of shoes, and lunge into the family room.

"Kara!" I grab her shoulders, stopping her in her tracks as she paces across the family room. "What do we do? Where do we go?"

She holds up a finger, breathing deeply and bending at the waist for what feels like hours. Finally, she straightens. "That was a long one."

"Five minutes!" Erco calls. He stands in the middle of the room with a huge pink bag over one shoulder and a terrified look on his face. "We need to go!"

"Everyone calm down." Kara waddles to her husband. "We have plenty of time. First babies always take a long time."

Famous last words.

"Do you have my bag?" Kara asks.

Erco proudly displays the chic, pink bag. "Right here."

With a shake of her head, she pushes past him toward the guest rooms. "That's *Larin's* purse, Sweetie. The delivery bag is a black duffle."

Erco drops the massive purse on the coffee table and darts past his wife. "I'll get it! You get in the bubble."

I take Kara's arm and lead her down the hall to the security office. "We can take the elevator, so you don't have to walk down the stairs."

"Thanks, Tree, good thinking."

I wave my holo-ring at the security office door, and it slides open. I wasn't sure it would—last time I was here, I didn't have access.

Vanti stands inside, wrapped in one of the virtual work pods. The invisible supports snake around the user's frame, keeping them in the optimum work position, while forcing the muscles to work so you don't get flabby and tired. Or something like that. I wasn't really paying attention when she described the system.

I usher Kara past Vanti, glancing at her open screens as I go. "What are you working on?"

She shakes her head and does a doubletake. "Is it time?" She swipes her screens away and disengages the system. "Why are you—oh, the elevator."

Last time we were on Kaku, we had to use the emergency escape hatch to, well, to escape. I never knew we had an old-fashioned elevator in the house until then. There are float tubes in the service areas to allow staff to move heavy items—and large quantities of food—to the upper floors, as well as others in the public areas of the house. But the elevator is closer.

I stop suddenly. "We can access it without doing the self-destruct thing, right?"

She pulls open the door to the break room. "Yeah."

The tiny room holds a counter with an AutoKich'n, a small sink, and a closet marked Supplies. Vanti shuts the door behind us and presses the access panel. "I have to approve it, since you didn't activate code zero, zero, zero, destruct, zero." She flicks through a couple of screens, and the floor vibrates.

We descend, then Vanti opens the narrow closet door, revealing access to the garage rather than supplies. We maneuver Kara and her enormous belly through the tight opening and into the dim, cold room.

"Over here!" Erco calls, his voice echoing weirdly through the low-ceilinged room. He stands beside the family bubble with the door open and a proud grin on his face. Then, the smile falls. "Wait, I can drive over there."

"It's not that far." Kara waddles across the hard floor. Halfway across, she stops. "Contraction. Time?" She breathes slowly and heavily, leaning against my arm.

"Four minutes and thirty seconds!" Erco yells as he runs toward us.

"Get the bubble!" I call.

He stops, dithers for a second, then races back to the vehicle. By the time he gets the bubble to us, the contraction has ended.

"Where's the bag?" Kara stops, one foot on the bubble's step, hands gripping the door frame. "That's not the right bag!"

A gray duffle lies in the middle of the bubble's floor. We all turn to stare at Erco.

"That's the only one I could find!"

"Seriously? The delivery bag is sitting on the bench at the end of our bed with a big tag that says 'baby' on the strap." Kara removes her foot as if to get it herself, but I stop her.

"Get in the bubble. I'll get the bag." I race away, passing Elodie and Leo as they run toward the vehicle. "Wait for me—I'll be right back."

I bound up the steps two at a time, landing in the back hallway. For a second, I panic—I haven't been in this part of the house in ages, and I'm not sure which room Kara is staying in. I try the first door, but it's locked.

Zark. I take a deep breath and move on to the next one. That first door was Hy-Mi's apartment, I suddenly remember. He took the last suite, so he was less likely to be disturbed by visitors.

The next door opens, and it looks like a clothing store exploded inside. Colorful fabric hangs from every piece of furniture. I notice Elodie's orange sweater draped on a wall sconce and move on to the last room.

This one is so orderly, it's like no human has ever set foot inside. The bed looks like a coin could be bounced on it. Since Kara left the family room hours ago, I can only assume Erco took the time to straighten the sheets and blankets. He's really rattled.

The big black bag sits on the bench, right where Kara said it would be. A bright pink streamer, about half a meter long and as wide as my hand has the word "FREYA" printed in huge black letters.

Channeling my inner Erco for a second, I hesitate. Kara said the bag was labeled "baby," not "Freya." What if I get the wrong one? I flip over the pink streamer, revealing the word "BABY."

I get back to the bubble in record time, heaving the bag into the center of the vehicle. "Baby," I gasp as I sag into my chair.

"Perfect," Kara says. "Oh, here comes another one!"

"That was only three minutes!" Erco howls.

Vanti hits the controls, and the steps fold up into a door. The bubble spins silently, then launches up the access ramp with a smooth rush.

While Kara pants in the back, with Elodie and Erco taking turns telling her to breathe, Vanti overrides the autopilot and presses the accelerate button. We flash past the estate walls, slipping out of the gate before it's fully open. The dark jungle whips past, barely visible in the bubble's external lights.

"You know where to go?" I ask quietly.

Vanti nods. "Mapped it out when we first got here. It'll take about ten minutes. She isn't going to have that kid in the bubble, is she?" Her face tightens, and one eye twitches a fraction.

"Are you worried you'll have to deliver a baby?" I keep my voice low, but the four in the back are paying no attention to us.

"Delivering it here wouldn't be my first choice." She keeps her eyes on the road, the trees now zinging by in a single green blur.

"I think Elodie could handle it." I glance over my shoulder. Erco is hunched in his seat, his eyes glued to the stopwatch holo hovering in his hand. Elodie sits between him and his wife, rubbing Kara's back and whispering to her. Leo is on Kara's other side, grimacing as she squeezes his fingers. Kara whimpers, then relaxes, and the other three relax with her.

"Almost there," Vanti says, her tone clipped and professional. "Just a few more klicks."

"We'll make it." Kara pants raggedly, then takes a sip from the water pac Leo offers. "Won't we, Freya?"

The baby doesn't respond.

CHAPTER SIX

"SHE'S IN THE BIRTHING SALON." I smile at O'Neill's image in my palm. "They said it could be hours before the baby actually gets here."

He swipes at his eyes and yawns. "Where are you?"

I bite my lip. "In the benefactor's suite. I might have name-dropped to get Kara into the best room, and they insisted we use this lounge. Apparently, Mother's donations made this whole wing possible."

"And what happened to the cat?"

I'd told him about Apawllo when I called before going to bed. "I don't know. I assume he's sleeping in a box in Elodie's room." Although I don't remember seeing the furry black menace when I looked for the bag. "I'm going to let you go. I'll call in the morning."

O'Neill stifles another yawn. "Thanks. I have a full day tomorrow. Sorry I can't be there with you."

"It's just a bunch of waiting. See you soon. Love you." I put a finger against the hologram, as if I could stroke his cheek.

He smiles. "I love you, too." The hologram dissolves.

"Did you say something about Apawllo?" Leo points at Elodie's huge pink purse. "He's right here." He opens the bag, and a furry, black head pops out. The cat looks around the lavishly appointed lounge, yawns, and drops back into the bag.

"You brought him with you?" I plop beside him on the couch.

"Not me. That was Elodie. I don't know why she thought he couldn't stay home alone." Leo leans back and closes his eyes.

"I'm surprised you came." I hold up a hand as one eye opens. "That wasn't meant to be judgmental—I'm just surprised you didn't stay back to make a welcome home breakfast or something."

"Well, for one thing, we won't be home in time for breakfast. And secondly, we've become a little family over the last few weeks. I'm practically this kid's uncle." Leo closes his eye again.

I put my head on the couch's thick armrest. "Wake me when I'm an auntie."

AN ENORMOUS CLAW hooks into the back of my sweater, lifting me off the ground. My neckband tightens around my throat, choking me, and my legs swing wildly. A blur of brown and black passes beneath my feet, then the claw retracts, and I fall. Huge golden eyes blink, coming close as I tumble in slow motion. A fuzzy, lime-green ball appears beneath my feet, with a dark, circular opening.

The rumbling shakes the sphere as I fall through the opening, and a deep voice growls, "Good human."

"Gah!" My eyes fly open. A furry black paw swats my nose, and golden eyes narrow. Apawllo reaches out to swat me again. I shove his paw away. "Get, cat. I'm not your owner."

"Aw, isn't he cute?" Elodie scoops up the cat and scratches his ears. "He woke you up so you could meet Freya!"

I bolt to my feet. "She's here?"

On the other end of the couch, Leo raises his head, his turban askew. "What time is it?"

Elodie beams. "She arrived at four-fifty-three! Three point six kilos. Fifty-two centimeters. She's beautiful."

"But what time is it now?" Leo rubs his eyes.

"I dunno, maybe sixish? If you want to see the baby, you can go in." She smiles and drops into the lounge chair on the far side of the room. "Can you hand me my purse before you go? I have some treats in there for Apawllo."

I lug the pink monstrosity to her. "What did you bring? This weighs a tonne." I set it on the floor beside her chair.

"Just some left over cioppino. The mini fridge is what makes it so heavy." She opens the bag and pulls out a large, shiny red box with rounded corners and a silver handle on the side. The control panel on top reads 3°.

I shake my head and follow Leo out of the room. "She packed a fridge for the cat?"

He glances over his shoulder. "While you were working on the tree thing." He opens another door and gestures me through.

Kara's suite is almost as plush as the benefactor's. Big windows look over a lush park painted pink in the sunrise. A small table with two chairs sits in front of the windows, as if the occupants might want to enjoy a pleasant brunch. The top-of-the-line AutoKich'n probably makes an excellent blintz.

"How are you? Where is she?" I make grabby hands at Kara as I surge forward.

"Don't wake the baby." She nods at Erco snoring in the reclining chair, then raises the blanket-wrapped bundle from her lap. "Freya, meet your Auntie Triana."

Big eyes blink up at me, and I'm in love.

FOUR DAYS LATER, Vanti and I take the corporate shuttle from the Ebony Beach landing pad directly to the private dock on top of SK2. Leo sits in the seat behind me, grumbling about going back to Lewei. Vanti dragooned him into helping us prepare.

"Just be glad you don't have to go." I release my seat restraints and stand to grab my bag from under the seat, narrowly missing head butting the flight attendant who tries to get it for me. "I told you when I got on—I can handle this myself."

The man backs away, bent over double—I'm not sure if it's because he's demonstrating his penitence in a manner expected by board members or if he's afraid I'll bash his head in the next time I move. Either way, the attitude makes me cringe. I don't want to be a terrifying specter of power.

Leo glances at the attendant and fights back a grin. "Maybe you'll fit in perfectly."

"I am not that person!"

"Yeah, I know. But you should pretend to be." He lifts his own bag and follows me into the station.

The float tube drops us to the Level 83 lobby. Vanti disappears to one of the lower levels while I show Leo to his room in Mother's compartment. It gives me great joy to know the caretaker from her Kaku estate is sleeping in her best guest room.

Elodie took Kara and Erco under her wing and moved the new family back to their apartment in Pacifica City. Her own place is a short T-bahn ride away, and she will make sure they don't need anything for the next two weeks. Although I was thrilled to be there for the birth, once I realized how much work a baby is, I didn't mind getting back to SK2 and my mission to Lewei.

We dump our stuff in our rooms, then I take Leo down to Level 82. "Have you been to SK2 before?"

He waggles his hand. "I flew in through here, of course, but I never left the port. Went straight from my interstellar transport to the dirtside shuttle."

"There's a flight from Lewei?" We reach O'Neill's office, but he's not there. I hide a sigh and take Leo to the conference room. Between my Morgan heir credentials and my maintenance access—which I *might* have hacked to retain after I left the MCC—I have access to everywhere on the station.

"I didn't come directly from Lewei. I was MIA for a decade, remember? I traveled the system, did odd jobs here and there, and eventually ended up at the Child-Hooper for culinary training. Then I worked at an estate on Sally Ride for a year before coming here. Hy-Mi wouldn't have hired me without experience." He drops into one of the comfortable rolling chairs. "Most of my traveling was aboard freight-haulers. I'd sign on to work cargo, and they'd always want to keep me when they tasted my cooking. Most freighters don't have great AutoKich'n maps."

"Was that before you went to the institute?" I dial a beverage from the AutoKich'n and raise my eyebrows at him.

"Whatever you're drinking. I learned to cook on Lewei, then perfected my best recipes as I traveled. Eventually, I decided to put that knowledge to good use and applied to the school. They like students who have some previous experience in the kitchen."

I hand him a glass and settle into one of the chairs. "What else do I need to know about Lewei?"

"It would help if I had some idea who you're meeting." He holds up a hand when I start to protest. "I don't need names, just what industry? What social status, government officials or private—that sort of thing."

I flick my holo-ring and bring up a non-disclosure agreement. "If you sign this, I can tell you more. It just says if you tell anyone what we talk about, the furies will hunt you down and burn the flesh from your bones. Or you'll go to prison on Sally Ride, which would be worse."

He chuckles. "I'm not telling anyone anything. I lived on Lewei—I know how to keep my mouth shut." He scans the document, then waves his hand through the signature icon. "Done."

"As long as you don't defect back to Lewei, I'm in good shape." I flick the file away and pull up another one. "Here's the brief I was given."

Leo pauses before accepting the new file, his eyes on mine. "I am never going back there."

CHAPTER SEVEN

WHEN MY STOMACH STARTS RUMBLING, we break for lunch. I wrinkle my nose at the AutoKich'n. "I need to get out of this room. Don't you?"

Leo gets to his feet, nodding slowly. "I could use a break. What did you have in mind?"

I smile and wave open the door. "I have a couple of favorites." I swing by O'Neill's office, but he's still missing. After shooting him a message, I take Leo to the Level 82 concourse. We bypass the door leading up to the penthouse lobby and take the public float tube to Level 11.

Since the station is a couple of hours ahead of Paradise Alley, it's now mid-afternoon, and the concourse is relatively quiet. Most of Level 11 is work-force housing, with a few shops and eateries in the center. The Happy Poel is deserted.

The burly man behind the counter nods when we enter, his eyes flicking to my guest and back. "The Happy Platter?"

"Thanks, Ye'an."

We take one of the tables by the window, which looks onto the concourse. The chairs creak when we sit, and the floor feels sticky. The plastek tablecloth is yellow with darker stains here and there and a hole melted in one corner. Leo slides a finger along the scorched edge and raises an eyebrow at me.

I wave an admonishing finger. "Wait for the food. And if you come here again, only order the pierogis. The rest is just so-so."

"I try not to judge a restaurant by its tablecloths." He leans back in the chair, making it groan again, then quickly sits upright. "Or its furniture."

We sit in silence for a while, each of us checking our messages. "Ty says he'll meet us for dinner." I glance at the time. "In about three hours. Oops—we won't be very hungry."

Leo laughs. "Are you kidding? When are you ever not hungry?"

"Fair enough."

Ye'an approaches, his hand wrapped in a fold of his apron. He clutches a huge platter holding a dozen different pierogis, some steamed, some baked, some fried. He drops the hot plate on the table between us and points with the chopsticks clutched in his other hand. "The sweezenberry ones are new. Try that sauce with 'em." The sticks flick to a small bowl holding pink sauce, then drop to the table with a clatter.

Leo picks up a pair of chopsticks. "I thought these were Shinese, not Poelish."

I shush him with a grin. "Just go with it."

We demolish the pierogis, barely speaking as we eat. Leo leaves the third sweezenberry one for me. I nod my thanks as I dunk it into the pink sauce.

"I wonder why they gave us an odd number of those?" Leo nods at the fried pastry as it disappears into my mouth.

I take my time enjoying the last one before answering. "The platter is supposed to have twelve. That was an extra because I'm such a good customer."

"And because *ze malutka* and I go way back."

I glance up in surprise at the tiny woman standing beside our table. She looks ancient, with a wrinkled face and tiny body swathed in voluminous wraps. "*Księżna*, my friend Leonidas." I'm not gifting her with his real identity. "Leo, this is the *Księżna*. She's the leader of the Poelish community on SK2."

"You are from Lewei." The old woman's voice is stronger now and devoid of her usual heavy accent. She pulls out a chair and sits, her various scarves and skirts drifting around her.

Leo and I exchange a look. "Why do you say that?" I ask.

She shrugs. "He is obviously Ervin Sidorov-Zhang. He looks just like his pictures."

"The most recent pictures of Ervin are from bad surveillance cams more than a decade ago. This is Leo." I lean my forearms on the table. "Is there something you wanted, *Księżna*?"

"I wanted to tell you to be careful. Lewei is not a safe place for a 'capitalist' such as yourself." She folds her hands in her lap and gives me a bland look.

"What makes you think I'm going to Lewei?" My trip is not exactly secret, but we've kept it quiet. Only the upper echelons of SK'Corp are supposed to know about it.

Of course, this is the leader of the *Sprzężaj*—the local mafia that runs this level and many of the other parts of the station. She makes it her business to stay informed. She shrugs again. "I have my sources."

"We know Lewei is not a safe place." Leo's eyes flick from the *Księżna* to Ye'an and to the door as if evaluating our exit route. "Everyone knows that."

"You better than most, perhaps." The *Księżna* pats my hand. "The *malutka* would be safe enough in normal times, but my sources tell me now is not a good time to visit Lewei. The recent unrest there…"

When she doesn't continue, I grasp her hand. "What unrest? Security hasn't unearthed anything lately."

"Maybe I should have phrased it differently. By the time you arrive, there will have been some recent unrest."

Leo's hand snaps out and grips the old woman's arm. "Are you saying something is going to happen in the next few days that will endanger Triana's safety?"

When he touches her, the wrinkles seem to fall away from her face, revealing a much younger woman. She yanks her arm away, and the old woman reappears.

"You're wearing one of those programmable visual disruption fields." Leo takes her arm again, and she grows younger. "Like the one Vanti gave me when we were at the embassy."

I stare at the no longer old woman. "Who are you?"

Her lips twitch. "I am the *Księżna*. My given name is Sonia—I'm Ye'an's cousin. You should ask your fiancé about me."

"O'Neill knows about you?"

"I helped him with his first investigation—the assassination of Don Smith."

Leo raises his eyebrows, but I don't respond. I remember Don Smith. He was the chair of the board before Mother, and his murder caused her to clamp down on my activities. In some ways, that was the last straw that caused me to run away. "O'Neill investigated that murder?"

"He and his friend Vanti. You didn't know?"

"I didn't know either of them back then." I shake my head. "Doesn't matter. Why are you wearing the PVD? And why did Leo touching you disrupt it?"

"I have a disrupting loop built into my holo-ring." Leo waves his hand at me. "I learned to be careful ages ago."

Sonia grimaces at Leo. "I need to watch out for those." She turns to me. "The *Księżna* is old—everyone knows that. We have to maintain that illusion to command respect. The PVD allows different women to play the role— always members of my family, but not always me. We're the ones who gave that technology to Vanti, by the way. Although I have to admit I like the upgrades SK'Corp built into it. The original only aged the wearer. Now you can look like almost anyone. If you're going to Lewei, you should get one."

I'm not sure if she's talking to me or Leo. It wouldn't make sense for me to wear one—I'm the official representative of SK'Corp. They know what I look like.

But I might want a disguise if things get dicey. "Where might I come by one of those?"

"For a small fee, I might be able to—"

Leo cuts her off. "Vanti has them."

"Vanti likes to keep me on a tight leash. Having one she doesn't know about—you won't tell her, will you?"

He looks at me for a long moment, then shakes his head. "I'm not your keeper, but I advise you not to pull any tricks on her. Vanti can't protect you if she doesn't know where you are. Or who you look like."

"I know." I tap my fingers on the table, then turn back to the *Księżna*. "Do it. I'll need it quickly. I'm leaving Monday."

She pulls a scrap of paper from one of her many draperies and slides it across the table. "Leave that with Ye'an, and you'll have the device within the day."

I place my hand over the paper, not looking at it, and nod. "Thank you, *Księżna*. May all your pierogis be hot."

She cackles as she rises. "I like the sweezenberry ones better cold." With a whirl of her black-on-black ensemble, she disappears through a door at the rear of the compartment.

"Let's get out of here." I palm the paper and shove my hand into my pocket as I rise, not quite as smoothly as Vanti but a credible attempt.

The concourse is busier now, full of that heavy, "why did I agree to take the mid-shift" attitude so common in the lower levels of the station. Later tonight, it will be full of partiers desperate to shake off the work week.

We take the float tubes up to Level 64, where the feeling is different. Up here, there are more tourists, fresh off the cruise ships to see the wonders of SK2. There are also wealthier people who seem to be better at hiding their unhappiness under piles of consumer goods. I angle across the concourse into Radial 6, where the crowds thin. Then we turn right into Ring B.

"Where are we going?"

"Cash machine." I push through an unmarked door into a spartan but comfortable waiting room. We've barely stepped inside when the inner door opens, and a hand waves us through.

"There are cash machines all over this station." Leo frowns at the generic prints on the wall as we cross the room.

"Not like this one." I enter the inner office and greet the small woman seated behind the desk. "Good afternoon, Sera."

Leo looks around the room, which contains only a desk, two chairs, and two "Visit Kaku" posters. His eyebrows come down, but he says nothing and closes the door behind us. Then he takes up a position beside it, like a bodyguard.

He does a good impression. Leo is a tall man, with broad shoulders. His body is hidden beneath the loose caftan he prefers to wear, but there's no hint of softness to him. The turban and dreadlocks give him a slightly foreign appearance, and his expression is foreboding.

I sit and turn to the woman. "I need a large sum of cash." I slide the slip of paper across the table. I hesitate for a moment—I probably should have looked at it before I handed it to her. Too late now.

The woman lifts the paper and peers at the reverse side. "Are you sure?"

Before I can voice my confusion, she turns the paper over. It says, "1 credit and a favor."

CHAPTER EIGHT

Zark. The *Księżna* has always preferred to deal in random favors to be named later—it's a pretty nice piece of leverage to have over someone. Do I want this device badly enough to make that promise?

"Sorry, wrong paper." I make a show of checking my pockets, then give up. "I must have left it in my other pants. Can you do twenty kay?"

The woman nods, although twenty thousand is a large sum, even on SK2. She flicks a holo-screen to me, and we spend the next few minutes swiping and waving files back and forth.

Finally, I send the last one, and she reaches into a drawer and pulls out a stack of paper credit notes. She counts out less than half of the wad and pushes them across the table to me. I count them, pass a hundred credit note back to her and pocket the rest. With a nod to the woman, I walk past Leo and out the door.

In the hallway, Leo grabs my arm. "Was that a money launderer?"

"I 'purchased' a number of different items from several different accounts, and she refunded my money in cash. Is that laundering?" I pat my bulging pocket. "I'm glad I have you as protection with this much paper on me."

"Yeah, that's pretty much the definition of money laundering. Does Ty know you do this? Or Vanti?"

"I've never mentioned it to them." I try for nonchalance. "I'd prefer you don't, either."

"Don't you know how dangerous it is?"

"Dangerous how?" I head for the radial, and Leo falls into step beside me. "I'm not worried about blackmail—she stands to lose way more than I do. And

35

all the upper levs use her. She doesn't deal with drug dealers or gamblers. Well —some of the upper levs use her to hide their gambling. But she's not working with any of the illegal casinos or bookies."

"How do you know?"

I stop at the edge of the concourse. That's a fair question. Am I sure she doesn't do those things? "That woman is a cousin of one of the board of directors. Fairly distant, but everyone knows she's related. The board will protect her—as long as she isn't doing anything egregious—and all the top-levs use her."

"You know 'everyone is doing it' isn't a legal defense, right?" When I start to protest, he waves me off. "Next question: if the *Księżna* wants a favor, why did you get the cash?"

"I'm going to try to renegotiate the terms. She probably won't go for it, but it's worth a shot. Plus, I hear Commonwealth credits are useful on Lewei."

"They're also illegal." Leo puts a hand against my back, urging me toward the float tubes. "If they find them on you, they'll confiscate the credits and probably throw you into Xinjianestan."

A tremor of fear goes through me. Everyone has heard of the Xinjianestan "educational camp." People who get sent there never return. Or if they do, they come back broken. "You couldn't have told me this before I got a massive wad of cash?"

"I didn't know what you were doing!" Leo pinches the bridge of his nose. "Luckily, we haven't left the station yet. You can stash it somewhere safe, and it's all good."

We take the float tube up to Level 82 and stroll down the carpeted corridor to the conference room. I pause as we pass O'Neill's office. He might be inside, but I don't want to interrupt him if he's busy. I'll see him in less than an hour. "We should get back to work."

"Agreed." He opens the conference room door. "When are you going to—"

"That was a long lunch." O'Neill gets up from his chair as we walk into the room.

"Ty!" I throw myself at him, marveling—as always—that such a perfect, shiny man wants to marry me. "I've missed you so much!"

When I finally break away from our long kiss, we're alone. "Where'd Leo go?"

O'Neill looks around the room and shrugs. "Dunno. He's a big boy—he can take care of himself. Where have you two been?"

"We went to The Happy Poel for a late lunch. We're still on Sierra Hotel time."

"I'm glad you're back." He runs his hands down my sides, and I suddenly remember the large wad of cash in my pocket. I'm not trying to keep any secrets, but if he notices it, that might spark some uncomfortable questions.

I pull away. "He hasn't spent much time on SK2. I hope he doesn't get lost."

O'Neill laughs and pulls me close again. "I'm sure he can remember your mother's place is on the top level."

His hands slide around my waist and down to my hips, dangerously close to my stuffed pocket. Can I sneak the credits out and hide them somewhere in the room? I reach down, trying to concentrate while returning his head-spinning kiss. I get lost a few times but finally get the cash out of my pocket.

Then he lets me go and steps back. "Did you have more work to do, or do you want to go upstairs?"

I put my hand beside my leg and turn away from him just a bit to hide my stash. "Let me see if Leo's waiting." I finish the spin and hurry to the door. Leo's not in the hallway. I turn back, careful to keep the money hidden behind my body. "I guess we're done. Can you get off work this early?"

"I work around the clock. I don't have to be in the office for all of it." He strides toward me and throws an arm around my shoulders. "Let's go home."

I slide my arm around his waist, the cash clenched in my fist. He'll notice if I pull back to stuff it back into my pocket. But someone else might notice a fat wad of credits in my hand. As we stroll down the radial, my mind spins, proposing and rejecting increasingly ridiculous schemes. We swing into the concourse, and his jacket flaps against my hand, the edge of a pocket catching on my finger. Without thinking about it, I shove the credits into his pocket and clamp my hand over the lump, hugging myself closer to his side.

Ty's arm tightens around my shoulders, and he leans over to kiss my cheek. All my worries fade away.

But only for a second. We step through the blank door in the center of the open concourse and wave our holo-rings at the guard desk. The man behind it snaps to attention when he recognizes us and nods. "Good evening, Sera, Ser."

"Everything all right, Huber?" O'Neill pauses when I would have walked by with a quick reply.

"Yes, ser. No anomalies to report." Huber fidgets with a stylus, tapping against the desk at a rapid tempo.

O'Neill's eyes drop to the man's hand, and the tapping stills. "You sure everything is okay?"

"Yes, ser. Nothing unusual today. Oh—one odd thing." He glances at me and hunches his shoulder as if that will prevent me hearing. "Sera Huatang came up a few minutes ago. She wasn't drunk."

O'Neill's lips twitch. "That is unusual at this time of day. Thanks for the update." He urges me toward the private float tube behind the desk.

We step out in the penthouse lobby. A woman in a plain black dress plays the grand piano in the center of the room. Fresh flowers nod in the matching urns set between the doors. Directly across from the float tube, the door to suite A slides open as we approach.

"Leo says Commonwealth credits are illegal in Lewei," I say casually as we cross the foyer to the living room.

"Is that why you stuffed a wad of cash in my pocket a few minutes ago?"

I stop in the middle of the room and turn, my face going hot. "You noticed that?"

He bites back a smile. "I'm a trained security agent. Noticing pickpockets is Agenting One-oh-one." He pulls the bundle of credits out and whistles. "That's a lot of loot. Definitely going to get you landed in Xinjianestan if you take it to Lewei."

"I wasn't stealing—I was putting it *in* your pocket."

He holds out the money. "Do you want me to hang on to this?"

I take it. "No, I'll put it in my lock drawer."

"Do I want to know where you got it?" he calls as I start up the stairs.

I pause and turn halfway around, looking down at him. "It's mine."

He puts a hand over mine on the banister. "I didn't think you stole it. I'm just wondering if I should worry about how you withdrew it. I suspect if I checked your bank account, I wouldn't see a large withdrawal."

"You can check my bank account?" He shouldn't be able to do that—unless Mother gave him access.

"No, of course not. Unless I found a maintenance tech who knows how to 'find' things in the system." He grins.

"I'm the only maintenance tech you're allowed to find." I lean over the railing to kiss him. "And I got it the same way Gloria got the cash for her escorts last week."

Gloria Huatang has been after Ty since she first laid eyes on him, but once we announced our engagement, she changed tactics. The latest appeared to be an attempt to provoke jealousy and involved a pair of twins she'd recruited and decked out to resemble O'Neill. In a creepy, not-right way.

He puts his hand over his eyes. "Don't remind me—I can't unsee them." His hand drops. "Just because Gloria uses that service does not mean it's a wise move."

"You know about that?"

He taps his chest with a forefinger. "Board security, remember? I keep up on all the top-levs' shenanigans."

If he's calling it a shenanigan, it must not be too dangerous. I file that information away as I caress his cheek. "I'll be right back."

In my room, I lock the cash in my secure drawer. My bag still sits on the bed. Normally, the staff would have unpacked it as soon as I arrived. Maybe my constant demands that they leave my stuff alone have finally been heeded.

The bag moves.

Maybe the staff have declined to unpack my bag because it's possessed by demons. I take a step closer to the bed. The bag moves again. Just a wiggle, as if the demon has decided he needs a more spacious habitat but can't get the zipper undone.

I gingerly grasp the plastek tab and pull the zipper open. A cloud of black fur and claws explodes from the bag, scattering dirty underwear across my bedspread.

I close my eyes for a second, then activate my message system. "Elodie, I have your cat."

CHAPTER NINE

"*ALLEY-LOOYA!*" Elodie cries. "I was wondering where he went. Why did you take him?"

"I didn't. He was in my bag." I stare at the seething pile of angry cat currently shredding my favorite panties. "He wasn't there when I packed, so someone must have put him in later."

"Who would have done that?" Elodie's face scrunches up in confusion. "Leo is with you—do you think he wanted to take Apawllo with him?"

"He could have packed him in his own bag. This seems more like a prank. I wonder if Vanti did it."

"Does Vanti do pranks? She seems way too serious for that." Something wails in the background, and Elodie's head spins. "That's Freya—I gotta go. Can you send Apawllo home?"

"I'll figure something out."

The baby's voice gets louder. How can one tiny human make so much noise?

"I'll talk to you later, Triana!" Her face disappears as the comm bubble pops.

I stride to the door and open it. "Out."

The cat looks up from the remains of my dirty laundry and narrows his golden eyes. Without breaking eye contact, he puts his claws through the delicate fabric one more time. Then he leaps to the floor and strolls past me, tail arched over his back.

I growl as he struts past, but he wisely ignores me. We walk down the plas-

41

glas stairs together. I wave at Leo and Ty seated in the living room below. "Did you bring a stowaway, Leo?"

O'Neill does a double take. "Is that a cat or a bear?"

"I didn't bring him." Leo scratches his short beard. "Does Elodie know he's here?"

"She does now." I cross the living room and drop to the couch beside O'Neill. "This is Apawllo, Elodie's cat. I found him in my bag."

"How did you not notice a cat that big inside your bag?" O'Neill makes a kissy sound. The cat rubs against his legs, purring.

"He can't have been in there. Someone must have put him into my bag after we arrived." I glare at Leo.

He holds up both hands. "Not me. I don't really like cats." Apawllo's ears twitch, and he deserts O'Neill and leaps into Leo's lap. "Did he understand that?"

"I'm pretty sure cats don't understand Standard. But they always seem to love people who don't like them." O'Neill puts his arm around me and gives me a little shake. "I just realized we've never had this important discussion: are you a cat person or a dog person?"

I'm caught in a staring contest with the cat. I rip my eyes away from his mesmerizing orbs. "Generally, I like both. This cat doesn't seem to like me, though."

"Then he should be on your lap, right?" Leo pushes Apawllo's backside, but the cat doesn't budge, continuing to glare at me.

"You know who else doesn't like cats? The Ice Dame." I look around the room, as if she's hiding somewhere.

"Good thing she's out tonight." O'Neill makes the kissing sound again, but Apawllo kneads his claws into Leo's pale yellow-and-white-striped caftan. "I hope he doesn't shed on the furniture."

Leo pushes at the cat again to no avail. He lifts the cat, carefully removing the claws from his clothing, and sets him on the floor. The cat spins around and wiggles as if preparing to spring, but Leo jumps to his feet. "Hah, no lap for you." Then he holds the skirt of his robe away from his body. "He doesn't seem to shed at all. See, no fur."

I flick my holo-ring and contact Hy-Mi. Surprisingly, the system goes to message. "Hy-Mi, I need to arrange to have something sent back to Pacifica City. Can you set that up?"

"Hy-Mi is on leave." O'Neill grabs my hand. "I'll take care of it."

I stare at O'Neill for a second, then turn back to my holo-ring. "Never mind. I didn't know you were gone. I'll figure it out. Have a nice vacation." I sign off and turn to Ty. "When did that happen?"

He raises his eyebrows, lips pursed. "I'm not sure. First I heard of it was this afternoon. I had to grant higher access to Spencer."

"Who's Spencer?"

"Hy-Mi's assistant?" His brows come down in a how-could-you-not-know look. "He's worked for the company for five years."

"I never talk to his assistants—except when he's on vacation, which isn't often." Hy-Mi has always felt more like family than employee. "In fact, it's more like never. He did take a few days off when we were on Kaku for the wedding planning. But I think the last time I spoke to his assistant, it was a woman named Raquelle."

O'Neill shakes his head in amazement. "Raquelle left years ago—while you were at the Techno-Inst. Poor Hy-Mi doesn't get much time off, does he?"

"No, and it's usually planned well in advance." I drum my fingers against my leg. "Something must be wrong."

"Are your spider-senses tingling?"

"What are spider senses?" Leo asks.

I glance at the time and get to my feet. "Old joke," I tell Leo. "And it's spidey, not spider. Let's go to the dining room—dinner should be ready."

Leo laughs at me, then pats his stomach. "I don't think I could eat a bite."

The cat meows loudly.

"I know what we can do with the leftovers."

CHAPTER TEN

"Since this is our last night on station, how about we go out for a drink?" It's Sunday night, and I haven't managed to visit Ye'an to renegotiate the deal for the PVD. "I haven't been to the Shuttle Dock in ages."

Vanti looks up from whatever she's reading—probably *Secret Agents Quarterly*—the top ten undercover tricks. Number ten: Fake nose sunglasses. I giggle.

She's staring at me. She obviously said something, but I was so preoccupied envisioning her with a plastek nose and moustache that I didn't hear her.

"Sorry, what?"

"That was my question." She goes back to the holo-screen. "Why would you want to go to that dive?"

"Did someone say dive?" Leo comes down the steps, flipping his dreadlocks over his shoulder. He's wearing a lime green robe today and no turban.

"We're talking about dive bars, not diving." Vanti doesn't even look up from her reading.

"I love a good dive bar. I haven't seen one up here. If we're going, I want to change." Leo swings around, then glances back and pauses. "We are going, right?"

I give Vanti a narrow-eyed glare. "Yes, we are." I make shooing motions at him, and he disappears.

Vanti does a great impression of rolling her eyes without actually doing it. "If you insist. I need to get another agent."

I moan. "I don't need two babysitters!"

"If Griz were here, I wouldn't worry about it."

If "Griz" were here, I would go to the Shuttle Dock without Vanti. Ty would be okay with that—he knows I know every centimeter of the station and that I'm perfectly safe on Level 4 as Triana. But Vanti has spent most of the last six years on Kaku, and she's not taking any chances. I wish he didn't have to work tonight. "You keep saying he's not on your team. But you treat him like he is. Which is it?"

"He's not on my team." She flicks her screens closed and stands. "He's a skilled agent, so I can use him in a pinch. But you two together are a disaster waiting to happen."

"Oh, come on. We aren't that bad." I head for my room before she can change her mind.

"At least Elodie isn't here," Vanti mutters. "She's the real wild card."

———

"Hey, Elodie's going to meet us at the Shuttle Dock," Leo announces as we step into the float tube to Level 82. He's changed into jeans and a T-shirt and has tied his dreads into a low ponytail.

Vanti groans, but I grin. "What's she doing on the station?"

"Apparently, she had some kind of job interview."

"On the station? On a Sunday?" Vanti asks.

Leo shrugs. "No idea. You'll have to ask her."

A short, serious-looking woman waits at the desk beside the float tube exit. She's chatting with the guard on duty.

"Sera Morgan, this is Perry-Ann Winters. She's been with SK'Corp for seven years and has been assigned to the station for six of those. She'll be running rear-guard." Vanti flicks a file at the short woman.

Winters glances through the file, then her dark eyes snap to me. She sizes me up and moves on to Leo, then back. "Good evening, Sera Morgan."

"If you're going with us, you need to call me Triana." I hold out a fist.

She looks surprised, then knocks her knuckles against mine. "Call me Win."

"This is Leo." I jerk a thumb at him. "We're going down to the Shuttle Dock for a couple drinks."

"I thought it was *a* drink," Vanti says.

Leo laughs. "A drink always morphs into a couple drinks, which frequently becomes too many drinks."

I think back to the night Leo was kidnapped in Paradise Alley. That was definitely the progression of events. "We're meeting our friend Elodie on Level 4."

Win's eyes widen into a hopeful-puppy-dog stare. "Elodie-Oh?"

My brows draw down. I've never heard anyone call her that. "Do you know her?"

"I wish. Do you?"

"I'm not sure we're talking about the same person. Who is Elodie-Oh?"

Vanti opens the door and does a quick scan of the concourse. "Win. We're moving."

"Roger that, Vanti." Win's face goes blank, and she points at Leo. "You first, then Sera Mor—Triana. I'll bring up the rear."

We parade across the concourse single file like a bunch of ducks following their mother. Vanti stands at the entrance to Radial 3, beside the float tube. Win takes up a position on the far side of the tubes near Radial 4.

I grab Leo's arm before he steps into the tube. "One of them will go first."

A couple comes to the mouth of Radial 4, and Win puts out a hand to stop them.

Leo stares from one agent to the other. "This is kind of conspicuous. I mean, ridiculously conspicuous. How are you going to pass for Triana when you've got the Giggle Sisters stopping traffic?"

"You're right, this is never going to work. Come on." I grab his arm and drag him to Vanti. "Get Win over here."

Before Vanti can activate her internal comm system, Leo sticks his fingers in his mouth and blows a shrill whistle. Vanti and I slap our hands over our ears while Leo waves Win over.

"Thanks." I make a show of reaming my ear with a finger.

Leo smirks. "It works."

I turn to the agents. "Since we're going to Level 4, we need to be inconspicuous. Just four friends, out for a drink. No stopping people from getting too close or blocking off Radials. We've done this before, Vanti. Remember the cupcake truck on Sally Ride? Or the night in Paradise Alley?"

Vanti points a finger at me. "That night in Paradise Alley is exactly why we're being so careful. Leo got kidnapped."

"But that was on Kaku. And it was his father's *Spiitznatz* who grabbed him. No one on SK2 is going to kidnap me. They know that would be hazardous to their health. Leo and I went to Level 11 by ourselves on Friday. What's changed?"

"I didn't know you were going. Griz said you'd be in the conference room all day."

I wave that away. "Whatever. We were down on 11 and didn't have any problems. Let's just go down together, get a drink and come home." And at some point, I will sneak away to get my PVD from Ye'an.

Vanti and Win exchange a silent look. I know they're talking on a private channel, but I can't hear anything. Their lips don't even twitch. After a long pause, Vanti sighs. "Fine. One drink." She glares at Leo.

"Sure. One." Leo winks at me and hurries into the float tube before they can move.

Vanti darts after him, and Win herds me in behind.

On Level 4, the noise ratchets up. The concourse is full of people, eating and drinking at the tables spilling across the open space, shopping in the well-lit stores, arguing in alcoves that provide no privacy. Across the way, a scuffle breaks out and quickly dissolves as the slightly tipsy break apart their very drunk friends.

Vanti strikes off across the space, arrowing through the crowd. She must have a death glare on her face because people do double takes and melt away, leaving a wide corridor before her. Win pushes me and Leo in behind, like the caboose on Vanti's anger train.

Elodie has commandeered a table in the center of the bar. As we approach, three rough-looking men move in on her. They gesture at the chairs, but she shakes her head, pointing at us. They talk, then one of the guys punches his friend in the bicep. The friend moves to the next table, rubbing his arm. The remaining two guys pose on either side of Elodie for a picture.

Vanti pushes ahead of me and stops by the ringleader. She doesn't say anything, but her glare speaks volumes. The two guys back away.

"I don't like this position." Vanti climbs onto a stool across the table. "By the wall would be better."

"Good evening to you, too," Elodie says. Vanti ignores her.

I hug Elodie and take the chair next to her. "What was that all about?"

"They wanted the table."

"What about the picture?" I punch my order into the table menu and raise my eyebrows at Leo. He leans across and taps one of the beer icons. "What are you drinking, Vanti? And where's Win?" I spin the stool, but the short woman is not in evidence.

"Win is sweeping the room. She's checking the bathrooms and placing sensors. I'll have a lemonade." Vanti's eyes swivel around the room, never stopping. "Non-alcoholic."

"Of course." I turn back to Elodie. "Why did those guys want a pic?"

"I've developed a bit of a fan club."

CHAPTER ELEVEN

ELODIE SMIRKS IN A SELF-DEPRECATING WAY. "Thanks for sending Apawllo home."

"Don't change the subject. You have a fan—"

"Elodie-Oh!" Win has reappeared, and her eyes are trained on Elodie. "It's really you! Will you sign—" She breaks off to search her pockets for something.

A mechanical arm slides overhead, stopping above our table, then lowers to deposit our drinks. We take them off the tray, and it zips away.

"What is this Elodie-Oh business?" I hand Elodie her drink. She whips out a pen and signs the coaster with a flourish, then gives it to Win.

"Win, focus!" Vanti hisses. She must be really put-out, to say that out loud instead of via their comm system.

Win's face goes pale. She tucks the signed coaster into her bra, then takes up a position beside my chair, facing away from the table.

The guy who was punched by his friend reappears beside us with a stool. "Sorry it took so long, Elodie-Oh." He pushes the chair up to the table and disappears into the crowd.

"Someone please tell me what's going on." I point at the chair. "Those guys wanted our table but ended up bringing you another stool?"

"She's Elodie-Oh!" Win gives me a look that can best be described as a what-side-of-the-swamp-do-you-live-on look. She flicks her holo-ring and pulls up the V-Time app. "She's viral."

A series of vids swirl across her palm, all of them featuring Elodie speaking to the camera. I can't hear anything she's saying—I think the audio is connected to Win's implant. Win laughs and points at one of the vids.

"Win! Focus," Vanti snaps again. Win blushes and swipes away the app. She resumes her not very subtle guard position behind my chair.

"I kinda got famous." Elodie blushes as another guy stops by the table.

"Sorry to interrupt. Can I—" He waves his hands incoherently.

"Sure. Gimme some love!" She wraps an arm around the guy and squishes her cheek against his. They both smile, and a light flashes. She releases the guy and waves the picture from her holo-ring. "There ya go."

I shake my head and message Kara: Did you know your mom is a V-Time star?

Kara: Didn't you?

Over the next two hours, I nurse my drink while Elodie gets pictures taken with her legions of fans. Vanti and Win try—and fail—to intimidate all of them. Vanti's jaw gets tighter as the night goes on, and she snaps at Win each time the other woman lets her guard down. Before Leo can order his third beer, I put a hand on his arm. "This isn't much fun."

"I'm having a good time. Watching those guys work up the courage to talk to Elodie is hilarious. Look at that one." He nods at a guy near the bar who appears to be having a discussion with himself. Finally, he nods, picks up a napkin and marches toward us. He gets halfway across the room, then stops, swings around, and returns to his place at the bar, wiping his hands on his pants and throwing the crumpled napkin on the bar.

"I still need to get up to the Happy Poel. That was the whole reason I wanted to come out."

"Why didn't you say so? I thought you just wanted a drink." He raises his voice. "Hey, guys, I'm hungry. Triana introduced me to this amazing pierogi place up on 11."

Real subtle, Leo.

Vanti's eyes narrow and dart to me. "That place is a *Sprzężaj* haven."

I widen mine at her and smile in what I hope is an unconcerned grin. "They make great pierogis, though."

She looks away, checking nearby tables for terrorists and kidnappers for the nine millionth time. "If you want to do it, we can go."

"Really?" I glance at Leo. I fully expected her to say no. But I don't need an audience while I renegotiate my deal. "Excellent. Let's do it."

Elodie stops for two more pictures on the way out of the bar. In the concourse, fans seem more intimidated by Win and Vanti and keep their distance.

"How are you taking those pics?" I ask as we follow the redhead to the float tubes.

"*CelebDrone*." She nods upward. "It's tiny but has a great lens."

"*Celeb*—you aren't working with *CelebVid* are you?" The notorious paparazzi firm has been stalking me for most of my life. A few months back, they intercepted a vid Kara sent her mom—one I'd originally sent to Kara. Since then, I've beefed up Elodie's security, but the idea that she's on their payroll chills me.

"No, those people are evil." She waves at a young couple who point in our direction. "*CelebDrone* isn't affiliated with them—although they use *CelebDrones*, too.*"

"They can't hijack yours, can they? I should probably look at your security settings."

She pushes me into the float tube. "Don't worry about it. I had someone check it."

"Who? I thought I was your go-to gal." We waft up to Level 11 and get out.

"Yeah, but you're busy these days. Erco found a co-worker who knows their stuff. She went through everything, and we're good."

There are lots of security specialists at SK'Corp, so I can trust Erco with this. "Okay, but let me know if you want a second opinion."

"Maybe when you get back." She pushes through the door of the Happy Poel and squeals. "This is so cute! My viewers will love it!" She checks her hair in the window, then flicks her holo-ring.

Vanti puts a hand on her arm. "You might want to check with the *Księżna* before you start filming." She nods at the ancient-looking lady sleeping in the corner. "Come on, I'll introduce you."

"You guys get a table," I tell Win and Leo. "I want to talk to the proprietor. If pierogis will freeze, I might take some to Lewei."

Win nods as if this makes perfect sense. When she turns away to choose the most defensible table, Leo makes a face at me, then follows her.

I step up to the tall counter. The front is covered in kitschy magnets from every planet in the Commonwealth, including a couple I have donated over the years. The edges of the plastek counter are curled, and a wide stain marks the center of one section. Behind the counter, Ye'an stands in front of the stove, frying something.

"Do you have your payment?" The big man asks without looking up.

"About that. I'm not in a position to promise a favor at this time."

Ye'an peers at me from under his heavy eyebrows. "That's what the *Księżna* said you'd say. No deal."

"But I can offer a great deal of cash—"

"No deal. One credit and a favor. That's the offer." He scoops some pierogis out of the oil and tosses a couple more in.

"But I'm not just me anymore. I can't promise something that might impact the company."

"I guess you don't want this item then." He shrugs and plates the pierogis, wiping his fingers on his apron. He picks up the platter and moves toward the open end of the counter.

I put a hand on his arm, stopping him. "I will offer a personal favor. Nothing to do with the company."

He looks me over, then pushes past to dump the plate on an occupied table. After a brief conversation with the occupants, he drops three pairs of chopsticks and stomps across the room to the *Księżna*.

Elodie is showing the old woman some vids, and she's cackling like a maniac. After a brief conversation with Ye'an, she holds up a finger at Elodie, who takes a few steps away. Ye'an leans close to exchange a quick whisper with the *Księżna*, then he returns to the kitchen.

"One credit and a personal favor." He holds out his hand. "Last offer. Take it or leave it."

I check over my shoulder, but Vanti is out of sight. Must be checking the bathrooms. Win stands by the door, ostensibly on guard, but she's completely focused on Elodie, who is filming. I pull a credit coin out of my pocket and place it in Ye'an's palm. "Deal."

He reaches into his own pocket and hands me a tiny capsule. "Done."

CHAPTER TWELVE

MONDAY MORNING, Ty, Leo, and I meet Vanti in the Level 82 concourse. She gives me a quick once-over, nodding in approval at my understated but elegant slacks and blouse. "We're taking the corporate cruiser to Lewei. Your luggage has already been stowed."

I haven't travelled in the SK'Corp ship in a long time. When I was younger, Mother took me with her to Sally Ride and Armstrong a couple of times, but since I've returned to the family business, I haven't had the opportunity to use it.

The ship is small and fast. It can carry up to twelve passengers in six nicely appointed staterooms. It's much more expensive than the Pleiades line fast transport we took to Grissom, but Pleiades doesn't fly to Lewei. Plus, as the official representative of Morgan Industries, I have an image to uphold. Taking a commercial ship wouldn't convey the sense of wealth and power we're going for.

The other advantage of taking our own ship is Leo can come along. He doesn't feel safe landing on the planet but doesn't mind riding along if he can stay in orbit on our Commonwealth-flagged ship. This way, I can access his expertise in real-time via ship to dirt comms.

All ships—with the exception of the SK'Corp executive shuttle—dock on Level 40. Long arms extend from the cylindrical station, providing spaces for commercial and private dirtside shuttles, massive interstellar cruise liners and everything in between. We hop on the slideway that takes us to the end of Bravo arm.

The arm is transparent—except for the floor—and provides an amazing view of the ships currently docked, the stars beyond, and a glimpse of Kaku off to the right. Two cruise ships and three cargo haulers hang from the access tubes protruding from the sides of the long terminal. We pass a trickle of tourists returning to their vessel. At the end, we meet an additional layer of security.

I tug O'Neill's arm and point through the plasglas at a pale peach-colored ship with maroon and lime stripes. An arrangement of seven stars decorates the bow, near the passenger embarkation tunnel. "Isn't that the CSS Morningstar?" We sailed on the Morningstar last year when we went to Sally Ride and made friends with some of the crew.

He nods, but his attention is completely focused on his holo-ring. It's a good thing I'm steering him, or he'd run into something.

When we reach the end, I wave my holo-ring at the kiosk, and the two agents snap to attention when they see my identification pop up. "Good morning, Sera Morgan," the taller one says in that fake-cheerful, brown-nosing voice I hate.

To paraphrase my mother, I am Morgan now—I guess I'll have to get used to it.

"Good morning." I step through the gate and wait while the rest of my entourage gets identified and scanned for everything from weapons to spare sticks of gum. I guess they don't worry about anything *I* might be carrying, since I *am* Morgan.

I'm learning to hate that phrase, but sometimes it has advantages.

We board the ship, and the steward flicks a welcome packet to our holo-rings, then shows us to our cabins. Mine is the large forward suite with a bedroom, living room, and conference room with a separate door to the hallway. I take my duffle bag—I insisted on packing and carrying it myself—into the bedroom and dump it on a luggage stand. There's a bureau and closet, but for the six-day trip, I'll probably just live out of the bag.

I wander back into the living room. A small but well-stocked AutoKich'n is built into a cupboard by the door. A large screen fills one wall, with plush furniture grouped around it. I flick my holo-ring and wave it at the screen. The huge stretch of black lights up with the words, "Welcome, Sera Morgan."

I switch the screen to the external cams, so I can pretend it's a window, and move on to the conference room. This boasts another AutoKich'n and a table for twelve. A note in the welcome packet tells me we can eat here or join the crew in the "mess" for meals. In addition to the six suites, there's a tiny gym which acts as a recreation space as well.

A bell chimes. The screen beside the door indicates it's the captain.

"Enter." I flick the welcome package away and turn to face my guest.

A tall woman with black hair and generous proportions enters. "Good morning, Sera Morgan. I am Carol Philpott. Welcome to the *Black Panther*."

"Named after the superhero?"

She laughs loudly. "How did you know?"

"I love *Ancient TēVē*."

"I don't know anything about *Ancient TēVē*, but I was raised on stories of the Black Panther. When this ship was commissioned, and I was installed as the first captain, I asked if I could name him. Most of the corporate ships are just numbers."

"And they said yes?" This doesn't sound like the SK'Corp board to me.

She smirks. "No, but I call him that anyway. No one questions it. Well, almost no one." She waves a graceful hand at me.

My turn to smirk. "I'm probably not your usual passenger. May I meet the rest of the crew?"

"Of course, but they're busy until we launch. Our departure is scheduled in twenty minutes—if that's enough time for you?"

"I'm ready whenever, but I can check with the rest of my team." This earns me a surprised blink. I try not to smirk again, but I love subverting expectations. Top-levs never do anything quickly unless it's to their advantage. "Do we have to strap in or anything?"

"It's always recommended when departing a station but rarely enforced."

"You're good at that."

"Good at what?" she asks blandly.

"Pointing out the stupid habits of top-levs without saying they're stupid."

She laughs again. "My mental health depends on it."

"Feel free to let loose while I'm here."

Her face goes blank. I get a sense she's totaling up scores and making decisions based on criteria I don't understand. She nods graciously, then pauses by the door. "If you would like to come up to the bridge after launch, I'd be happy to introduce you to the crew and show you around the ship, sera."

"Thank you, captain."

Note to self, Triana: SK'Corp employees are not going to be friends with the boss, no matter how charming you are. Good thing I made friends before I became Morgan—otherwise it would be a lonely life.

I wander back into the lounge, thinking about what "being Morgan" means and how lonely my mother must have been all these years. Always representing the family. No one to let loose with. She has Hy-Mi, but as close as he is, he's still an employee, not family. No wonder she clicked with R'ger so fast when he came back into her life. He was the only person who knew her as Imogene, not Morgan.

I flick my holo-ring, sending the launch countdown to my team. "The captain recommends we strap in. Come on up to my cabin if you want to watch the launch on the big screen."

Within a few minutes, Ty, Vanti, and Leo have gathered in my stateroom. The screen shows the tail of a cruise liner parked in the next berth, and the curve of Kaku below us. We're parked perpendicular to the long arm, facing the planet. The station is turning, of course, but it's slow enough that the movement isn't visible. The planet below is in full daylight, with the reddish desert interior of Kaku's main continent filling most of the curve.

Someone knocks on the conference room door. I wave it open without leaving my seat on the couch and call through. "We're in here."

Vanti greets the agents, then turns to me. "Sera Morgan, this is Theodore Young." She indicates a man with brown hair and a goatee. "And Estelle Liandra." She points to the older woman with a square body and gray hair. "They're part of your security detail." She turns back to the newcomers. "Where are Nash and Cris?"

"They're in their cabins," Young says. "We're running a twelve-hour rotation, so they're going to use the trip to adjust to the time change. Shift change will be at ten am local, since that's when we arrive at Lewei."

"We'll hold a team briefing once we're out of Kakuvian space. Tell them not to go to bed yet." Vanti waves at the chairs by the small table. "You can watch from here, if you want."

The two exchange a look, and Liandra responds. "We'll go and unpack. We'll come back to the conference room when you're ready."

"Excellent." She watches them march back out the door. "You'll meet Perseus Nash and Pat Cris later."

"They seem like fun," I say sarcastically as I flick my holo-ring to bring up the in-flight restraint system. It's a function of the artificial gravity, but with its own power system, so it won't go down unexpectedly. Unless that power system fails. I prefer a physical harness when flying, but I guess most top-levs don't want to muss their clothes.

"They aren't supposed to be fun." Vanti pulls a pair of straps from somewhere inside the armchair she's sitting in and buckles them across her lap. "Their job is to protect you, not have a drink with you." She narrows her eyes at Leo and Ty, sitting on either side of me on the couch.

I point my thumbs at the two men. "*Their* job is to have a drink with me. Kind of. Where'd you get that harness?"

"You have to stick your hand through the gap between the cushions. No one ever uses them, so they're hard to find."

Ty pulls a strap out of the couch and hands it to me. "Sec agents always strap in, but we rarely fly in this compartment."

We get our belts sorted and latched, and I twist around so I can lean against O'Neill's side while watching the big screen. Since we're docked on the end of the arm, we won't have to back out—the ship is small enough to push laterally, then turn into the exit corridor. As a countdown in the top right corner approaches zero, the captain's voice comes over the speakers. "All passengers, welcome to the *Black Panther*. We will depart Station Kelly-Kornienko in thirty seconds. Although we anticipate a smooth departure, please engage your restraints. All systems green. Departure in twenty seconds."

When the clock reaches ten, a different voice counts down. She reaches zero, and the clock disappears from the screen. After an interminable pause, the view on the screen begins to rotate. The cruise ship disappears from our view, and the curve of Kaku grows thinner and rises as we angle downward. Soon, we can see only the stars of deep space.

The ship will dive toward the "southern" end of the star, to the jump belt. Once we reach it, the jump beacons will guide the ship's computers to send us to the right location, based on our speed and angle. We'll jump out at the "northern" end of our destination's primary. The longest part of the trip is getting to and from the jump belts. The actual jump takes no time at all.

The captain's voice comes through the speakers again. "We have departed Kakuvian space. Flight to the jump belt will take two point three Kakuvian days. The countdown clock is accessible via channel three." As she speaks, a new countdown appears on the screen. "You are free to move about the ship."

We unlatch our harnesses and tuck them back into the couch cushions. Vanti disappears into the conference room, shutting the door behind her.

I stare at the closed door. "Does she not want us to know what arrangements she's making?"

Ty shakes his head. "You can attend the meeting if you want. You have to remember most top-levs want nothing to do with their security detail. They just want to show up and know they're protected."

I slide my arms around him. "I only care about my security detail if it's you."

Leo clears his throat. "I guess I'm going to go back to my cabin."

I lean back in O'Neill's arms. "I'm going to get a tour of the ship in a bit—if you want to come. Then I guess we should get back to my Leweian culture lessons. Or maybe we deserve some time off."

"Call me for the tour." Leo waves as he exits.

O'Neill's arms tighten around me. "What shall we do in the meantime?"

I grin. "I'm sure we can think of something."

CHAPTER THIRTEEN

"Uн, guys?" Leo's call comes through my audio implant. "Can I show you something?"

It's late evening on our first day out of Kaku. Leo and I got a tour of the ship, then we spent the afternoon playing board games and watching vids. After our week of intensive studying, it was a welcome break. Now we're winding down for the trip to Lewei.

The flight will be long and tedious. The Kaku end is fast, but once we're in Leweian space, we have to comply with Leweian rules. That means our speed is restricted. In addition, the star Lewei orbits is hotter, so Lewei's orbit is larger. Even at top speed, it would take longer to reach the planet. At Leweian speeds, it will take a week.

"What do you want to show us?" I'm in my jammies and ready to do some serious snoozing. "And who's us? Do I need to put real clothes on?"

"Well, you might not want to traipse through the ship naked, but there won't be any celebrities, so wear what you want. Just come to my cabin."

When I reach Leo's cabin, Vanti and O'Neill are already there. Both are fully dressed and look as if they've been staring at holo-screens too long.

I touch Ty's cheek. "You should get some rest."

"Vanti and I noticed a strange anomaly in the security system—we're trying to figure it out." He knocks on Leo's door.

It slides open, and Leo stands in the opening, wearing one of his loose caftans. "Good, you're all here. Look what I found in my cabin tonight." He steps back and points at the bed.

Apawllo blinks at us, then goes back to licking his nether region.

"You brought Elodie's cat?" I stare at the animal, noting the scar on his face and chewed ears. It's definitely Apawllo.

"I didn't bring him. He just showed up."

"We sent him back to Kaku. We have a signed receipt." Vanti flicks her holo-ring, presumably to show us said receipt.

I touch her arm. "I don't think the cat cares about the paperwork—he's clearly here. Besides, Elodie said she got him back. How'd he get on the ship?"

Leo leans close to us, checking over his shoulder to see if the cat is listening. Spoiler—he isn't. "I think he's following me."

I burst out laughing. "Right. The cat bought a ticket on a shuttle to SK2, then snuck aboard this ship because he can't bear to be away from you."

"I don't know why he's here, but I definitely didn't bring him."

O'Neill steps between us. "It doesn't matter why he's here. What matters is how he got on the ship."

"This would explain the anomaly we noticed." Vanti taps her lower lip. "An extra life sign, but smaller—a cat would look like that strange echo rather than a human."

"That doesn't explain how he got aboard." O'Neill looks at the cat. "He seems comfortable here, but if you don't want him, he can stay in my cabin. I like cats." He winks at me. "And dogs."

Leo huffs out a sigh, but a little smile plays at the corners of his mouth. "I guess he can stay here. We can hang out together while you're on the planet."

———

SEVEN DAYS AFTER JUMP, we finally approach the station orbiting Lewei. This station looks old—faded markings, pock marks, singed panels.

I stare at the station on the screen. "It looks dingy. Kind of depressing."

"What would you expect from a Leweian station?" As we've gotten closer to his home planet, Leo has become quieter. Like the station, he looks depressed.

"You really hate it here, don't you?" I ask.

He drums his fingers on the conference room table. We've spent most of the flight going over Leweian customs and courtesies, so I won't accidentally insult anyone. "It's a police state. Why would anyone like it?"

"Yeah, but you were the premier's son. Surely your experience of Lewei was less—" I wave my hands. "Less negative?"

He gives me a level stare. "Why did you run away from SK2? You're as close to royalty as I was."

"Good point. But different reasons. I wanted freedom."

"Me, too."

"And to follow my own dreams…"

"Me, too."

"And an escape from the constant demand for material possessions and power."

"Okay, you got me on that one." Leo snorts as he gets to his feet. "We don't have mass consumerism like you do. We get police brutality and retraining camps instead. Much better."

I hold up both hands. "You win. I'd rather live with conspicuous commercialism than either of those things."

We put away our files and meet Vanti and Ty in the lounge for the arrival.

"What have you been working on?" I ask Ty as I strap in next to him.

"More of the same. Reviewing maps, looking at agent reports, analyzing the news—such as it is. The Leweian government keeps a pretty tight lock on information. Most citizens have no idea what's going on in their own city, much less the rest of the planet. Except on Luna. We'll visit there before we leave. It seems to be a little more relaxed than Lewei."

We watch as the ship closes on the station. It's huge—bigger than SK2 and kind of junky looking. In fact, it resembles the house next door to Sierra Hotel—an estate owned by the Leweian government. The mansion there has so many additions tacked on, it looks like a child's toy. This station has the same hodge-podge appearance. And although it looks neglected and dingy, a swarm of ships constantly moves around it. The *Black Panther* slows, still well beyond the traffic pattern.

"This is the captain. Lewei Station requires tractor beam docking, so I am relinquishing controls to them. I highly recommend you strap in. They aren't known for being gentle."

I tighten my belt, and the others do the same. "Good thing Mother sent me."

Vanti nods. "Your lower-lev mentality could be useful on this venture."

"Was that a compliment?"

"More a statement of fact." Her lips twitch—the biggest smile I've seen since we started this trip.

The ship jerks as if some giant has just grabbed us. For a while, nothing seems to happen, then the station grows to fill more of the screen. As we approach, it becomes obvious many of those smaller ships are repair skiffs. Everything seems to be under construction.

"Is that because they're adding on or because everything is broken?" I ask.

"Broken and repaired in a sub-standard fashion." Leo shakes his head, his voice subdued. "Slap a patch on it and call it good. No one ever addresses the larger underlying problems."

Our speed continues to increase, the station growing larger and larger until we can see only part of the spiderweb mishmash of modules and connecting tubes.

With a jerk, we change directions, all of us thrown against our restraints. A forgotten coffee mug slides across the table and crashes to the floor. Luckily, it's plastek, so it doesn't shatter. The view on screen swings around to a docking arm, and we decelerate rapidly. We lurch forward, then our artificial gravity catches up, and the ride smooths.

"I don't think the ship's gravity was built for this kind of abuse," Ty mutters.

"Most Leweian ships don't have artificial gravity, so the station doesn't care," Leo says.

"They don't have it?" I turn to him in shock. "You mean they fly interplanetary trips in free-fall?"

Leo shakes his head. "The interstellar ships have gravity. Or they use thrust to create gravity. But you forget—most of these ships never leave this planet's orbit. They'll fly to the station or Luna, but that's it. And you don't need gravity for that."

The ship shudders as we seem to ram into the docking arm. Captain Philpott announces our arrival and, before she turns off the comms, mutters something about never flying here again.

"I guess it's a good thing most of the business can be done virtually after this." I unlatch my belt and stand. "How long do we have?"

"We have thirty minutes to debark, then Philpott needs to vacate the berth. You're ready, right?"

I nod. "I didn't really unpack. I assume someone will unload the cases in the cargo hold?"

"The crew has probably already moved it to the air lock. One last check—if you need it—and let's go."

Ty and Vanti head to their cabins for a last look. I peek into the bedroom and bath while Leo checks the conference room.

He meets me in the lounge. "Looks clear."

"Thanks for coming along. I hope you aren't too bored up here." I give him a swift hug.

"Better up here than down there." He squeezes me and releases.

"See you in a few days. Feel free to use the lounge while we're gone." I shoulder my duffle bag and point to the cupboard by the door. "I left you some chocolate."

He grins. "You know I don't eat that stuff! It's not on my surf-season meal plan."

I shake my head in despair. "You won't be surfing for the next two weeks, so I think you can cheat a bit." Not eating chocolate is an abomination. I will break him of that depressing habit. Or maybe the stress of this trip will.

I meet Ty and my security team in the airlock. Captain Philpott stands by the hatch. "I don't like this station, and I don't like leaving you here. I've heard nothing but bad about Lewei."

"You've never been here before?" I ask.

She shakes her head. "This is kind of a big deal. Commonwealth citizens are not normally welcome." She beckons Vanti and O'Neill closer. "This ship is built to launch from the dirt, so if you get into trouble, I will come get you. It would probably make you *personae non grata*, but at least you'd get out alive."

Vanti gives a jerky nod. "Noted. Thank you, Captain. See you in a few days. Team, translators on."

"If the ship can land, why did we stop here?" I whisper to Ty as I activate the Lewei-Standard translator downloaded to my holo-ring.

"The Leweian government controls access to the planet through this station. They don't want visitors landing. Plus, if they don't know we can land, that gives us the upper hand if we need it. Which we won't." He glances at the captain. "I think she's being a bit pessimistic. I would have recommended against this trip if I believed it was dangerous for you."

He might have tried to veto the trip, but what the Ice Dame wants, the Ice Dame gets.

The captain hits the controls next to the hatch, and the internal door shuts behind us, sealing us into the airlock. Then the hatch to the station opens with a hiss. "Safe travels."

Vanti knocks her knuckles against the captain's and steps into the station. O'Neill and I follow, with my security team arrayed around me.

CHAPTER FOURTEEN

A SHORT, opaque tunnel ends with another airlock. We cycle through and step onto the cold metal plates of the docking arm. Stale air wafts over us, carrying a whiff of fuel, lubricant, and old sweat socks. Unlike SK2, this terminal doesn't have a scenic view. The gray metal of the floor extends overhead in a low arch. Small windows puncture the wall at regular intervals, but most of them are scratched and blurry. If they have a space junk repelling system like SK2, it must let the finer stuff pass through.

Or maybe they need to wash the inside, a voice in my head whispers. The space janitor still lives there.

As the other passengers notice my security detail, they dart out of the way, clearing a path for us. Even on SK2, where top-levs are treated like royalty, we don't see this level of deference. In fact, it looks more like fear.

Vanti leads the way, with my team around me. Young pulls a wheeled vehicle piled high with our luggage. Back home, that would have been unloaded to the cargo deck and delivered to our hotel.

We stop at the end of the arm, where a security team blocks the way. Each passenger empties their pockets and sends their luggage into a dark tunnel. The people are scanned with a hand-held wand, then walk through a lighted gate. They stop in the middle on a small platform that pivots in a full circle as they raise their arms. An elderly man in the machine loses his balance and falls, catching himself on the gate. The guard lunges forward, yelling unintelligibly.

I reach out and grab O'Neill's hand. His warm fingers close around mine, reassuring and strong. As we approach, the people in line step out of the way, allowing us to move ahead of them.

"It's okay," I say to a woman. "We can wait our turn."

Vanti glares over her shoulder at me and mouths, "Morgan."

Oh, yeah. I'm supposed to be the Ice Dame. I lift my nose and push past the woman I just smiled at, feeling like a jerk.

Young starts loading our luggage onto the conveyer belt while O'Neill and Vanti empty their pockets. The woman supervising stares at the pile of items Vanti deposits into the little bin, her eyes going to Vanti's sleek uniform with each new addition. I know exactly how she feels—Vanti should look like a lumpy sausage with all the gear she's carrying, but not a single bulge protrudes.

The Leweian woman picks up a folded knife. "This will be confiscated."

Vanti flicks her holo-ring and swipes the file toward the woman.

The Leweian steps back in alarm, hands coming up in a defensive position.

"The Lewei government has granted my team certain liberties, including our weapons. We've only brought what they approved. It's all in the file." Vanti raises an eyebrow that clearly says, "Your move."

"What file?" The woman puts her hands on her hips and glares.

Vanti's lips press together. "I just sent you a file, but I guess our tech is incompatible. There should be a representative meeting us here to clear all of this." She opens the file and shows the holo-gram to the woman.

Her eyes widen at the ghostly screen floating over Vanti's palm. "That is—"

"So cool!" a young man behind me exclaims.

The woman glares. "I do not have an authenticated copy of this order, so I cannot comply with it. My procedures require me to confiscate any items on the forbidden list." She taps a sign on the wall beside her station.

Vanti consults her file. "Can you call Ser Randolph T'ien? He's supposed to be here to escort us through this mess."

The woman doesn't budge. "No one is allowed back here but terminal security. Your party will meet you at the main concourse."

I tap Vanti's arm. "Maybe you can send the offending articles back to the ship, and we can get them delivered later?"

She turns her glare on me instead of the security guard. "I need my weapons. My job is to protect you."

"We both know you don't need a little folding knife to do that." I give her a nudge with my elbow. "You are the weapon."

Vanti's glare wavers for a second, then she turns back to the guard. "This isn't over." She swings around and points at Nash. "Take everything she rejects back to the ship and meet us inside. Snap to it! Our docking slot is gone in eleven minutes."

The man leaps forward to sort through the items in the bin.

While they work on that, I move to the next station. Being Morgan means I don't have to carry anything myself. Oh, who am I kidding? I can't carry anything in this outfit—some genius made it without pockets. I need to find out where Vanti does her shopping.

A woman with a wand approaches me and asks me to raise my arms. I comply, smirking a little as I think how my mother would have responded to this indignity. She'd probably be stewing in the ship, paying overage fees for taking up a berth beyond the thirty-minute slot, and refusing to move until this Randolph T'ien showed up.

We get through the gauntlet, which dumps us into a huge open space. Like the concourses on SK2, this one has shops around the perimeter and float tubes at strategic locations. Unlike SK2, the ceiling is low, and the center of the area is full of stalls and tents, similar to the markets on Armstrong. The noise is deafening and the smells overwhelming—sharp spices, cloying florals, the faint fishy odor of *terkfiske*, and a metallic, mechanical smell, all fighting with a steamy haze of grilling meat and caramelizing onions.

"They're cooking, right in the middle of the station." Vanti stares at the tents in amazement. "That's a huge safety issue."

"Depends on how they're cooking." O'Neill takes my hand again, now that we're through security. "Induction grills are safe."

"I see flames over there." Vanti nods at the jumble of people and tents thronging the room.

He puts a hand on her shoulder and juts his chin across the concourse as he speaks. "Emergency egress pods are there, there, and there. Let's just stay focused on the mission and leave the local customs alone."

Vanti flushes—something I didn't know she even did. She shakes off Ty's hand and squares her shoulders. "Right. Where's that escort?"

A slender man with dark hair, pale skin, and gray eyes approaches, bowing slightly. "I am Randolph T'ien. You must be the SK'Corp team. Welcome to Lewei station."

Vanti steps between me and T'ien. "This is Sera Morgan. I'm Vanti, chief of her security. Your rent-a-cops back there tried to confiscate our equipment."

"Rent-a-cops?" T'ien's face doesn't change, but he bows again. "You mean the terminal security team? My apologies for any inconvenience. I know you had an official exemption. I shall see that they are punished."

"I don't want anyone punished." I step forward, angling next to Vanti.

"They were just doing their jobs. But you might want to figure out why they didn't get the memo."

Vanti steps between me and T'ien again. "And I want my team's gear. We sent our personal items back to the ship, but they confiscated my weapons case." She waves at the cart beside Cris. The stack of luggage looks as big as it did before, but if Vanti says something is missing, it's missing.

T'ien bows again and taps the device strapped to his wrist. "I will open an investigation immediately."

"What is that?" I point at the wrist-device. A wide strap secures a rectangle to his arm. It's about four centimeters wide, six long, and thicker than looks comfortable.

"It's my NexUs Cuff or NCuff. It's a communications device that allows me access to the NexUs—our information mesh. I believe it's similar in function to your holo-rings." He holds out his arm, so I can inspect the device.

Words scroll across the screen, tiny but legible. It might be similar in function, but if files can only be displayed on that miniscule screen, I'll stick with my ring. "How convenient. May we connect to your NexUs?"

T'ien's face remains impassive. "I will look into it."

That means no, then.

My audio implant pings, and Vanti's voice comes. "We need to remain in direct contact range at all times. No one gets more than two klicks away from Runner."

The security team all murmur agreement. I seethe. I still haven't mastered talking through my audio implant without moving my lips or being audible, and T'ien is standing less than a meter away.

And I can't believe they're still calling me *Runner*.

"If you're ready, Lady Morgan, I'll escort you to the deorbiting shuttle." T'ien sweeps his arm to the right to indicate direction.

"Thanks, let's do it."

His eyebrows twitch, as if he wants to comment on my slang but won't. I silently rejoice that I provoked a reaction.

As we walk, T'ien launches into a history lesson about the great Leweian Empire. I let the monologue wash over me—it's almost word-for-word what Leo told me over the last few days. Instead, I focus on the new sights around me.

We leave the concourse and step into another gray tunnel. A steady stream of people pass by on our left, as if the tunnel is divided into lanes for pedestrians. There are no markings visible, but no one strays across the center.

They wear subdued colors, in only three or four different styles—a hip-length tunic with slim-fitting pants, a wider, knee-length tunic or dress with pants, a button-down shirt tucked into wide trousers, and on the young, shorts with a T-shirt. Different collars provide a touch of variety, but otherwise, the clothing is bland and unoriginal.

The people's faces are also uniform—downcast eyes, mouths drooping at the corners, gray and hopeless. A group of teens thunder past, moving quickly and talking in low voices. They've decorated their clothing with bright color splotches, but only one of them cracks a tiny smile when he meets my eyes.

Fun place.

We leave this tunnel for another, narrower one, then move into a second concourse.

I interrupt T'ien's monologue. "Why is the shuttle to the surface so far from the dock?"

His eyes flicker with annoyance. "There are shuttles to the surface from many different locations on this station."

"So why didn't we take a closer one?"

"This is the shuttle used for out-system guests." His eyes flick over me, as if assessing my wardrobe—and my intrinsic worth. "It's the nicest."

O'Neill chimes in over the audio. "They don't want interstellar visitors to have easy access to the planet."

T'ien holds up a hand as we approach a gate guarded by a sour-faced woman. "Let me make sure they're ready for you."

The two hold a low-voiced discussion, then T'ien returns to us. "Just a few more minutes. Would you like something to eat?" His arm sweeps outward.

This concourse is as cluttered with tents and stalls as the first one. The smell leans more sweet than savory here. The clientele appear to be better dressed—I see nicer-looking fabrics and fewer frayed seams, although everyone still wears the same basic styles.

My stomach growls in response to his offer, but the sound is covered by the rumble of conversation. I open my mouth, but Vanti beats me to the punch. "We're fine. We ate before we left the ship."

Normally, I'd tell her to speak for herself and get one of those gooey-looking rolls, but this is foreign territory. Maybe there are things I shouldn't eat here. Besides, I don't think I have any form of currency. I left my Commonwealth credits on the ship since I don't want to go to prison. I make a mental note to ask Vanti about some cash.

We stand in an awkward huddle, with my security team scaring off anyone who would dare to approach. Not that anyone looks even mildly interested in us. We stand in a little island of empty space while the locals ebb and flow around us, none of them approaching the gate. If anyone was thinking of taking this shuttle to the planet, they've given up and headed off to find another.

T'ien launches into part two of his history lesson, but I wave him off. "Tell me about Luna."

He freezes for an instant, then recovers. "What would you like to know?"

"I've heard it's a semi-autonomous district?" Leo warned me this question could provoke a number of responses, and I feel like poking the beast.

"That's a common misconception. Luna is a province within Lewei, just like Chengdu, Belgistan, and Sheffield. It just happens to exist on the moon rather than the planet."

I hide a smile—T'ien is spouting the party line as Leo predicted. According to Leo, the reality is a little less cut and dried. Luna, which is made up of several domed cities, gives its citizens a bit more freedom than the rest of the planet enjoys.

T'ien makes another sweeping gesture. "They're ready for us."

We troop to the security gate. It scans us as we pass through the two-meter-long structure, which leads to a small lounge. Rows of ugly black plastek chairs divided by a wide corridor fill the space. The small windows are as blurry here as the terminal where we docked. We file between the chairs and follow T'ien through a doorway and into an airlock. The Leweian closes the hatch behind us and cycles the system. The far door opens, and we move into a utilitarian shuttle. It looks almost identical to the waiting room, with black plastek seats in two rows and tiny, blurry windows.

"Take any seat you like—we're the only passengers on this trip." T'ien strides the length of the craft, then knocks on a door. When this opens, I catch a glimpse of the pilots' compartment.

"We sit backwards in this thing?" I take a seat near the door and fumble for my seat restraints. The frayed straps hang over my shoulders and latch with a tarnished buckle. "At least they have real seatbelts. Five-point harnesses seem like overkill for a drop to the dirt, though."

"They don't have artificial gravity on these, remember?" O'Neill sits next to me and buckles in. "As for the backwards seats—maybe it makes the G forces easier on the passengers?"

"Have you seen anything so far that looks like it was done to be easier on the general population?"

He puts a finger to his lips, and his eyes travel to the overhead and down the walls. Good point—Leo said we should assume every word was being monitored and recorded. I wish again I'd mastered our sub-vocal comms because they're encrypted. I keep trying, and the skill keeps eluding me.

I thread my fingers through Ty's and lean against his arm for comfort. This place is cold, strange, and a little bit scary. He slides an arm around my shoulders and squeezes in wordless comfort.

CHAPTER FIFTEEN

WE RIDE IN A BUBBLE—WHICH they call "autos" here, but I like bubble better—through a busy city. I try to follow our progress on the static map I'd downloaded before we left the *Black Panther*, but I'm too accustomed to an app that does it for me. The hotel appears to be centrally located—if we are where I think we are.

The city is huge and unbelievably crowded. Even New Sydney, the largest city on Sally Ride, doesn't have this many people. Tall buildings seem to brush the sky, their sides brilliantly reflecting the other buildings around them. Our bubble zips through town on a series of bridges strung along the buildings. From a distance, they look like a fragile network of gleaming ribbons hanging from glass prisms.

Below, people throng the wide streets in a monotonous but ever-changing sea of muted colors. They move in and out of the buildings and down stairways and float tubes to what I presume is a subway system. Sunlight peeks between the high buildings, flooding streets with warmth in the few places it reaches the ground.

The bubble takes a side bridge and heads directly for the side of one of the massive, glittering structures. Before we smash to our doom, a door slides open, and we glide inside. The bubble slows, and the door shuts behind us, leaving us in a lighted tunnel. The walls are unadorned gray tile.

Before I can comment, the bubble slides out into a long, tall room with floor-to-ceiling windows on our right. Sunshine beats down onto the shining floor that stretches to a high desk on the left. Intricate glasswork in gemstone colors makes it appear we've arrived in a kaleidoscope. We glide to a halt behind another vehicle, and the door opens.

T'ien steps out of the bubble and sweeps his arm again. "Welcome to the Zhengzu-Maryought Hotel. If you'll follow me, I'll expedite your reception."

Vanti exits the vehicle, her head on a swivel as she assesses the location. A scattering of people wander the long lobby, most of them moving from the bubbles ahead of us toward the desk. She points at Young. "You're with Runner. The rest of you, unload the bubble. Triana, exit the vehicle."

I grimace at Ty as I follow directions, stepping into the brilliant sunlight. He moves to my right side, taking my hand in his. He always walks on my right in uncertain circumstances—since he's right-handed, this leaves his dominant hand free in case of attack. Vanti closes in on my left, and Young falls in behind. I don't bother looking—I can hear his shoes clacking on the polished floor. Plus, it's not my job to keep track of him. I'm supposed to look aloof and unconcerned.

T'ien announces my name to the perfectly coifed woman behind the counter. She nods and bows, then produces one of the wrist devices. "This NexUs Cuff will provide you with communications and function as your room key, Lady Morgan. Please press your thumb against the screen to activate it."

I stick my thumb on the thing, leaving a smudge on the screen. "Does my whole team get these?" I stretch the band and slide it over my left hand.

"Of course." She passes a handful of the devices to T'ien who distributes them to the others. "You're on the eighty-seventh floor. The drop chute is to your left—the second one is an express to the upper floors. The Ncuff will guide you to your room. If you require anything, press the red service icon, and a staff member will assist you. Thank you for staying at the Zhengzu-Maryought."

A small army of uniformed attendants have shouldered the agents out of the way to unload our luggage. Liandra attempts to pull a case from the grasp of one of the hotel staff, and a tug-of-war ensues. While Vanti breaks up the fight—Liandra takes possession—T'ien leads the rest of us toward the float tubes—or drop chutes, as the locals call them.

We step out on the eighty-seventh floor and follow T'ien to the suite. It looks almost identical to every high-end hotel suite I've ever visited, with a shared living room and multiple bedrooms with en suite baths. This suite has four rooms, with an adjoining 2-room suite accessible through a small hallway on the left. Tasteful art hangs everywhere, with heavy drapes pulled across the entire far wall.

Vanti checks all the rooms, then assigns me the front right. "It has a real window, which could be a security issue, but we're probably safe up here. We'll set an alarm on the glass."

T'ien glances up from the fruit basket he's rearranging. "The windows are made of triple-pane indestructible plasglas and are locked from the inside. There's also a force screen to keep out bugs. And larger pests."

Vanti nods. "The back room has a virtual window with the same view, but the shared wall with the hallway is a higher security risk. Griz, you'll take that one. I'll take the back room on the other side." She turns to the other agents and points at the hallway. "The four of you can bunk in the other suite. We'll use that living room as our command center and the empty bedroom—" She breaks off as she glances at T'ien who's now fussing with the flowers beside the AutoKich'n. "Cris is senior, so she can have it."

I smile at T'ien. "Thank you for your help. Will we see you again?"

"I am at your disposal for your entire visit. If you'd like to rest, I'll return this afternoon to escort you to tonight's dinner." A worried frown crosses his face. It's a good piece of acting, but his previous impervious blandness makes me doubt the sincerity. "It would be best if you stay within the suite until that time. There have been some..." he makes a small moue of distaste, "minor disturbances in recent days."

I widen my eyes at him. "Disturbances? Is it dangerous?"

"Mere inconvenience, but we don't want our honored guest subjected to that. Please, remain here, and I'll return to escort you later." He bows and marches out the door. It clicks loudly behind him, but I'm not sure if it's just the latch or he's locked us in.

I turn to the others, but Vanti lays a finger to her lips. "You look tired, Sera. Perhaps a nap before lunch would be in your best interest. Let me show you to your room." She pulls a device from one of those invisible pockets and flicks her holo-ring as she walks. I follow her into the front bedroom.

The view is spectacular. Our hotel is one of the taller structures, and we're near the top. The drapes have been pulled back, and the city stretches out before us. The bubble bridges gleam in the sun, twisting through the skyscrapers like ribbons of light. Lesser buildings range around us, like minions protecting their master. In the distance, at the edge of the sprawling city, the sea gleams greenish blue.

"Sunset will be fantastic from here." As I speak, Vanti moves around the room, waving her device and stabbing icons on her holo.

"Why don't you tell me what you'd like for lunch, then take a nap?" She moves into the bathroom and out again. "Take your shoes off, relax."

With a shrug, I sit on the bed and pull off my flats. I'm not taking a nap until I know what's going on, though, so I follow her back into the living room.

The door chimes, and a soft voice announces, "Your luggage has arrived."

Vanti tucks her device away and make shooing motions at me. I retreat to the bedroom, leaving the door ajar, so I can peer through the crack. The army of hotel employees troops in with our luggage. They move soundlessly, depositing cases and bags in response to Vanti's whispered directions. Mine are piled outside the door—probably to maintain the fiction that I'm napping.

When they've left, she swings the bedroom door wide and holds a finger to her lips. The other four agents swarm over the cases, each of them waving tiny devices. They open the bags and remove the clothing, scanning each item as well as the insides of the bags.

Nash clears his throat. "I wonder if we can view the Rangers versus Nebulas game?" He pulls the lining away from the inside of the bag and removes a small item. He raises the tiny circular device so we can all see it, then gingerly sets it on the counter.

Liandra moves to the counter and flicks open her holo-ring. The others continue the discussion about the game—I think it's la grosse. Or maybe field golf. A new team is mentioned each time an agent finds a device in the luggage. When they've completed their scan, they replace the devices and stack the cases in a corner of the room, with the smaller bags inside the larger ones.

Liandra nods. "We're clear. I've set up an AI-guided program sending a false audio signal to their surveillance system."

"We have those? How have I not heard of them before?" I plop onto the couch next to O'Neill. "And how did you get those scanner things through security?"

Vanti tosses one into my lap. It looks like a hair ornament. She takes it back and shows me how to activate it. "Most of them came through in your toiletries case. The plain one was in my hair."

"Uh, guys?" Cris stands by one of the larger hard-sided cases. The open top hides the contents from the rest of us.

The others look up at the strained note in her voice. "What is it? Did someone compromise our gear?"

Cris pulls at a strand of her hot pink hair, then reaches into the case. "Did someone pack a cat?"

CHAPTER SIXTEEN

WE ALL STARE at the fur draped over Cris's arm. Apawllo droops, like a ragdoll in a child's arms. His eyes are half-closed, and he's purring.

"What the—" Vanti glares at the other agents. "Is this some kind of prank? Some planets levy heavy fines for bringing in animals—here on Lewei, they'd probably throw us in Xinjianestan! Who did this?"

"And why didn't Leweian security find him? Surely their system scans for life signs?" O'Neill shoves his hand through his thick hair. "And those cases are airtight. I can't believe he didn't suffocate!"

No one has an answer.

"I guess we'd better let Leo know—so he isn't searching the ship for the cat." Vanti stalks toward the empty bedroom.

Cris follows her, carrying her pile of clothing. "I'm sleeping in here? Why did you say I'm senior?"

Vanti shakes her head. "Remember, they're listening to everything—or trying to. I told them you're in charge so they wouldn't know Nash is senior. Misdirection. And no, you aren't bunking in there. That's going to be our communications room."

While Vanti and her team set up their gear, O'Neill and I check out the entertainment system. The large windows in the lounge become a huge vid screen at the flick of a button—much like the window in O'Neill's old compartment on SK2.

I run a sweep of the decades-old gear with the security device Vanti gave me. "It's clean." The hand-held control remote is a thin, rectangle with a touchscreen interface. "Their technology is about a generation behind ours." At home, I can control virtually anything on the station with my ring.

"Their *affordable* tech is a generation behind ours." O'Neill takes the small, boxy thing and taps the screen. "Their government—and the ultra-wealthy who do business with the Commonwealth—are likely to have more advanced stuff. From what I've read, they've 'borrowed' almost everything we have."

If this hotel—which clearly caters to the wealthy—doesn't have the more advanced tech, then who does?

I lean back and close my eyes. Most of the "entertainment" we've paged through has a heavy cultural indoctrination component. An app on my holo-ring also indicates a low level of subliminal programming. I can run a filter, if there's anything worth watching, but at this point, it seems to be mostly morality plays and sports.

My audio implant chimes with O'Neill's ringtone. "It's safest not to talk about anything important outside the communications room. The crew has scanned the suite, but we could have missed something. In there, they'll have real-time scanning and jamming. And try not to be too negative about the local government. They're a bit touchy."

"Leo told me." I say the words as quietly as I can, but O'Neill narrows his eyes at me.

"Don't use his name."

My fists clench in irritation. I need something I can write on—but that would leave a record...I pull up my holo-ring message system and send him a text: *It's not his real name. And I don't know any of your secret code names except my own. Which reminds me—could we please change it to something less insulting?*

"Yes, ma'am." He kisses my cheek and stands. "I'll talk to Vanti. Why don't you take that nap?"

Is he brushing me off? Trying to get me out of the way like a typical top-lev, so he can get in on the fun with the other agents?

I'm not tired.

Even texted, it sounds like a petulant child, but I don't care. I'm the boss—these people all work for me. And I want to know what's going on. I get up and stalk to the bedroom opposite mine.

As I reach for the doorknob, O'Neill's hand closes over mine. "Wait—we don't want to open the door if they're in the middle of a sensitive conversation." He taps the wood with one knuckle.

The door swings open, and Vanti motions O'Neill inside. When her eyes hit me, something crosses her face, but the emotion is banished so fast, I don't get a good read. Is she happy I'm taking an interest or mad I'm getting in the way?

Knowing Vanti, it's probably both.

But I'm not going to let her exclude me. I push past her and step inside.

The room has been transformed. Tables loaded with equipment stand along either side of the bed. A series of holo-screens show the inside of our suites from every angle—when did they install those cameras?

"Where did all of this come from? They checked our luggage." I stare at the holo-projectors and tiny boxes with blinking lights.

"The cameras are theirs." Vanti points at the different views of the living room, the bedrooms, even the baths. "We've tapped into their system, and we can add feeds to hide our activities. But most of the time, it's easier—and less detectable—to just leave their gear running."

"I don't want them watching me shower!" I glance at the other agents carefully avoiding my gaze. "I don't want you watching me shower, either!"

Vanti chuckles. "Our AI will run a loop when you're in the bathroom. The Ice Dame insists on it when we travel. We have an avatar. Young, show her."

Young flicks his ring, and the closest screen changes to one of the bathrooms. I stare, amazed, as I walk in. When I start taking off my clothes, I wave both hands at Young.

"Turn it off! That's not any better than watching me—it is me!"

"I assure you, it isn't." Young watches the screen. Other me has turned her back to the cam, and she's standing in a position that is visible from the waist up. She wraps the towel around her body, then turns and steps into the shower, keeping most of the important bits hidden. She disappears behind the tiled wall, leaving the towel hanging on a hook.

"And you're telling me there isn't another cam in that bathroom? I can't believe our hypervigilant hosts would leave me any privacy."

Young eyes me silently for a second, then turns to Vanti.

Vanti nods. "Show her."

He flicks his ring, and the view switches. The outline of a woman showering is vaguely visible through a thick fog. "It was tricky, but we figured it out. We have the avatar run the shower for a few minutes before getting in, which makes the fog believable."

"We have tech that could see through that fog." I cross my arms and stare at Young.

"We do, but we don't believe they do." He shrugs. "It's the best we can do."

"What happens if they have that tech?"

"They'll see an avatar of you showering." Young blanches under my intense glare. "It's the best we can do. It's not really you."

I try to hide my elation at the success of my death glare. I've gotten so used to Vanti ignoring my crankiness—it's nice to know the Ice Dame attitude will work on Young. Although he's probably afraid he'll lose his job, so it's not very nice. "It just looks like me. Exactly like me." I squint through the fog. "But with bigger boobs?"

Vanti laughs. "The avatar was made from your last medical scan—it's exactly like you."

I glance at O'Neill. His face has gone a bit pink, and he's studiously avoiding my gaze—which is tough considering the size of the room.

"I guess if we don't want them to know what we're doing, it's the best we can do." I turn to Vanti. "You never told me where all this gear came from. They confiscated our stuff."

Her lips quirk into her famous not-smile. "We let them find all that tech so they wouldn't find the real stuff. It was concealed between the layers of the suitcases."

"The cases they searched and hid bugs inside?" I ask.

"Those exact ones. The trick to hiding stuff is making sure they find something—then they'll give up looking. They found our obvious equipment—and sent it back to the ship. They also found our "hidden" gear when they placed the bugs. That stuff is set to self-destruct if anyone tries to activate it or take it apart. Not in a fire and explosions way but data-burn. The real stuff was hidden deeper. And some of it came on our bodies."

"But you took all your weapons and things out at the scan." I had watched her—and marveled at the number of devices she had hidden on her body.

"That was the obvious stuff. I always have more. It's standard procedure." She turns to the team. "Who here has a weapon?"

All of them—even O'Neill—raise a hand.

Vanti pats my arm. "It's our job to keep you safe, and we take it very seriously."

CHAPTER SEVENTEEN

VANTI and her crew continue tweaking their system. O'Neill begins working on a report. I decide to take a nap, just like Avatar-Me. Who knew being Morgan could be so exhausting? Or so boring.

In my last stint as the family representative—the Families Meeting on Sally Ride—I ran away after two days. That's probably where I'd gotten my embarrassing callsign. O'Neill had brought me back—and likely saved me from a grisly death at the hands of a serial killer. Then Vanti and I had gone AWOL in a cupcake truck.

So much more fun than this.

When the door chimes, I'm dressed and ready for anything. Without Hy-Mi's Dress Success app to guide me, I'd picked comfortable but classy slacks and a light tunic.

Vanti gives me the once over. Her eyes flick over my hair and clothing, then she nods. "It will have to do."

"Maybe you can review my wardrobe later?" I ask hopefully. "Without Hy-Mi to set it up, I didn't know what worked with which."

She tries to hide her excitement behind a jerky nod and waves the door open. Vanti has a surprising love of fashion.

T'ien doesn't attempt to enter the room but bows from the hallway. "Good evening, Lady Morgan. May I escort you to dinner?"

I wait for Vanti to check the hallway, then step out to join them. "Of course. I confess, I haven't looked at my schedule—are we meeting anyone from Xiughen tonight?"

Vanti answers before T'ien can. "No, tonight is scheduled for recuperation from the journey. Your first meeting is tomorrow morning."

T'ien's jaw tightens as if he's suppressing a smirk. He probably finds it amusing that Commonwealth top-levs require so much recovery time after a seven-day cruise aboard a luxuriously appointed ship. Not that he's seen the ship, but I'm sure he can imagine.

"Where are we going?" I ask T'ien.

"The hotel has a very nice restaurant." He stops at the drop chute. "You'll have the opportunity to see more of the city tomorrow, so I thought we'd stay here for tonight."

I glance at Vanti. She'd said our movements would be carefully monitored and controlled. Keeping us in the building makes that easier. Time to test the limits. "I'd like to take a walk outside after dinner."

"I'm sure that can be arranged." T'ien's eyes flick to the top of the drop chute—as if he's making eye contact with a hidden cam.

I resist the urge to glance at Vanti again and step into the chute.

We emerge and cross the huge lobby where we checked in. T'ien leads us to a dim, cavern-like corner where Leweian letters spell out a name over a red-lit doorway. I flick my holo-ring and bring up my visual translator. Apparently, we are eating at the Delicious Foods Café.

A man standing behind a small podium welcomes T'ien and takes us through an empty dining room. Crisp white tablecloths cover every table. The carpet underfoot is thick and woven in a colorful pattern of whirls and dots. The plush chairs match the carpet. The host shows us to a large table in the center of the room, claps his hands to summon a waiter, and departs.

Vanti details Nash and Liandra to take places by the kitchen and front door. The other two agents must have stayed in the room—I wasn't paying attention. Vanti, O'Neill, and I sit, and T'ien orders wine and meal "number seven."

Dinner is unimpressive. We could have gotten better food from the Auto-Kich'n in just about any college dorm room. According to T'ien, the kitchen staff went to great lengths to prepare a "standard Commonwealth meal" of hamburgers with barbeque sauce and fried chicken. The side dishes—a very wet cabbage salad and some square noodles with cheese sauce—are equally poor. I almost wish they'd served us *terkfiske* instead. One could expect them to know how to make that properly.

I eat a few bites of each, trying to suppress my gag reflex. After a long gulp of water, I turn to T'ien. "I imagine this style of food isn't common here. Where did your chefs study?"

T'ien launches into a long monologue about the most impressive state-run culinary schools and the breadth of knowledge the Zhengzu-Maryought chefs have gained by serving previous visitors from outside Lewei space.

I smile politely and try to focus on his voice instead of the unappetizing food.

When he offers to order dessert, I decline. "I would like to go for a walk, however. You don't need to escort me—my security detail will—"

He interrupts before I can finish the thought. "I would be happy to show you around my city. But it's so much better to first experience Lewei City during the day. Perhaps we can save the sightseeing for morning?"

"Yes, of course. But I just want a quick walk around the block—you know, some fresh air." I stand and move toward the exit. My team closes in around me.

We exit the still-empty restaurant and stride across the highly polished lobby floor. A pair of bubbles sit empty in the shallow trough beside the windows. I stop, turning on my heel. "How do we get out of here?"

"Drop chutes. We're on the tenth floor." Vanti points at the lifts.

T'ien leaps in front of me. "Please, Lady Morgan. I highly recommend you wait until tomorrow to go outside. There's nothing to see right now."

I pivot and stare out the windows. The bright lights of the city sparkle around us, the occasional passing bubble shining bright stripes across the gleaming glass.

"It's beautiful. I just want to—"

"Please—" T'ien is breathless, and a faint sheen of sweat glistens on his brow. Why is he so nervous? Will something bad happen to him if I get out? I've heard the Leweian government can be ruthless with their employees.

I relent. "Never mind. I can see it all tomorrow. What time will you meet us?"

T'ien swallows hard and bows to me. "Please, allow me to see you back to your suite." He holds out an arm toward the drop chutes.

"Of course." I precede him to the chutes and up to my room. At the door, I cut off his obsequious nonsense. "Good night." I turn and leave him in the hallway. Safely caged in my suite for the night. I hope he doesn't have to sleep in the corridor to make sure I don't sneak out.

THE NEXT MORNING, T'ien arrives at eight-thirty, accompanied by a team of six. "They are here to provide escort for your team. Lewei City is vast and easy to get lost in. We will make sure you don't." Each member of my team is assigned an escort.

"Liandra and Nash will stay here today," Vanti tells him when it's obvious we're a few agents short. "Liandra isn't feeling well—maybe the unusual food." She doesn't look at T'ien as she says this. "Nash will look after her." And the cat.

When we reach the lobby, the extra escorts disappear—probably to the hotel's surveillance center to keep an eye on Liandra and Nash. The rest of us take a bubble to Xiughen's corporate headquarters.

We slide away from the hotel, twisting along the sky-bridges into an area of the city that looks more uniform. Here, every building is tall and square, with no ornamentation. Xiughen's headquarters bears the name across the top floor but otherwise appears identical to the edifices beside it.

The bubble pulls inside the ninth floor and stops in a lobby similar to the one in the hotel, although less flashy, and with a lower ceiling. A group of corporate drones greets us and takes us to a conference room on the top floor.

I spend the next three days in endless meetings, making trivial conversation with executives at different companies. I find it odd that they've all worked together to set up my visit, but O'Neill points out they aren't really competitors. None of these corporations manufactures the same things—they aren't even in the same arenas. Here in Lewei, the state controls which companies flourish and which flounder. There is only one bubble producer, one drop chute company, one major software developer.

I never get my walk outside. T'ien and his team meet us each morning. We travel via bubble, never once setting foot on the street with the throngs of pedestrians. Each corporate headquarters has a private bubble bridge leading into its lobby. For all I know, the whole city smells of *terkfiske*, but I remain sealed inside my special, high-end cocoon.

After the third day of meetings, I request a private night in. "I'm exhausted from the meetings, T'ien. I hope you don't mind." I don't wait for his reply but let the door slide shut on his bowing figure. "He's probably happy to have a night off babysitting us."

Vanti gives me a stern look and points at the communications room. I drag my feet on the carpet, feeling like a reprimanded child as I follow her inside. "What?"

Vanti swings the door closed. "We can't gather information if we're stuck in our suite."

I wave my arm at Cris and Young sitting in front of their dozens of screens. "Really? Because it looks like you're doing a pretty good job of it. Besides, that's not my problem. My job was to meet the bigwigs. I've done that. I'm tired of doing it. It's not like T'ien was ever going to let us out anyway."

"Since when did that stop you?" Vanti drops to the bed to pet Apawllo. He kneads the blanket and purrs.

I hold up a hand. "I'm on my best behavior. I'm being a good little Morgan. If you want to sneak out and look around, go for it, but don't expect me to bail you out. I was given very explicit instructions not to get into trouble."

Vanti gives me a sad smile. "Wow, you've really committed to this whole thing, haven't you?"

"Besides, what information do we need to gather? I'm here to do a meet and greet. You're here to protect me."

"Dame Morgan always wants complete intel on any prospective partnerships. Part of our job is to get that. You didn't think all this surveillance was just for you, did you?" Vanti waves her arm at the agents focused on their holos.

"How am I supposed to know what your orders are? I may be 'Morgan,' but I'm a mushroom Morgan—kept in the dark and fed a refined diet." I consider storming out of the room, but that's what the old me would do. I'm trying to be the new, better Triana. "What's Ty been doing all this time? Isn't local research his job?"

O'Neill hasn't attended most of the meetings. He rides with me to every new company, then disappears with his escort and the host's security personnel. At the end of the day, he meets us at the bubble. When I've asked, he hasn't been forthcoming with details.

"He's been doing his best, but he's stuck with an escort, just like the rest of us." Vanti fidgets with a budvase full of plastek flowers.

I narrow my eyes at her and cross my arms. "What do you expect me to do about that? Am I supposed to sneak out like I used to, so you have an excuse to follow me? Is that why you were so eager to come on this trip—you thought I'd give you cover for a clandestine snoop around the city?" I'm so angry I could spit, but that reaction was firmly trained out of me at age five.

Vanti's been lecturing me on behaving myself while subtly provoking me to get into trouble since day one. Looking back, every time I've bolted, she's been behind me, poking at the constraints, reminding me of the freedom I've lost. Seen from this angle, her whole career has been as much about pushing me outside the limits as it has been about protecting me.

But what should I do about it? Because the reality is, no matter how hard I try, I'll never be Morgan like the Ice Dame. Someday, I'll pick up the full responsibility, but that day is decades in the future. With current health care, my mother easily has another hundred years ahead of her. Am I supposed to be the heir for most of my life, just waiting around for her to die? Do I want to spend the next eighty or ninety years like Don Huatang's son, trying to please my mother and pretending to be the perfect heir?

As mad as I am at Vanti, she's offering me an out. "Fine. Let's go exploring."

Vanti's secret little smile spreads across her lips. "There's the space janitor." She heads for the door.

CHAPTER EIGHTEEN

I PUT my hand over the doorknob. "Ty comes too."

Vanti groans. "Really? Usually, you run away *from* him."

"I've never run away from him. Well, okay, once, on Sally Ride. Or maybe that was twice—but it was the same trip, so it only counts as once. Either way, I'm not running away from him anymore. If we go, he comes with us." I brace my feet and grip the doorknob tightly. Vanti could overpower me easily, but there are two other agents in here, and their job is to protect me, not their boss.

I think.

"Fine." Vanti waves a hand at me. "Go put on some dark clothes."

I open the door. "I'm not sure I brought any."

"You did."

I give her retreating back my best death glare.

"I saw that."

"No, you didn't."

O'Neill looks up from the files spread virtually around him. "Do I want to know?"

I look him over. He's wearing dark pants, a snug black T-shirt, and athletic shoes in a dark material. Was he planning on sneaking out himself?

I look around the room, as if scouting for a hidden camera. "I'm going to bed."

O'Neill's brows draw down, then he holds up a finger. Probably a call from Vanti.

I go into my bedroom. Vanti was right—I find a thin, dark pullover and leggings tucked in the bottom drawer. I don't remember packing those, but maybe Hy-Mi's assistant threw them in as lounge wear? I slide my legs into the pants and discover a hidden pocket along the seam. Maybe Vanti brought them for me. I open the sealed pocket and find a small toolkit—the kind I usually carry for unexpected hacking jobs. Definitely Vanti's work.

When I return to the lounge, O'Neill gives me a hard look. "Do you really want to do this?" The words come through my audio implant.

"Don't you?" I whisper back.

His eyes light up, but his voice doesn't change. "I don't want to put you at risk. Ever."

"If you're going to try to wrap me in cotton wool and top-lev security my whole life, this isn't going to work." I wave a hand between us, to indicate our relationship.

He heaves a sigh and pulls me close. "I know. But I'm not sure this is a wise move. You've heard Leo's stories—and read the reports—on Leweian secret police."

"If they throw us in Xinjianestan, Mother can negotiate to get us back."

"Wow, that's super comforting." He looks away for a second, then turns back, resigned. "If you're determined to go, you aren't going alone. What's the plan?"

"Ask her." I nod at Vanti as she enters the room.

She darts past us without a word, disappearing into my room. When she returns, she's carrying a flowing silk wrapper with big pastel flowers. "Put that on."

I slide the robe over my black clothing and fluff my hair. "Now what?"

"We're going to the roof for some air." Vanti leads us out of the suite and to the drop chutes at the end of the hall. Rather than stepping in, she turns aside and opens an unmarked door beside them. Stairs wind up into the gloom above. "Turn on your cam disruptor."

I activate my holo-ring and flick the app. The glow from the ring provides enough light to follow Vanti up the steps. O'Neill falls in behind me.

"Maintain silence from here on," Vanti says through my audio implant. "You really need to learn to use the subvocal." A laugh runs through her words, as if she enjoys my enforced silence.

I clench my teeth and speak under my breath. "You mean like this? Surprise, I've been practicing."

Vanti pauses on a landing to look down at me. Her brows are raised, and she makes a mocking bow. "Well done. That was almost soundless."

We reach the top. Vanti waves her hand at the door.

To my surprise, it slides open. "Why did that work?"

"It's an emergency exit. If a lower floor were to catch fire, guests would have to evacuate upward. We might find it a bit more difficult to get back inside." Vanti peers at the locking mechanism. "I could prop it open."

I shake my head and point. "Don't. There's a reader here. If this circuit doesn't close, I'm betting it will set off an alarm. In fact, we might have already done so." I look closer, shining my light on the mechanism. "Hang on."

I pull the tiny tool kit from the hidden pocket and use a universal cable to attach an adapter to the circuit. Then I use a near-field link to connect my holo-ring to the adapter and worm into their system. "I've added our credentials to the master key loop."

"Will they be able to track that back to us?" O'Neill asks.

I shake my head as I disconnect my gear. "I put in an anonymous relay. Their system will only record the equivalent of 'user x'. If they happen to be watching in real time when we come back, they'll see an unknown user open the door and might come looking. By the time they get up here, we should be back in our suite. And the chances that they're watching the lock logs on this particular door are pretty small. This is the kind of thing you check if an alarm sounds."

I swing the door shut and listen for the lock click. "And now the alarm won't sound. And the cam has fritzed, too—in case you were wondering." I grin.

"I'd forgotten how handy you can be." Vanti takes a deep breath and looks around the rooftop. "Take off your robe—that was just to make us look less suspicious if someone stopped us on the stairs. I'll stash it in my backpack. And tuck your hair into that." She tosses me a dark beanie made of thin material.

I slide the silk off my shoulders and hand it to Vanti. In our dark clothing, we blend into the deep shadow cast by the drop chute house. She crouches to unzip her backpack and stuff the silk robe inside.

Luna is full in the sky, casting bright light and dark shadows across the flat roof. Another mechanical shed sits at the far end of the long narrow building —the top of the other drop chute and a second stairway, no doubt. A low wall runs along the edge. We approach, stepping over cables and rain puddles. The damp plastek squeaks under our feet as we move.

From the edge, the view stretches out before us, seemingly unlimited. Most of the buildings are shorter than ours, but their tops are brilliantly lit with company names and aircraft warning lights. The bubble bridges shine as they loop out of the shadows, then twist away into darkness. In the distance, moonlight glints on the sea.

Our building has lights set into the outside of the low wall which illuminate the top meters of the deep chasm between this building and the next. Far below, more lights cast cones of brilliance amid the darkness of the pedestrian street. I glance over the side and immediately grab O'Neill in reaction to the vertigo. His arms close around me.

"Take off your Ncuff," Vanti says through the audio. "We'll leave those here."

We pull off the devices and hand them to Vanti. She drops all three into a dark bag and cinches the top shut. Then she tucks it behind a loose piece of flashing along the edge of the drop chute house.

"Now what?" I ask.

Vanti hands me a grav belt. "Now we fly."

"Where did you hide these? I didn't see any in the luggage." I clip the belt around my waist while the others do the same.

"Special delivery." Vanti taps her controls and lifts off the ground.

"Delivery? You ordered them from a local vendor and had them delivered to the hotel?" I match her altitude.

O'Neill chuckles. "She had Captain Philpott send a drone." He rises beside me.

"A drone? From the ship? You had this planned?" I look from one agent to the other. "If you were going to drop a drone, why bother with the comm gear hidden in the suitcases? Why not send it that way?"

Vanti flicks her holo-ring, and something tugs at my belt. "I'm tethering your belts to mine. We can talk while we move." She swings toward the shadowed side of the building, and we follow.

"To answer your question, the drone was a backup plan. If the gear got damaged or confiscated, the captain would send down the drone." O'Neill's voice is warm and comforting in my ear. "It's small—about the size of Apawllo's carry crate—so it doesn't trigger their planetary protection systems."

Vanti snaps her fingers. "I should have sent the cat back to the ship in the drone."

Without warning, she drops over the side, taking us with her. My heart leaps into my throat. We seem to free-fall for a few seconds, then level out. In the shadow of the building, Vanti and O'Neill are virtually invisible. I look at the hotel—either none of the guests have their curtains open, or the windows filter the light from inside. It rises beside us as a dark hulk.

The cap Vanti gave me must project camouflage to my face. I can't see even a hint of my skin in the reflecting wall. I try to fly closer, but my belt doesn't respond to my command—it's tethered to Vanti's.

I look at the others—or where I think they are. "Where are we going? You must have a destination in mind—I don't believe you brought all this equipment just to give me a joy ride." I get the impression of them exchanging a look—they're probably chatting on a separate call, deciding what to tell me. "Why did you want me along anyway? You've been doing this since we got here, haven't you?"

Vanti sighs. "Of course we have. Griz's job was to evaluate the political environment as well as the physical security of visitors to Lewei. Can't do that with a minder dogging your steps. I've been helping with that after hours."

"We should have brought her along earlier—being able to unlock the roof door from the outside is stellar," O'Neill says.

"You're the one who didn't want her coming. And I had no problem picking the lock."

"You didn't want me to come?" I repeat.

"Being ignorant of our activities was safer for you." O'Neill moves closer and puts a hand on my shoulder. "To be honest, I didn't want to bring you tonight—it's too big a risk."

I groan. "So, all that crap about being Morgan—"

"Is still one hundred percent true." Vanti's voice is flat and brooks no argument. "Your primary job was to represent the brand. But I knew you'd want a little fun before we left. Plus, we can use your help."

And there it was. She wanted to keep me safe—except when it was more convenient to have me along. Whatever they were investigating was more important to Vanti than my safety—which she kept saying was her highest priority.

I've always had a sneaking suspicion about Vanti's dedication to SK'Corp. O'Neill swears she's completely reliable, but she's done too many iffy things—especially when it comes to me. "Who do you really work for, Vanti?"

"What?" O'Neill and Vanti both swing around to stare at me. This is slightly unnerving, since we continue to fly into the darkness at a high rate of speed. I hope Vanti has programmed the belts for building avoidance.

"She's obviously got a priority higher than my safety—that's always been the case." I stab a finger at O'Neill. "*You* wouldn't have taken me into that building in Pacifica City where Wil had the explosives. Or into Shikumen Palace knowing there were enemy operatives on the premises. *You* wouldn't have let me join you in a cupcake truck on Sally Ride. You *didn't* let me investigate the bank in Paradise Alley with you. Even Gary Banara recognized it when he talked me into the basement of the Leweian embassy. He told me *Vanti* asked for his help, not you. Vanti is a cowboy, willing to risk my life to achieve her objective. There's no way SK'Corp would assign me a security team leader if they also gave her a higher priority, so that priority must come from somewhere—someone—else. Who is it Vanti? Who do you really work for?"

As we slip out of the shadows and across a deserted street, the moonlight shines on their faces. O'Neill's is bleached and strained as he stares at Vanti, his mouth set. "She's right," he whispers. "She suspected before, but I wouldn't believe it. Who is it, Vanti?"

Her lips press together, then she slips into darkness. We trail along, curving around another structure, crossing stripes of light and shadow as we progress across the city. This neighborhood is made up of smaller buildings. Most are only ten or twelve stories high, and there are several on each block, crammed tight together, perhaps sharing internal walls.

Finally, Vanti sighs. "I work for the Commonwealth. The SK'Corp job gives me access to places I would have difficulty getting to otherwise."

"Kakuvian Defense—like Gary Banara claimed?" I ask.

"Kind of—the KDD is a department of the Commonwealth Department of State."

"It's true?" O'Neill's voice is shocked. "You're a government agent posing as corporate security?"

A hint of remorse sounds in her voice. "Yes. And before you ask—I've been in their employ since the start. Before the academy. Now be quiet, we have work to do."

CHAPTER NINETEEN

VANTI IS A GOVERNMENT AGENT. It makes so much sense, I can't believe I didn't see it before. I've always suspected she was up to something, but I thought it was another job for SK'Corp.

"At least she's working for our government, not theirs," I say on a private call to O'Neill.

He doesn't reply. I put a hand on his arm, but he shakes me off. I try to push the hurt away. He and Vanti have been friends—and partners—since they joined the academy over a decade ago—long before he and I met. He undoubtedly sees this as a huge betrayal of trust.

"Where are we going?" I ask on the shared channel.

"We have a meeting with a local dissident," Vanti says.

"No! We are not taking Triana to meet a rebel." O'Neill's voice is cold and hard. "You can talk to him on your own. I'm taking her back to the hotel."

My belt jerks, as if an invisible hand has tried to pull me loose from Vanti's tether.

"I need her expertise," Vanti says, and the belt jerks again. "You can't untether her belt—or your own—so don't bother trying."

"Vanti, please." O'Neill's voice sounds strained. "Let's take her back to the hotel, then you and I can meet your contact. If they recognize her, they'll realize she's extremely valuable as a hostage. I won't let you put her at risk."

"Don't I get a say in this?" I ask.

"NO!" they both shout. The sound echoes back at us, bouncing across the narrow chasm between the buildings.

"If you get her killed, you'll lose your job," O'Neill says coldly. "Like you've lost my friendship. But I guess an undercover agent doesn't care about that."

"Can we talk about this later, Griz?"

"No, I think we should hash it out now, while flying through an enemy city on contraband grav belts. We could have talked about it at any time over the last twelve years, but it wasn't important to you then. I don't care what's important to you anymore. I care about what's important to me. And that's Triana's life."

"Look, I just need her to hack into something for me. I can drop both of you in a safe location and connect via near-field comms. I'm wearing an oc-cam, so you can see everything I see."

"If you needed a hacker, why didn't you bring Liandra?" O'Neill demands.

Vanti sighs. "Liandra would have asked awkward questions. Triana usually isn't so inquisitive. She's game to try something exciting. That's why she's an excellent cover. Although the first four years at the Techno-Inst were a little boring."

The grinding of O'Neill's teeth is audible.

We drop suddenly, angling toward a dark street far below. "The power's gone down," Vanti says. "Perfect timing."

"Leo said outages were common here, but I was starting to think he was joking." The lights had flickered a few times, but nothing more.

"Our hotel has a generator." O'Neill's voice is still strained. "The wealthy can't be subjected to inconvenience."

We touch down in the darkness. Vanti moves closer, so we can see her in the faint moonlight reflected from the building across the street. She points. "Can you break into that office building, Triana?"

O'Neill's hand closes over my wrist as he taps his grav belt with the other. "I'm taking her back."

"We're here now—maybe I can help first?" I consider mentioning the PVD I purchased from the *Księżna*—it will render me completely unrecognizable.

Before I can speak, Vanti puts out a hand. "I brought a PVD. She stays here, does her hacking, while I go and meet my contact over there. If anyone happens across her, they won't have a clue who she is. You can stay with her or come with me—your choice."

O'Neill snatches the item from her palm, then pushes me into a sheltered doorway. He stands in front of me, like a guard dog. "Easy choice—I'm with Triana. Tell her what you want her to do. When it's done, we're out of here. You're on your own."

Vanti's eyes droop the tiniest bit, then she wipes her face clean. She steps into the shadows on the other side of the entry. "Fair enough. Triana, I need you to hack into that building on the corner. Run a search on the whole thing —it should be clear. Then set perimeter alarms on the first three floors. I want to know when my contact arrives and from which direction."

"You could have done all of that yourself," I say on a private channel, trying not to look at O'Neill as I speak. "Why did you need me?"

"I want real-time monitoring. And you always think of something I don't. I need backup on this—I don't know these people, and it may be a trap. I was never going to put you in danger—you'll be safe here. But please, stay until I'm done. I might need you."

I don't reply—what am I going to say? O'Neill isn't going to provide backup—unless I'm safe in the hotel. Or unless I can convince him to over-look his hurt and betrayal. His sense of loyalty is intense—maybe I can convince him not to abandon his partner.

I glance up at the target building. It looks like every other building on this street. It doesn't appear to be alarmed—or the alarm hasn't been engaged tonight.

Of course—the power is off. But there's something running. The building's operating system is ticking away in the background. "How is the building system running if the power is out?"

Vanti looks up from her holo-ring. "Any building sophisticated enough to have a built-in operating system is going to have a battery backup."

Good point. "Then why is the alarm off?"

Vanti's eyes flicker. "Maybe you should pick a different building to hide in."

"Maybe we should leave." O'Neill puts an arm around me. "Let's get back to the hotel."

"We're here now. Give me that PVD." I take the capsule and twist the two halves. A faint frisson runs over my face—or maybe I imagine it. "How do I look?"

O'Neill grabs Vanti's wrist and raises it until her holo-ring casts its faint glow on my face. "You look completely unremarkable."

Vanti's lips twitch. "That's the point." She holds out a hand. "I brought one for you, too."

O'Neill snatches it as if her palm will singe his fingers. He twists the capsule, and his handsome features dissolve into a slightly less attractive face. Even with a PVD, it's hard for him to be anything but shiny. But at least he's not recognizable.

Vanti, on the other hand, looks like O'Neill's great grandma. Or at least a contemporary. She grins, showing off mismatched teeth.

"That's horrible." I look away. "I thought the plan was to be unremarkable."

95

"You two are supposed to be unremarkable. I'm just supposed to be unrecognizable." She fiddles with the device, and her apparent age regresses a few decades. Now she's merely old, like my father.

"That's cool. Is mine programmable, too?" I peer at the device in my hand.

Vanti's old head shakes negative. "Just the top-of-the-line ones. Go on, pick a building and get hidden. Here's the oc-cam link." She flicks her holoring, and mine vibrates as the link arrives. The ocular cam is hidden in a lens she wears over her eye. It transmits everything she sees directly to me.

I flick it open on the smallest setting to confirm her lens is transmitting. The vid shows two people I don't know standing in a dark doorway. I lift a hand, and the dark-haired girl raises hers. "That's us, I guess." Vanti turns to scan the street, and the view in my palm pans along with her.

I check the other buildings. All of them have operating systems, but none have their alarm set. Maybe they default to off in a power outage. Seems like an odd choice, but it also seems common. Just to be sure, I check the buildings on the street behind this one. Every place, as far as my signal will reach, shows the same. "That one is fine." I take O'Neill's hand and drag him across the street.

A quick flick and swipe opens the door, and we step into the dark lobby. There are four doors and a flight of stairs.

"Let's go up." O'Neill's whisper tickles my ear.

As he leads me silently up the steps, I scan the building. We're the only people inside—as one would expect with an office building at two in the morning. I connect to the building Vanti indicated and begin another scan, stumbling when I expect another step and there isn't one.

"Sorry." O'Neill slides an arm around my waist and guides me through the second-floor lobby, then up the next set of steps. "I'll warn you when we reach the top."

My legs burn by the time I finish working on Vanti's building. I tap open the oc-cam vid. She's still standing in the doorway across the street. "You're cleared to enter the building. I've checked all the floors and set up a perimeter. Oh, and there's a basement, so I checked that too."

"Nice work. I'm going in."

A door opens, and wind brushes my cheeks. "Where are we?"

O'Neill pushes me over a threshold. "Roof. I want a clear line of escape."

I rub my aching quads. "We should have flown up."

Lawn chairs and folded umbrellas clutter the roof. Someone obviously uses this space as an employee lounge—or maybe for parties. We skirt around a broken table, making for the low wall that guards the edge.

We reach it before Vanti enters the building, but even though I followed her progress via the oc-cam, I can't see her on the street below. She manages to blend into the deep shadows like a chameleon. I slide down to sit against the wall, leaving O'Neill to watch for bad guys, hoping the faint glow from the holo isn't visible from the street. In the dim light, the faint hologram shows remarkably well. "She's inside." I reactivate the perimeter alert behind her.

A new voice interrupts. "Turn off that light and put your hands over your head."

I bite back a scream as a shadow steps away from the stairway door.

CHAPTER TWENTY

IGNORING THE COMMAND, O'Neill spins. He points a mini blaster at the shadow. "Who are you?"

The figure by the door stops. It wavers, then speaks. "I'll ask the questions." The voice is high and shaky.

"Drop it." O'Neill takes a step closer to the figure, his blaster held steady. "Vanti, we have a bogey."

Moonlight vibrates on the other's weapon as it shakes. Clearly, our adversary is terrified. O'Neill closes in and takes the thing from her unresisting fingers. He slides the heavy metal into his pocket and jerks his weapon toward the corner of the roof. "Over there—by the edge."

The woman backs away, her arms held out from her body. She's wearing a long, baggy coat over slim pants and a dark top. A hood leaves her face in shadow.

"Stop there. Triana—pat her down. Don't get between us. You remember how to do it?"

On screen, Vanti has paused, her back to a wall in a room with one window. "I'm good—help Griz."

"Got it." I gulp and flick my holo-ring to standby as I rise. Watching the target carefully, I cross the roof and step behind her. Her body trembles under my searching hands. I remove a wrist device from her arm, a small pocketknife and some cash from one pocket, and a flat, rubbery circle with a piece dangling from the other. "What is this?"

The woman can't seem to tear her eyes from O'Neill's mini blaster. "What is what?"

I step back and hold the rubbery thing off to the side where she can see it. She swallows hard. "It's a zero gravity whoopie cushion."

"What is it, really?" O'Neill demands, his voice low and threatening.

I turn the thing, so the moonlight hits the writing. "It says it's a zero gravity whoopie cushion."

The woman sounds defensive. "I work for Luna City, Limited—a novelty company. It's our biggest seller."

"That doesn't explain why you're accosting strangers on a roof in the middle of the night." O'Neill jerks his head at me. "With a weapon that shouldn't be available in Lewei City."

I cross the roof to his side, shoving the confiscated items into my hidden pockets as I go. These pants are amazing. Which makes me stop—what if she's wearing pants with hidden pockets? "Wait, I need to search her again."

"Take the coat off this time," O'Neill says as I approach her. "Who are you?"

"My name is Katie Li." She shrugs out of the coat, letting it fall to the roof.

I run my hands down the seams of her pants and lift her sweater. She shivers as the wind whips a salty breeze at us, and I squash my compassion. She held a gun on us. She needs to be searched. I finish and pick up the coat, checking the pockets. Nothing. "I think she's clean."

"Keep your hands where I can see them, Katie Li." O'Neill glances at me. "Anything else?"

I shake my head. "Nope, just the pocketknife and whoopie cushion. Not even identification."

"That's on my Ncuff." She shivers in the wind. "I really am Katie Li."

"Can I give her coat back? It's cold up here." I lift the thick, wooly garment.

"She should have thought of that before she accosted us." He pulls something from a pocket and hands it to me. "Tie her hands."

I take the slip ties and move around the woman again, securing her hands behind her back. "I'd better check on Vanti."

"Vanti can take care of herself." O'Neill points the blaster at a rickety lawn chair. "Sit down, Katie Li."

Katie sits while I pull the oc-cam vid up again. Just then, an alert pings my audio. "Vanti, you have company. Coming down from the roof. One person. Looks to be male."

"Was he waiting up there, or did he just land?"

"I don't know! You didn't ask me to watch the roof. I didn't see anyone on the scan, but I didn't see this woman, either." I glance at O'Neill. "She's not wearing a grav belt."

O'Neill's eyes narrow as he stares down at her. "How did you get up here?"

"The same way you did—the stairs. I've been up here for hours. Nick wanted me out of the way. But you locked the door when you came up, so I had to—" She waves at the mini blaster. "It was stupid. I should have just waited until you left, but I kind of panicked. Nick is going to kill me."

"Who's Nick?" I swipe through a couple screens, watching the man sneaking down the stairs in the other building. "Vanti, he's on the second floor."

"Roger that. I'm ready."

"Who's Vanti?" Katie looks around, as if she expects to see another person.

"Never mind." I didn't realize I'd said that aloud. This girl has thrown me off my game.

Who am I kidding? I don't have a game.

"Who's Nick?" O'Neill repeats my question.

"I'm betting Nick is Vanti's contact, and Katie was sent to distract us," I tell O'Neill, being careful to speak silently through the comm link.

"Agreed. Keep an eye on her building." He stares down at the woman, then raises his voice. "Who is Nick?"

"Nick Beckett. He's my friend."

"And where is he now?"

She starts to look over her shoulder—toward Vanti's building—but stops with a jerk. "I don't know."

"Do your friends often leave you sitting on a rooftop in the middle of the night while they wander off alone? Doesn't seem like much of a friend."

Katie's shoulders slump and tears glint in the moonlight. "No, of course not. This is different."

O'Neill lets the growl leave his voice. "Different how?" He almost sounds sympathetic.

"I—I can't tell you." Tears slide down her pale cheeks, and she takes a deep breath. Either she's an excellent actress, or she's really scared and miserable.

Maybe both.

My alerts ping again. "Vanti, you have two new bogeys approaching from the sub-basement."

"There's a sub-basement?" Vanti sounds chagrined.

"Yeah, but I found it. The entrance is behind the heating equipment in the regular basement." I swipe and flick through the building's system, hijacking cams as I go. "They're coming up the stairs right now. I recommend you leave."

"There's only two of them? I can take two. And my new friend can help."

"Are you sure he's a friend? He might be with the other two."

"No, we're alone!" Katie says.

I look up in surprise. "Did I say all that out loud? Again? Zark! Vanti, the girl says they're alone, but I don't know if you can trust her." I glare at Katie.

"We are alone! If someone is sneaking in, Nick needs to know!"

"That's your job, right?" I turn away from her, glancing up at O'Neill. "Do you think Vanti needs help? I'll be safe enough here."

"I told her she's on her own. I'm not leaving you—especially with a potential adversary."

I put out a hand. "Give me the blaster. I'll watch the girl—you go help Vanti."

He wavers, obviously torn even though he swore off his partner. "She can get help from her real boss."

I get up and move a little closer. "She doesn't have anyone to back her up—if she did, they'd be here instead of us. She needs you, Ty. I don't want to come between you and your best friend."

"You aren't what came between us—her dishonesty did that all by itself."

"She's still on the same side we are. Do you really want to leave her to the Leweians?" I swing around to point at the girl. "Is that who you are? Leweian secret service?"

The girl's eyes go wide. "No! At least… I don't think so."

"How could you not know? Don't—"

O'Neill cuts me off. "She's trying to stall us." He hands me a stunner. "Watch her. Wait for me. If we don't come back by sunrise, get Hy-Mi to start extradition."

I grab his arm. "Extradition? You think they're going to throw you in Xinjianestan?"

He pulls me in for a fast, hard kiss. "I don't know who they are. But if we don't want to get caught, I need to help Vanti now." He drops me and lifts off the roof, arrowing toward the building on the corner.

"He can fly?" Katie shoots up from the lawn chair and stares into the darkness.

"Grav belt." I jerk the stunner at her. "Sit down, there, where I can see you." I watch through the holograms to ensure she complies, then focus on the cam feeds.

A tall, broad man looms over Vanti. He's just a bulky shadow in the dim room, but I get the impression of muscles and a square jaw.

"Nick!" Katie whispers, staring at the reverse side of the holo. I flick on the audio, low but loud enough she can hear, too.

"Who's coming?" Nick asks. He has a beautiful voice—deep, warm, with a faint burr. I'm not sure if he's speaking Standard or if our translators are that good.

"Unknown. I recommend we vacate, now."

"Agreed." The guy turns as Vanti rises toward the ceiling.

I toggle my audio connection. "Vanti, O'Neill is en route."

"Negative—wave him off. We're out." She's skimming along the ceiling, headed for a doorway. The tall man disappears through it.

"Ty—"

"I heard. I'm covering the exit."

I don't have a visual on O'Neill, so I lurch across the roof to peer over the low wall. I barely register Katie moving up beside me. While we've been here, the moon has set, and there are no streetlamps in this part of town. The thick darkness fills the chasm between the buildings like ink. "Where are you?"

"Directly across from Vanti's building."

I focus on Vanti's oc-cam again. She and the tall man have reached a narrow lobby—I vaguely remember her clearing it as she entered, but we were busy with Katie at that point, so I barely noticed.

A vehicle enters the street below, its lights cutting through the darkness. In Vanti's view, Nick jerks back from the door. "Let's wait until they pass."

The bubble purrs down the street and stops at the corner, right between Vanti and O'Neill.

"Triana, can you get me inside this building?" O'Neill asks. "I need to—"

Before I can answer, the place explodes.

CHAPTER TWENTY-ONE

NOT A LITERAL EXPLOSION. Lights slam on from every direction, their force almost physical. Figures clad in black armor and helmets pour into the street like ants converging on a sugar cube. Voices yell, weapons flash, someone screams.

That might have been me.

I duck behind the low wall, pulling Katie down beside me. "It's a trap! Who's out to get you?"

"I don't know!" Katie wails.

I slap a hand over her mouth. "Shut up!" I peer at my holos. Vanti is walking out of the building. Nick walks ahead of her, his hands aloft. As they emerge, a pair of agents push O'Neill toward the small group. No one seems to have heard us.

A crusty female voice speaks. "Three of them. The two shorter ones came here to meet the big guy—look at their clothing. That's not Leweian. There should be one more—three of the security team were missing when we deported the Morgan woman."

They deported me? How's that possible? I'm right here.

"PVD." The acronym comes through my audio—Vanti's amazing gift in play again. Even Ty can't match her for talking without appearing to talk. Apparently one of my security team used a PVD to masquerade as me. I'd bet Liandra—she's closest to my height.

I try to put a call through to the rest of the team, but it doesn't connect. Too far away, locked up somewhere, or on their way back to the ship?

"Why are they here?" The speaker, a short, tank-like woman, swaggers to

Vanti, her helmet under her arm. Her short gray hair stands up from her head in a brush-like bristle, and her narrowed eyes are almost lost in a sea of crow's feet. "Why are you here?"

Vanti doesn't respond.

"The rest of your team has been ejected from the country. You three will be detained and questioned." She raises a hand and waves it in a complicated signal. Three more helmeted agents converge on the group. They grab arms and hustle the agents to three separate bubbles. Vanti watches them take O'Neill, giving me a good look at the vehicle. Unfortunately, it looks like every other vehicle on Lewei.

The oc-cam feed goes dark.

"Vanti, are you still there?"

Vanti's voice comes through, faint but strong. "I am. They've blindfolded me. Follow us—you're our only hope."

I wonder if she knows that's a misquote from *Ancient TeVe*. Probably— Vanti knows everything.

I twist around onto my knees and peer over the low wall. I should be able to track them via the audio link—provided I'm close enough. Can grav belts keep up with Leweian bubbles?

One of the vehicles pulls away from the building. With a flick of my wrist, I send a tracking tag to each of them, hoping one of them is able to worm into their operating system and stick. Fortunately, they appear to be moving in the general direction of the hotel. I turn to Katie.

"They're going to start searching buildings soon. We need to get out of here." I pull out the pocketknife I took from her earlier and cut the slip ties binding her wrists. "I'm going to trust you only because the enemy of my enemy—"

"—is my friend." She nods at the street. "How are we going to escape?"

"We're going to fly. How much do you mass?"

She gulps. "You mean like your friend did? I can't do that."

"You have to." I crawl away from the edge until I'm sure I won't be visible from the street, then stand. "Come over here." I flick my grav belt and check the settings. Trust Vanti to get military grade equipment. "Unless you're a lot heavier than you look, we should be fine."

"I'm sixty-five kilos."

I pause in adjusting the belt to look her up and down. "How is that possible? You're tiny!"

"I live on Luna—but I've always wanted to travel. I work out every day, so I can withstand this heavier gravity."

"Sounds like a lot of work." I stretch the belt to its full length, then hand her one end. "Put that around you and give it back to me."

She complies, her hands shaking as she transfers the buckle to me.

I click the buckle shut and start to tighten the strap. "Turn around—we're going to fly back-to-back."

"Are you sure this is going to work?" Her shoulder blades tremble against my ribs.

"No." I hit the lift controls, and my feet rise off the rooftop.

Katie gasps.

I twist around, trying to see over my shoulder. "Are you okay?"

"We're flying!"

I'll take that as a yes.

The door to the stairway slams open.

"Time to go!"

"Wait, where's my coat?" She struggles behind me. "I can't leave it here."

I spin us around and peer into the darkness. The pile of wool lies on the ground halfway between us and the edge of the building. "Hold on!" I flick the controls to drop us closer to the roof and spin, so Katie is facing forward. "You get one shot—grab it!" I lean back, so Katie is flying face down as we speed toward the edge.

"Halt!" Voices shout from the stairway. Dark-helmeted figures spill from the door, their weapons aimed at us.

"They're going to shoot!" My fingers hover on the belt's controls.

"Got it!" Katie shrieks.

I yank us to the side and up as the first round of shots blazes out of the muzzles, narrowly missing us. Someone screams—not me this time. Then we shoot over the edge of the building and plummet toward the street below.

Another shout echoes up from the ground, then several gasps and yells. I hit the controls again, bringing us around in a tight arc, and we rocket away into the gloom, Katie's coat flapping behind us like a cape.

At least that's how I imagine it. We probably really look like a large, clumsy bird trying to carry too much nesting material to a nearby tree.

I adjust our altitude upward and tweak the settings, so we're upright. Wind whips against my cheeks, bringing tears to my eyes. Our brief altercation on the roof has given the vehicles time to disappear into the dark street.

I fly faster, heading in the same direction the bubbles were going, boosting my holo-ring receiver to full scan.

Nothing. How did they get away so quickly? In this part of the city, the bubbles run on the roads—the shining, looping sky bridges are many klicks away. I rise higher—maybe the buildings are blocking the signal.

Still nothing.

I need a network connection. "Do you have some kind of secret lair?" I call over my shoulder.

"What?" Katie calls back.

"Never mind."

I set my belt to return to the hotel. They won't expect us to go there, and we need somewhere to regroup while we figure out how to rescue our friends.

We touch down on the roof of the Zhengzu-Maryought as the sky begins to lighten. I unfasten the grav belt and let one end drop, stepping away from Katie. "Are you okay?"

She scrubs at her cheeks—wiping tears away. "I'm okay. Why are we here? We should have followed them." She swings her coat over her shoulders and wraps it around her body.

"I tried. I've got a tracker on the bubbles. I need to connect to your network—my comms won't reach more than a couple of klicks." Plus, I need to find out what happened to my team.

"That woman said your boss was deported."

"My boss—" I turn away, fiddling with the grav belt. I'd forgotten she doesn't know I'm Sera Morgan. And thanks to Vanti's PVD, I don't look like Annabelle. "You stay here—I'm going to sneak into the suite. Maybe they've left something behind."

I use my holo-ring to pop the rooftop door open. Katie crowds into the stairway after me. "I thought you were staying up here?"

"I don't want to get left behind." Her voice drops to a whisper I don't think she intends me to hear. "Again."

"Fine. Stick close to me. Is anyone going to be looking for you? Do they know who you are?"

"I don't know."

"Have you been seen in public with this Nick person?" I start down the steps. "Keep your voice low." I wish she had an audio implant.

"No, I met him here. I mean—people have seen me with him on Luna." Her voice trembles.

"Why are you here? What's your official reason for being on Lewei?" I stop a few steps above the landing and turn to look at her.

"Tourism. I always wanted to see the planet—I was born here. So when Nick arranged for me to—"

I cut her off. "Nick arranged for you to come? Then we have to assume they know you're with him."

"But they don't know we're together."

"Have you ever heard the phrase 'follow the money'? If they can track who paid for your ticket, they know you're together."

"But Nick's undercover—he sent me cash to pay for the ticket. There's no connection—"

I cut her off again. "Perfect." I pull my tool kit out of my hidden pocket and open it. Inside, there's a small capsule—the PVD I bought from the *Księżna*. I hold it out to Katie. "Twist this, then tuck it into your bra."

She stares at me.

I grab the two ends and twist. She gasps. I twist it back. "It's your disguise. Put it into your bra—it's a convenient place to hide it and gives the best coverage." I hand her the capsule.

She twists the ends, and her curly dark hair morphs into gray-streaked waves. The brown eyes transition to gray, and her cheeks sink in. She looks like a younger version of the *Księżna*. I think back to the discussion with "Sonia." She probably has dozens of these—she said different women play the role. I should have specified a different face, but no one here is going to recognize the *Księżna* of SK2. I hope.

"Tuck that away, and let's go."

CHAPTER TWENTY-TWO

THIS EARLY IN THE MORNING, the hotel hallways should be deserted. I open the stairway door a crack and peer down the hall. The door to my suite is open, and the hum of cleaning bots filters to us. They don't waste any time at the Zhengzu-Maryought. If I could connect to the building's network—

The NexUs Cuffs! I pull Katie's from my pocket and tap the screen. "Do you know anything about how these things work?" I connect my holo-ring to the device.

She shakes her head. "I really am just a call-center girl. Can I have it back?"

I hand it to her, then sit on the bottom step to start looking for a back door. "If I can break into the system, I should be able to find a cam on one of those cleaning bots and see what's going on in the room."

She straps her device to her arm. "Why don't I just walk down the hall and look?"

"What if they see you?"

"I'll say I got off the drop chute at the wrong floor by accident." She taps her Ncuff. "I'll send you a connection request—so we can stay in touch."

"On an open line?"

"There are millions of people wearing these things—they can't track everyone." She opens the door again.

I grab her arm. "Actually, they can. And they're definitely tracking mine—I'm a foreigner."

Her eyes go wide, and her mouth forms an oh. "You shouldn't use it at all!"

"Relax. That's why I'm not wearing it. Let's just go look."

We walk down the hallway. The door to my suite is still open. As we pass, we casually peer through the opening. A vacuum zips across the floor, but no human cleaners are visible. Voices emanate from the front bedroom. A faint whiff of smoke and burned wire tickles my nose. I pause and look closer. There are singe marks around the bedroom door. I grab Katie's arm and hustle her back to our stairway.

The door clicks shut behind us. "Was there a fire?" Katie whispers.

"I think my team had a self-destruct in the comm room."

"Comm room?"

I shake my head. "Never mind. We aren't going to find anything in there." I drop to the steps and cradle my head in my hands. How are we going to rescue Vanti and O'Neill?

"Hello there. Who are you?"

I look up, startled. Katie crouches at the top of the next flight of steps, a hand reaching downward. A familiar black furry face butts at her fingers.

"Apawllo!"

The cat purrs and presses his head against Katie's stroking hand.

"Is this your cat?"

"Kind of. He must have gotten left behind when they evicted the others."

"That's sad." She lifts the tag hanging from Apawllo's collar. "This is odd."

"What?"

She rubs the tag between her fingers. "It doesn't have his name. It's just a blank disk."

"Give me that collar. He didn't have that before."

Katie unbuckles the collar and hands it to me. While she strokes the cat, I examine the tag. It's thicker than an engraved tag needs to be. On any other cat, I'd assume it was simply a tracking chip. But Apawllo didn't have one— unless Elodie bought it before he followed Leo to the ship.

My heart sinks. It's a scannable identification chip. Faster and cheaper than implanting one under the cat's skin. I wave my holo-ring over the tag, and a message pops up. Probably "Call Elodie-Oh if you find this cat." I flick the icon.

Vanti's voice emerges from my holo-ring. "Protocol Omega Three. Enter password."

"What's protocol omega three?" Katie asks.

I close my eyes. "I don't know."

Now what? I look at the message screen. There's a blinking symbol—if I swipe through it, I can speak the password, and the message will unlock. Which would be great—if I knew the password. There's also a tiny number three at the bottom. That's probably the number of tries I have before it self-destructs.

"Why don't you know? Weren't you trained for this?" Katie sits on the step, Apawllo purring in her lap. Her shoulders are slumped, and she leans against the wall as if she's tired.

"Not—" I shake my head. Vanti wouldn't leave me a locked message without giving me the key. She's always prepared. She had the forethought to use the cat—a cat she didn't know we'd have when we left the ship—so she must have improvised at some point. She'll have improvised the password, too. I have the password somewhere—locked in a memory or hidden in my clothes. I just have to figure out where.

"This isn't standard procedure. I need to think." And a cold stairwell is not conducive to this kind of thought. "Do you have a bolt hole somewhere?"

Katie's brows come down. "A hidden base? No, I don't. I'm not an agent. I don't have those kinds of resources."

I rub my forehead. I'm going on a full day without sleep, and I'm hungry, which makes me slow and cranky. "Where are you staying?"

Her face clears. "A hostel on the west side of the city. It's affordable."

"Did Nick book it for you?"

She shakes her head, her eyes downcast. "He told me to travel on my own —less chance of anyone connecting us. He didn't even want to know where I was staying until after his meeting today. He said it's safer."

She obviously would like to be *connected* to Nick. I wonder again why she's with him. Obviously, he's using her for cover, but why is she letting herself be used? By the look on her face, I'd say it's the oldest reason in the book. She's in love with him.

He's a *forking gas.*

I put a hand on her shoulder. "Let's go to your hostel—do you think they'll have room for one more? We can figure out what to do after we've found a safe place to hide." My stomach growls loudly. "And some food."

She stands, hefting the cat. "I don't know if they'll let us bring Apawllo in with us."

I give the cat a narrow-eyed glare. "He'll be fine. He's good at getting into places he doesn't belong." The cat glares back for a second, then starts licking a paw.

I dust my hands together and start up the stairs. "First things first—we need to get out of this hotel without anyone seeing us. For that, I need my Ncuff."

"I thought you said they'd be tracking it." She lugs the cat up the steps behind me.

"You don't have to carry him—he can walk."

The cat hisses.

"I don't mind. He's keeping me warm."

The temperature in the stairwell is cool but not unpleasant, and she's wearing a thick coat. "You're cold?"

"Luna City is warmer than this—the plants that extract oxygen from the rock produce a lot of energy."

When we exit the stairs, bright sunlight stabs into our eyes. I squint against the glare, blinking rapidly. Behind me, Katie gasps. I turn to look at her. "What?"

She shades her eyes, staring at the sunrise. "It's amazing!"

I glance over my shoulder. The sky is painted in faint pinks and yellows, but we've missed the most vibrant colors. "I've seen better."

"I haven't. Ever. At least not that I remember." Tears roll down her cheeks, and she wipes them on the cat's fur.

"Don't stare at the sun—that could blind you. Are you telling me you've never seen a sunrise before?"

She shakes her head.

"You do have to get up pretty early." I stoop beside the structure covering the stairwell, feeling for the loose flashing where Vanti hid our Ncuffs.

"There aren't many places on Luna where you can see sunrise—and they're all in the more expensive domes. I went on a field trip once in school—we took a train to Lenisvad City, and we saw the sunrise, but it didn't look anything like that. No colors." She peeks over the cat fur at the fading streaks, then looks away quickly.

"No atmosphere. Ow!" My fingers hit a sharp edge, pain stabbing into my fingertips. I yank my hand back—thin red lines score the ends of two fingers. Blood begins to seep from one of them. I stick my finger in my mouth and use the other hand to pull the flashing away from the wall. "I found the stash."

Katie peers over my shoulder as I pull the black bag from the hidey hole. The flashing snaps back into place, leaving no trace of Vanti's cache. She is good. "Hang on—take these, will you?" I hand the bag to Katie without looking up and pull the plastek away from the wall again. A flick of my bloody finger brings my holo-ring to life, and I stick my hand into the opening to light the small cavern. "Nothing. I thought she might have hidden the password there."

"I can't believe you don't know the password. What kind of training screws up something that important?"

I open my mouth to explain I'm not a real agent, then think better of it. I don't know this girl—she might decide to sell me to the Leweians. Or the Lunians. Lunarions? Lunites? Whatever. "I'm kind of new to the team.

Protocol Omega wasn't supposed to be necessary, so they didn't cover it. I'll probably have to go back to the academy when I get home."

I stand and take the bag from Katie. The Ncuffs are identifiable by the color of the band—mine is white, while Vanti and O'Neill had black. I'm not putting mine on—I don't want them to know I'm still here. I slide the smaller one over my hand and tighten the band.

A tap brings up the screen, and it requests a thumbprint to activate it. Zark. I don't have Vanti's thumbprint. With a shrug, I press my own thumb to the screen—knowing Vanti, it's worth a try. There's the risk the system might report my print back to their operating system, potentially identifying me. But I don't think their tech is that sophisticated.

The screen blinks yellow, then green. "Welcome, Lindsay Fioravanti."

I yelp as the words scroll across the screen in Standard text. "I'm in!" How did she get my thumbprint to register on her device? I shake that question away—this is Vanti—who knows how she does most of the miracles she pulls off?

"Now what?" Katie leans closer. "Is the password there?"

I do a quick prowl through Vanti's files, but there's nothing, as I expected. "She wouldn't store it on a Leweian device."

"Then why did you need it?"

"So I can get us out of the building. We can't fly in daylight—too many people would notice. But I can hack into the system and get us out the service entrance." I pull out my toolkit and crouch beside the door to connect my gear to the device strapped to my arm. Then I wirelessly connect my holo-ring to my adapters. The firewall in my ring will keep anything the Leweians throw at bay—at least for a few minutes, which is all I need.

While I make a few tweaks, Katie wanders around the roof, staring at the landscape. "Don't get too close to the edge," I whisper-shout. "You don't want anyone on the ground to notice you."

"What about those kids in the next building?"

CHAPTER TWENTY-THREE

I LOOK up from my holo-screen, still crouched beside the drop chute house on the roof. "Kids?"

Katie points at the building behind ours. It's only two floors shorter, and two children stand in one of the top-most windows, staring. Katie waves the cat's paw at them, and they return the gesture.

"Katie, stop drawing attention! We aren't supposed to be up here."

"They're just kids. They aren't going to tell any—" She breaks off and hurries to me, stepping into the shadow in the lee of the little structure.

"What?"

"I think they went to get their mom."

I duckwalk around the corner, then peek over the low wall. Across the way, the kids have reappeared, and a woman stands next to them, squinting our direction.

"Perfect." I grimace to myself and finish the work.

"They're gone." Katie says as I put my tools away.

"Then let's get out of here before they send security looking for us."

"She probably didn't believe I was real—parents don't generally believe their kids' wild stories, you know."

I didn't know. I couldn't remember my mother ever paying attention to something I tried to show her, but Hy-Mi always did. And he always believed me—probably because he knew kids notice things adults don't, and as a top-lev, we always had to be on guard.

One of the many reasons I ran away. But I'm back now, and those lessons will stand me in good stead. "Let's get inside anyway—just in case." I stand and pull the door open.

We clatter down the steps to the penthouse level. A quick peek reveals the hallway just as deserted as before. I grab Katie's arm and drag her to the drop chute. My new programming allows us to bypass the lobby and drop to the service area in the basement. "Put the cat down," I hiss. "We need to blend in with the employees, and none of them bring pets to work."

Katie starts to protest, but I give her my best Ice Dame glare. Her face goes pale, and she drops Apawllo.

We step into depressing but organized gloom. Four dim lights hang from the ceiling of a large, dismal room. A dozen or so men and women lounge at tables, perusing things on their Ncuffs, or wander back and forth, loading carts with linens and cleaning supplies from the cabinets along the walls. A big, boxy machine dispenses what smells like mediocre coffee.

No one even glances in our direction as we arrive. Katie follows me out of the drop chute, and Apawllo slinks beside our ankles, his black fur making him nearly invisible in the poor lighting.

A man looks up from his wrist device as we walk past his table. "You two are late. Get your uniforms on. You need to be ready if someone calls." He jerks a thumb over his shoulder at a door and goes back to his device. Most of the cleaning is done by bots, but high-end hotels like to brag about their human staff. That staff mostly sits and waits—in horrible waiting rooms, if this hotel is the standard.

Katie and I exchange a quick look, then nod at the guy. "Sorry." We jog past him and through the door. Rows of lockers fill the next room, with benches between them. The splashing of water and chatter of muffled voices filter in from an internal doorway. I hurry across the room, checking between the lockers for another exit.

"At least there's no one in here." Katie pulls on a locker door, but it doesn't open. "Where are we supposed to get uniforms?"

"We don't want uniforms." I grab her wrist as she reaches for another locker. "We want to get out of here, remember?"

She twists away and tries another one. "Yeah, but we can blend in if we can find—ah!" She pulls a door open and reaches inside. "Look, two tunics." She tosses one at me and pulls another over her head.

"You've still got your coat on." I grab her collar.

She shrugs out of the coat and yanks the shirt on. "This will help us blend in until we get out of here. Put yours on."

The water shuts off, and a metallic rattling sounds from the shower room. With a panicked look at the door, I drag the shirt over my head. The blue is dark enough that our black pants don't stand out. Katie bundles her coat up and tucks it under one arm. "Come on."

I shut the locker and follow her out of the room, hissing, "Find the exit."

"Marquele, Randonere!" the man who pushed us toward the locker room yells, still looking at his wrist. "Get over here. Take towels to four-twenty-three."

No one moves.

The guy looks up and points at us. "What's your problem? Newbies get the first jobs. Just be glad you don't have to clean up vomit—that'll be later. I heard there's a bachelor party on seventeen." A chorus of laughter goes around the room.

Katie jerks her head at me and moves toward the cupboards near the drop chute. She opens one, seemingly at random, and pulls out a stack of towels, handing them to me. She takes a second stack, tucking her coat between two, and jerks her head toward the chute.

As we step into the lift, Apawllo reappears beside our feet. "Good kitty," Katie whispers.

We fly upward. "How did we become Marquele and Randonere?" I ask.

She taps the badge on her shirt, where something is written in Leweian script. "I'm Marquele, you're Randonere. Can't you read?"

"Not Leweian. We need to get out of here, not deliver towels." We reach the fourth floor, and I follow her into the deserted hall. "They didn't seem surprised we arrived via the drop chute, so the exit must be on a different level."

Katie nods and knocks on a door. "Housekeeping!"

The door opens a crack, then swings wide. A nude man stands in the doorway, dripping water on the rug. "It's about time!"

I shove the towels at him, averting my eyes.

"Sorry it took so long, Citizen." Katie's voice is cheerful. "Have a wonderful day."

The door slams shut, and I turn to Katie. "He was naked."

"And wet—which is why he needed the towels."

"You act like you see naked men every day!"

She hands me two of the remaining bath sheets. "Is nudity a big deal where you live?"

"One doesn't usually answer the door in the all-together, no."

Katie nods. "Interesting. Let's get out of here, shall we? There are probably two basement levels—we'll try the other one. That's got to be where the door is."

I tap my Ncuff and set the drop chute for the upper basement. We drop to a dark, deserted hallway. Cool air blows through the corridor, bringing a faint scent of sea salt and fuel. Katie points at a red sign over the door at the far end. "That says exit."

I grab her arm. "Wait. I want to connect to the network and try to find Ty and Vanti." I slide down the wall to sit on the cold floor and log into Vanti's Ncuff again. Using my adapter, I connect my holo-ring to the device and erect a series of firewalls. Then I use a one-way loop to worm into the hotel's system.

It takes twenty minutes to set up. Two other employees have trudged past us, not even looking in our direction even though the second one had to step over my legs to get past.

"You don't think they'll tell the boss we're hiding here, do you?" Katie bites her lip as she watches the second one step into the drop chute.

"What's he going to do, fire us?"

"He could send security to throw us out."

"Ooh, good call. I'm almost done." I finally make a connection and send a signal to my tracking tags. All three vehicles are in the same location, sitting a half-klick from the meeting point. "There." I mark the spot on my map and log out. "We need to find that place." Katie gives me a hand up, and I groan as I stretch my back. "I'm getting too old for this."

"You're like, what, thirty?"

"I'm only twenty-six!"

CHAPTER TWENTY-FOUR

WE DITCH our uniforms and the three hotel-provided Ncuffs behind a dumpster outside the back door. I tuck the bag into a pocket—it might come in handy later—and we trek up the narrow alley toward the street. Katie points at the end where a steady stream of pedestrians crosses without looking in our direction. "We'll turn right at the corner, then find the subway."

"Can we get some breakfast?" I rub my stomach, hoping to stop its insistent growling.

"We should have looked for pastries in the hotel—I don't have a lot of cash."

"I don't have any." I think longingly of the thousands of Commonwealth credits I left on the ship. Maybe Protocol Omega Three will give us access to some.

At the end of the alley, we merge into the stream of people. The "street" is a wide, paved section with occasional plantings. Throngs of pedestrians surround us, some hurrying, others sauntering along, backing up traffic. We pause at a corner where sunlight streams down between the buildings.

The mingled scent of hot food reaches us, faint and teasing. Grilled meats, tangy spices, sweet chocolate. Along the next section of street, small booths stand at regular intervals. Pictures of different foods hover above the stalls, and my mouth waters. The sun seeps into our shoulders, and I would stand here forever, if I could. Then someone jostles me, and my translator bleeps their cussing.

Katie takes my arm and pulls me to the side. "The subway is down here."

We rumble down the steps with a mob of others, and I follow her into one of the many tunnels branching off the main one. "The blue line is this way."

We step into a smaller tunnel that runs crosswise. Hot air whooshes through, bringing a wave of dirty oil and body odor. I clamp a hand over my mouth, trying to filter the stench through my fingers. A long train zips by, slowing as it enters the tunnel. It finally stops, and the doors open. A crowd pushes out, and Katie grabs my arm, dragging me against the flow into the train. Apawllo scoots through the doors just before they slam shut, and the train takes off again. We stand in the entry, clutching the vertical poles bolted to the floor and ceiling.

The train zips into another station, and a flood of people lurches off. Katie grabs me again and pulls me to a just-vacated seat. "We've got a long ride—may as well be comfortable."

I try to breathe shallowly as I fold myself into the hard seat. "This is comfort?" The subways and hyperloop on Kaku are pods of luxury in comparison.

She gives me a hard look and pulls the cat onto her lap. "It's not bad."

I must doze off, because the next thing I know, Katie is shaking my arm. "Next stop is us." She pushes through the crowds, carrying the cat under her coat. I clutch the back of her belt so I won't lose her, trailing along behind.

When the train stops this time, very few people get off. Katie pushes to the door, and we pop out like corks from sparkling wine bottles that have been shaken too hard. The doors close, and the train whooshes away, leaving the hot, stomach-churning stench in its wake.

This station is deserted. We clatter through long, echoing tunnels, encountering no one. A sliding stairway crawls to the surface. The dim, reddish lights of the tunnel are replaced by bright sunlight as we emerge.

"We're not too far from the hostel." Katie turns left and strikes out across a street. A bubble slows to avoid us, angry-looking words scrolling across the side of the vehicle, then shoots away.

"Did that bubble just yell at us in Leweian?" I point to the retreating vehicle. Coward.

She chuckles. "Yeah, it said to use the crossing bridges, but the next one is half a klick away. The hostel manager told me it's safe to cross anywhere. If we were closer to a busy street, it would be a different story."

The buildings sit back from the road, with narrow strips of foliage between them and a waist-high fence along the sidewalk. They're only five or six stories high here, and the warm sunlight pours down onto us. We walk, darting across nearly-empty streets and pissing off two more bubbles.

I stop on a corner, turning as though to look at the words scrolling along the top of a building across the street. "That's it."

"That's a porn shop," Katie says.

"Not the one I'm looking at. The third building down. The one with the bars on the windows."

"The porn shop has bars on the windows."

I glance at the window, then at Katie. "So it does. I mean the gray, depressing building down the block, not the purple building with pink trim and the curvy, female silhouettes in the windows."

"That's an LIA sub-station." She stares at the gray building.

"Stop staring. That's where the cars parked. I can try to connect to Vanti and O'Neill's rings, but I'm sure the bad guys took them away."

She gives me a blank look. "Rings?"

"Holo-rings?" I tap mine, and it starts to glow. "The thing I used to connect to the Ncuff."

"Oh, right. I've never seen one of those before today. Does everyone in the Commonwealth have them?"

"Yeah, and I'm sure your LIA people know that. What does that stand for, anyway?"

"Leweian Intelligence Agency. That's who Nick—" She breaks off.

"What? Is Nick LIA?" Perfect. Vanti, a Commonwealth agent, was meeting with an LIA agent. Does she know? Does she think he's something else?

"Kind of."

I grab her arm and shake it a little. "How can he be 'kind of' an LIA agent?"

She doesn't reply.

"Is he a double agent?"

Her eyes cut to mine, but she doesn't say anything.

"Which side are you on?"

"I'm on Nick's side."

"That is *so* not helpful."

She pulls away from me. "I don't know for sure, okay? When we first met, I thought he was LIA. But then I was picked up by the LIA for—something—and he got me out. Maybe he used his pull in the agency, or maybe... I just don't know. All I know is I'm on Nick's side."

Perfect. "Well, it doesn't really matter because I'm on Ty and Vanti's side, and I intend to extricate them from LIA prison." I need to contact the ship, so I can have "Sera Morgan" send a demand that her security personnel be released. Hopefully, Protocol Omega Three means someone has already done that.

I really need to figure out what Omega Three is.

"Let's find somewhere to make plans."

———————

KATIE POINTS across the street at the building. "That's the hostel."

The buildings all look alike, and I haven't learned Leweian script, so I don't know which number is which. The digits on this one look like a seahorse, a three-legged stool, and a spindly tree with two huge apples. I take a picture with my holo-ring in case I have to find it again on my own. "Won't it look suspicious if I don't have any luggage?"

She looks me over and bites her lip. "You look suspicious enough already." She yanks the beanie off my head and tucks it into her pocket. "Where's that bag the Ncuffs were in?"

I pull it out and hand it over. She turns away from the house, leading me to a small alley in the next block. A large blue dumpster with a triangular logo painted on the side stands beside a noxious smelling brown one. She opens the blue lid and paws through the contents.

"Is this what they call dumpster diving? I've never done it before."

Her lips pinch together, and she glares, then pulls a small box from the blue bin. "This is the recycling. See if you can fit that inside the bag—it will look like you've got something."

I shove the plastek box inside the thin bag, pushing and twisting the material into a somewhat rectangular shape.

Katie looks it over critically, makes a few more tweaks, then nods. "Carry it like it's heavier than it is."

I glance at the bag in my hand, then let my arm sag as if pulled down by the weight. "Like this?"

"It'll have to do."

We approach the plain gray building again. Two low steps take us to a narrow door set inside a tiny arch. A sign on the door tells me nothing except that next time I come to Lewei, I need a visual translator.

"Apawllo, you wait here," Katie whispers to the cat before she opens the door.

The cat curls up in a patch of sunlight, as if following her instructions. "Does he understand you?"

Katie shrugs. "He's your cat. But he seems pretty smart."

CHAPTER TWENTY-FIVE

WE STEP into a dingy hallway with a wood floor and gray walls. At the back, a tall desk stands guard in front of a pair of doors. Katie leans over the counter and looks through the open door to the right. "Good morning, Citizen Venderle."

"May I help you?" A short, plump woman with gray hair and a friendly face bustles out of the room, pulling the door halfway shut. "How did you know my name?"

Katie's brows come down. "I—"

I grab Katie's arm. "A friend of ours recommended your place. You *are* Citizen Venderle, aren't you?"

Katie's head swings around, and she gives me a confused stare. I drop my eyes to her neckline, then back to her face. We've both got our PVDs still active, and she doesn't look like Katie Li. I try to tell her this in my glare, but I'm not sure she gets it.

"Do you have a room available? I need a place to stay." I smile tentatively at the woman.

"This is a hostel, young woman. We rent beds, not rooms. You can have a bunk in the women's dormitory." She pulls a huge old-fashioned book from under the counter and lays it on the table. Paging through it, she reveals sheet after sheet of hand-written names and contact information. She reaches a half-empty page and spins the book around, offering me a pen. "Sign here."

Zark. I don't know Leweian script. "Actually, it's my friend, Treena Morris, who's staying here." I push the pen at Katie.

The older woman's eyes narrow, looking back and forth between us.

"What kind of shenanigans are you trying to pull? First you want the room, then she does. Which is it?"

"Sorry, it's been a long day. I misspoke." I nod at Katie again. "She's staying. Treena Morris."

"Oh, right." Katie takes the pen and prints something on the page.

"That will be four keis per night, paid up front. How long are you staying?" The proprietor holds out a hand.

Katie reaches into her pocket, then looks at me, panicked. "I—"

Zark, I took her cash when I searched her. "I have your money, dear. Remember? You wanted to make sure you didn't buy any more street vendor food." I lean closer to the old proprietor and lower my voice. "It's not good for her." I pat my stomach, then pull the wad of cash out of my pocket and give it to Katie.

The hostel woman's eyes widen at the sight of the wad, but she says nothing. Katie glares at me, then peels a note off the bundle and hands it to the woman. "Keep the change." She shoves the rest into her pocket. "Can my friend come in with me? To see the dorm?"

"If she's not registered, she can't come in." The woman tucks the bill away into her clothing, then swings around to point at a door on the right. "She can wait in the public room."

Now what do we do? Katie has two beds, and I have nothing. "Why don't you put your bag upstairs, and I'll wait for you here." I hand her the small bag and push her toward the inner door.

Katie nods uncertainly and follows the woman up the creaky steps.

I consider checking out the rest of the ground floor, but the woman left the stairway door open. I can hear her voice as she explains where the sanitary facilities are and how to set the lock on the security drawer. I don't want to get caught somewhere I shouldn't be, but the partially open door tempts me. I lean across the tall table and push it a little wider.

It's an office. A large, old-fashioned virtual bubble hangs above a heavy wooden desk. Worn spots in the carpet show Citizen Venderle must spend a lot of time at this desk—or the carpet is really old. A sparkling clean window looks out into a bright garden behind the house. A door in the far wall probably hides the woman's private quarters.

A stair squeaks, and I jerk back, hurrying to the lounge in the front of the house. When Citizen Venderle appears a few seconds later, I'm sitting on a wooden bench, paging through an ancient book. It looks like recipes, but I can't read it, of course.

"Tell me about yourself." Venderle positions herself in front of the open door, as if standing guard.

I shrug. "Nothing to tell, really."

"There's everything to tell. Your name, for example. You didn't mention it." She crosses her arms.

"Oh, I'm—" Zark, I don't know any Leweian names! I wrack my brains, trying to remember the name of even one of the women I met this week. "I'm Citizen Randonere. You can call me Randy."

Her nostrils flare, and her jaw clenches. Apparently, she doesn't approve of my nickname. Or maybe it's the informality that she doesn't like. "What do you do for a living, Citizen Randonere?"

"I work in housekeeping at the Zhengzu-Maryought. I took some time off to show my friend around town."

Her eyes light up at the hotel name, as if she's reassessing my potential financial value. It's the same look I saw on the faces of the Xiughen executives when I was introduced as Annabelle Morgan. Then her eyes narrow again. "And you didn't have room for your friend to stay with you?"

I hitch a shoulder as if embarrassed. "My landlady doesn't allow guests upstairs."

Venderle's eyes flicker as she recognizes the shot. "It pays to be careful."

Katie reappears behind Venderle. "All settled in. Do you want to do some sight-seeing?"

"Actually, dear, I have to go. I got a call from work while you were upstairs." I glance at Venderle, and her brows rise. "It was a text. One of my coworkers didn't show up, and they need me. Will you walk me to the station? We can meet this afternoon, after I get done."

Behind Venderle, Katie mouths something at me, but since I don't speak Leweian, I don't know what she's trying to say—another reason to get a visual translator next time.

I hope there isn't a next time.

"Of course," Katie finally says. "I'm kind of tired anyway—haven't adjusted to the time change yet."

I push past Venderle and hustle Katie toward the door. "It was nice to meet you, Citizen Venderle. Sorry I have to run." I shove the door open and drag Katie down the street.

"Now what?" Katie pulls me into the alley we used earlier and swings around. "Now I have two beds, and you have nothing."

I hold up a hand. "We'll switch PVDs. I'll become Treena Morris, and you'll go back to being Katie Li."

She puts her hands on her hips. "How is that supposed to work? You're much taller than me. She'll notice if Treena suddenly grows."

"No, she won't. People don't pay that much attention—unless you're really tall or really short." I point at her. "I mean, I hardly noticed how short you are until now. Besides, I'll slump. And not get too close to her. She already thinks Treena is kind of odd. Speaking of noticing things—why didn't she think it was odd that I don't speak Leweian?"

"They get lots of emigrants in Lewei City. She probably thinks you're from Tereshkova or Gagarin."

"Standard sounds nothing like Gagarian." I pull the PVD out of my bra and switch it off. "Give me yours."

She stares at me, her hand reaching toward my frizzy red hair. "I've never seen hair that color. Is it real?"

"Of course it's real! It would look way better than this if I paid for it." I tuck a loose corkscrew behind my ear.

Katie hands me her PVD. I tuck it back into place and give her a critical look. Her curly dark hair tumbles over her shoulders in luxurious waves. Even after a night out spying, it's smooth and silky instead of a frizzy mess—exactly the kind of hair I've always wanted. I could have Kara make mine look like that, of course, but a stubborn bit of me refuses to pretend. Besides, I had brown hair for six years when I was hiding from my mother. "How do I look?"

Katie's eyes widen. "Is that what I looked like? Yowza, you're old!"

"Treena is old. I told you, I'm only twenty-six. Let's get back in there. Give me fifteen minutes, so she doesn't wonder why we arrived at the same time." Without waiting for a reply, I turn and walk away.

CHAPTER TWENTY-SIX

IT'S HARDLY the ideal hideout. Residents are only allowed in the dorm if they're sleeping, so we're sitting in the front room again. Through the thin walls, Venderle's occasional conversations come through loud and clear. She's called a plumber, an electrician, and a roofer so far. There seems to be a lot of work getting done on this dump.

Don't get me wrong—it needs the work. But clearly, it's been disintegrating for years. Why is Venderle suddenly flush with cash? I saw her eyes light up when I handed the wad to Katie—she doesn't see that much very often. Maybe she plans to steal it.

"We should go somewhere else," I whisper.

It's late afternoon. We both slept for several hours, although I woke every time Venderle's footsteps squeaked on the stairs. She seemed to climb them a lot—maybe trying to get up the nerve to rob us. Luckily, Katie has the money, but Venderle thinks it's mine.

"You were supposed to meet—well, Treena was supposed to meet whoever you were playing this afternoon." Katie checks the open door for the seven hundredth time.

"Good point." I stand and raise my voice. "I must meet my friend, now. Randy gets off work in half an hour."

Katie blows out a long breath. "I'll walk to the station with you. I have to meet a friend, too."

I give her a "that sounds too suspicious" look which she ignores. Or doesn't understand.

She follows me out of the room, stopping to tap on the office door. "Citizen Morris and I are going out."

"Together?" Her eyes narrow in suspicion.

"No." Katie laughs as if this is the funniest thing she's heard in a long time. "No, just at the same time. Although, we'll probably walk to the station together. See you tonight!"

"The external locks engage at ten—if you're late, you'll sleep in the garden." She glares at both of us.

I don't have to feign my look of horror. Sleep outside—in nature? Ew. "I will not be late."

"Me, neither." Katie gives her a little finger wave. "Bye!"

We hurry out of the building and across the narrow yard, turning left as we leave the gate. Apawllo appears from nowhere, and Katie scoops him up. "Where are we going?"

I shrug. "Coffee shop? Library? Train station waiting room?"

"Coffee shop. We can afford two cups of black coffee."

"That wad of money you had looked pretty substantial to me. Why are you being so stingy?" I follow her up the street.

The neighborhood has come to life. Children play in yards, adults hang laundry from clothes lines, a man delivers a package. Bubbles slide silently down the street, flashing angry words at anyone who dares to step in front of them.

"It looks like way more than it is." Katie nods and offers a cheery greeting to an older woman pushing a cart full of grocery bags. The woman mumbles something and crosses the street as if to get away from the strange tourist. "I can't believe they don't have drone grocery delivery here."

"You do on Luna?"

She gives me a disbelieving look. "Don't you?"

I scratch my head. We do on SK2, but I'm not sure about dirtside. Leo takes care of all that at Sierra Hotel, and when we were in the Techno-Inst, we ate in the student dining hall. "Probably?"

"How could you not know? Don't—" she lowers her voice "—secret agents have to buy groceries?"

"I'm not really a secret agent."

"No kidding—if you were, you'd have figured out the Protocol Omega stuff by now."

I hold up both hands. "Whatever. Let's find that coffee shop. I'll pay you back if you buy us lunch."

We find a cafe on the next block, and Katie orders two beverages and a pair of small fruit pies. She hands me my food, and we go outside to sit in the courtyard behind the building. This is apparently shared by the other occupants of the building—in addition to three small tables, there's a sandbox, a small shed, and a half dozen laundry lines crisscrossing above our heads. The windows looking into the sheltered space are small, and most of them are open.

"I'm not sure this is much better than the hostel." I take a seat and flick on an audio disruption app from my holo-ring. If anyone is using tech to listen, they'll get interference and one word out of six. I bite into my pie. "Holy Zarquan, that is the best thing I've tasted in days."

Katie looks at hers suspiciously. "Really? I'd call it passable."

"I'm starving." I eat half of the pie and wash it down with some coffee. The beverage is hot but unsweetened and black. Yuck. "Okay, I guess we need to get down to business. How do we find the password?"

She taps her fingers against the metal table. "Have you searched through all your stuff? Did you check inside that bag?"

"You mean the one we left at the hostel? Yeah, I looked. Nothing. I suppose it could have been hidden in a seam. I don't think Vanti would have done that —she would have hidden it in something I was sure to find."

"So, it's probably on you." Katie looks me over. "Did she have access to your clothes?"

I stare at her, dumbfounded. Of course, Vanti had access to my clothes. I start searching through the secret pockets sewn into the leggings, putting items on the table as I remove them. The knife I took from Katie, my tool kit, a tranq-ring.

Katie snatches her knife and points it at the ring. "What is that?"

I explain how it can put a grown man out in ten seconds. "Just twist this and—" I mime slapping her shoulder.

She jerks away, even though I didn't touch her. "Sounds useful. If you don't mind getting arrested for assaulting someone."

"We only use them in extreme situations." I slide it on my finger. I hadn't even realized I had one with me. What else do I have concealed in these pants?

"What about that?" She taps the knife on my tool kit.

I glance around the courtyard to make sure no one is paying attention. My cam disruptor has been running since we left the Zhengzu-Maryought, but a quick check shows no surveillance active. Still, I set the case on my knee, under the edge of the table, and open it.

"This allows me to connect to systems and hack into them." I tap the items as I name them. "Wireless adapter, pliers, ultra-thin mag connectors, variable frequency disruptor, signal booster—hang on—what's this?" I lift a small, thin square. It's wrapped in foil, with bright red writing.

"It looks like candy," Katie says.

"That's exactly what it is." I tip it, so she can see the writing. "Dolce Amour is the most famous chocolatier on SK2."

"What's SK2?"

I ignore her. I didn't put this chocolate in my tool kit. It could be a gift from O'Neill—he knows how much I love this brand. I unwrap a corner and take a nibble. It's Dolce Amour's most expensive confection—the *Depths of Deep Space*.

A smile spreads across my face. "This is the password."

CHAPTER TWENTY-SEVEN

"That piece of candy is the password?" Katie's voice is flat and disbelieving.

With a grin, I unwrap the chocolate and hold it where she can see it. The thin square is a deep, dark brown, with glints of gold. "Yup. This is from my favorite chocolatier—it's the candy my fiancé buys when he thinks he's in trouble. Or when he wants to butter me up for something. So, you might think he hid it in here for me. It's the kind of thing he would do."

"But he didn't?" Katie makes a get-on-with-it gesture that appears to be universal in the galaxy.

"This particular variety is their most expensive, and it's the *only* one I don't like. It's too dark, and the flakes of gold creep me out. Who wants to eat metal?"

"Is it real gold?" She takes the candy from me, careful to hold it by the wrapping.

"Yeah, that's why it's so expensive. I think there's some platinum in there, too." I shudder. "Yuck. Plus, it's a stupid name. *Depths of Deep Space* was the best they could come up with? Obviously, Vanti planted this in my tool kit— she knew I wouldn't eat it, but if anyone found it, it would mean nothing to them."

"If someone found a piece of expensive chocolate in my stuff, they'd wonder who I stole it from. Commonwealth agents must make a lot more credits than most Leweians."

"Something like that." Under the shelter of the table, I make sure my ring is connected to my internal audio system. Then I pull the metal tag from Apawllo's collar out of another pocket and wave it over the ring.

Vanti's recorded voice says, "Protocol Omega Three. Enter password."

I whisper, "Depths of Deep Space."

"Incorrect password." The tiny three on the holo-screen changes to a two.

"Zark! That has to be it!" I look up to see Katie taking a bite of the chocolate.

She freezes, her wide eyes focused on me. "Was I not supposed to eat it?"

"I don't know—if the name wasn't the secret, then there must be something else!"

She sets the half-eaten square on her napkin, her eyes downcast. "Sorry. But you tasted it, so I thought..." She gasps.

"What?"

Katie holds up the foil wrapper. Inside, there's more printing:

"Chocolate <> love."

I try the authentication sequence again. "Chocolate is not love."

"Protocol Omega Three initiated," Vanti's voice says. "Please stand by."

"Is that what it says?" Katie taps the scrap of foil wrapping.

"I forgot you don't read Standard. How'd you know it was important?"

"It was printed on the inside of a chocolate that looked like it had never been opened. If that isn't a secret agent trick, I don't know what is." She carefully flattens the brightly colored foil. As she slides her finger over the writing, it disappears. "Ew, what if that got on the candy?"

"I'm more worried what would have happened if someone else had found the candy first. I'm sure it's safe enough—Vanti wouldn't waste good chocolate."

My audio implant buzzes, and a call connects. "This is Captain Philpott. Protocol Omega Three has been initiated. I am sending pick-up coordinates to your ring."

"Pick-up coordinates? No—we need to find Vanti and O'Neill!"

"And Nick," Katie whispers.

I nod in agreement as Philpot replies. "Protocol Omega Three instructs me to retrieve you immediately. These coordinates are the closest landing place. How long will it take you to get there?"

"I don't know." I swipe the coordinates to a mapping program, but I don't have enough stored data to find the location. "Where is this?"

"Stand by—sending map updates to your ring." A few seconds later, the map pops up, showing me the location and a route to it. "According to my data, you should be able to get there in twenty minutes via bubble or walk there in three hours. Do you have access to transportation?"

"We can take the subway. But we don't have a lot of money." I glare at my stingy banker.

"The subway is free," Katie says.

"Oh, right, we didn't have to pay before, did we? But I'm not meeting you until we get O'Neill and Vanti."

"Negative, Runner. You are to proceed to the retrieval point immediately." Philpott's voice is hard.

"Sorry, Captain, you aren't the boss of me. I'm not leaving without my team." I bite my thumbnail, thinking. "I need three—no, four grav belts and a signal to track them."

"Protocol Omeg—"

"Fork Protocol Omega Three," I snap. "I will rescue my friends. And you will get me the equipment I need to do it. Moore out." I swipe coordinates and a list of equipment to the captain and close the connection.

CHAPTER TWENTY-EIGHT

"Who were you talking to?" Katie asks as we cross a narrow grassy park on the way to the nearest subway station.

"Oh, yeah, you only heard my side of that." I slow down so the shorter woman doesn't have to run to keep up with me. "That was the captain of my ship. They're in orbit. She wants to pick us up, but we need to find the others first. I told her—"

"I heard. Where is she sending the stuff? And how?"

I hesitate. Katie Li is an unknown entity. She might be a dissident, or she might be a Leweian government agent. Or something else altogether. They don't need to know our technology.

On the other hand, I'm going to need her help to rescue Ty and Vanti. I'll have to trust her—to a point. "The captain has access to a drone that can deliver the gear we need."

Her eyes widen. "A drone? Like, fly stuff to us? Is the ship in orbit or somewhere on the planet?"

I shake my head. "That information is beyond my pay grade." I've heard agents say this, and even though my pay grade should entitle me to all the information, I've found this is not always the case. "But she'll deliver it tonight, after sunset."

"Where?"

"You'll see. First, let's get a real meal. That pie was a good start, but I'm starving. Don't worry, the captain is sending cash."

KATIE TAKES me to a street vendor selling stew and bread. The mouthwatering aroma of yeast and butter almost makes my heart stop. The man hands us two plastek bowls, each cradling a small, round loaf that's been hollowed out and filled with savory meat and vegetables. The center of the loaf sits to the side with a pat of butter melting into it. It smells heavenly and tastes even better.

"Are you sure we'll get more keis?" Katie asks as we sit on a nearby bench, scooping up our dinner. She drops a piece of meat on the ground for Apawllo. He looks away, bored, but when she reaches toward it, he bats her hand out of the way and grabs the morsel.

"Yes, it was on my list. Why are you so worried about cash? You had a huge wad of it."

"It looked huge, but those were small bills. That wad won't last very long." She pulls a bill from her pocket. "This is five keis. That bowl of stew cost twenty. I don't go home for another four days, and this has to last me until then."

"But the bed in the hostel was only four."

She shrugs. "Housing is cheap."

"What about your partner? Can't he cough up some more?"

"Where do you think I got this? I thought it would be plenty when he gave it to me."

"Your organization doesn't take very good care of you, does it?"

Her face tinges pink. "I'm not an official member of the organization. I'm kind of a civilian auxiliary. Usually, I'm 'cover'—to help him blend in."

"But he's not staying at the hostel, is he?" I rip off a piece of my now-empty bowl and take a bite of stew-soaked bread. Fantastic.

"No, he's not. This mission was different—I'm his backup plan, I guess." Katie plays with her stew, smushing a carrot with the spoon.

"What's the plan, then? What were you supposed to do if he got caught?"

Her shoulder twitches, and she makes a business of scooping out more meat for Apawllo. "I was supposed to send a message to his handler."

I freeze. I don't have any idea who Nick works for—if Katie has notified his handler, we could have Leweian agents descending on us at any moment. Or dissidents. I look around, trying to appear casual, identifying potential threats.

A man leans against a building, scrolling through something on his Ncuff. Every once in a while, he looks up. We make eye contact, and I give him the Ice Dame death glare until he looks away. Apparently, that works in all languages.

A woman with a baby stroller wanders by, nodding at me as she passes. The baby is hidden under a blanket—is it a baby or a weapon? I watch her in my peripheral vision as long as possible, turning slowly to keep her in sight until she goes into a store.

On the other side of the street, a pair makes out on another bench. Are they really that preoccupied with each other, or is it a cover to watch us?

"Did you?" I whisper.

Katie starts. "Did I what?"

"Message his handler?"

"No."

A wave of relief goes through me. "Why not?"

She gets up, tossing her half-eaten stew bowl in a recycler. Apawllo meows in protest, so she picks him up. I shove the last of my bread in my mouth, dump the plastek holder, and follow her across the park. "Why not?" I ask again as we head up the street.

"I don't like her. And you seemed to know what you're doing, so I figured we could rescue him ourselves."

Katie Li is either very gutsy or a complete idiot. Maybe both.

THE SUN DROPS behind the buildings to the west as I return to the hostel. Katie went back an hour ago, so it wouldn't look like we were together. I turn the knob on the old-fashioned door, grateful an Ncuff isn't required for access, since I don't have one. I should have asked Philpott to send me one of those, too. Although street vendors accept the paper notes Katie carries, the regular stores all work on the Ncuff system. Or at least I didn't see anyone using cash.

"How was your afternoon with your friend?" Venderle asks as I shut the door behind me.

I pause to dust my feet against the mat inside the front door. "She has to work again tomorrow, so we had to make it an early night. And I didn't want to sleep in the garden." I chuckle.

Venderle stares up at me, not laughing. "Good call. You look... different. Did you do something with your hair?"

I hunch my shoulders and bend my knees as I move closer, trying to disguise my height. "My hair? No, it's the same as it always was. I'd love to cover the gray, but it's not in the budget, if you know what I mean."

She pats the tight bun on the back of her head and gives me a disapproving look. "You should be proud of your gray—proof of a life well lived."

"Sure, sure." I look around the hallway, peering into the lounge, then past Venderle into her office. "Have you seen that young woman—the one I walked to the station with? I wanted to tell her we tried the street vendor she recommended."

Venderle jerks her head toward the closed door on the left. "She's in the garden out back, encouraging a stray cat." Her lips press together as if this is the height of depravity. "If that thing comes back after she leaves, I'll poison it. I detest furry things."

Yikes. I'm not a huge cat fan, but never trust someone who hates animals. "Thanks. I'll just pop out there and thank her for the recommendation. And suggest she shoo the animal away. It could have fleas."

Venderle nods regally. "Showing the wisdom of your years."

With a sickly grin, I push through the door. This leads to a small dining room. It looks like it hasn't been used in years—a layer of dust covers the table and chairs. But a wide, transparent door lets into the back garden where Katie sits petting Apawllo. I open the sliding door and step onto the low deck.

"Here you are. I tried that vendor you recommended. Excellent stew. Randy was really impressed." I cross the deck, my footsteps echoing. Standing with my back to the windows, I flick my holo-ring and turn on the audio disrupter again. "Venderle thinks you're encouraging feral cats to infiltrate her yard."

She takes the cat's face in both hands and talks to him in that voice people use for pets and babies. "Apawllo isn't feral, are you? No, you is a civilized boy." She glances up, and her tone changes. "All set for the drop off?"

"I hope so. I haven't heard anything from the captain, so I assume it's a go." I sit beside her on the bench. "I went back to the building where we lost them —there was yellow tape across the door and a couple of obvious law-enforcement types wandering the street."

"You went without me?" Her hand freezes on Apawllo's back. He waits less than a second before twisting around to bat her hand. The petting resumes.

"I also cased the prison again. There's a back door with an Ncuff reader and a cam. That's where we'll go in—I can fake the cam feed and use my gear to open the door."

She gives me a narrow-eyed look. "I thought you weren't an agent?"

I smile. "That's what I wanted you to think."

CHAPTER TWENTY-NINE

WE GO BACK INSIDE, to the lounge. Two other residents are there, playing a card game. Katie joins them, and I sit on the couch, paging through one of the many books. We don't have a lot of real books on SK2—too heavy—and Mother's library on Kaku is mainly for show. The books here are old, and I wish I could read them. Instead, I caress the pages and breathe in the musty scents of age and wisdom.

Precisely at ten, Venderle stomps to the entrance. Tumblers turn and the lock snicks. She pauses on her way up the hall to peer in at us. "I hope everyone made it home tonight."

We all reply in agreement, and she disappears into the office. I lean my head against the wall, listening intently as she moves through the small room behind me. Finally, another door opens and closes, and all is quiet.

All except the card game, that is. Someone cheers, others groan, and Katie rakes up a handful of paper bills.

Pounding echoes through the room. "Keep it down out there!" Venderle hollers through the wall.

The card players snicker. Katie gets to her feet. "Nice doing business with you folks, but it's bedtime for me."

"You can't win all our cash, then go to bed!" The two men jump up, too.

Katie shoves the bills into her pocket. "Someone has to end up with it."

"But that's not fair! You need to let us win some back!" The shorter guy's face turns red.

"That's not how poker works." The taller guy puts a hand on his buddy's arm. "She won, fair and square. Let's go to bed—and remember not to play her again."

The short guy continues grumbling but follows his friend into the hallway. "A little late to learn that."

"Good night!" Katie calls.

The taller guy waves, and the shorter guy shoots an angry glare over his shoulder as they climb the stairs.

I put my book on the table. "I'm glad they aren't sleeping in our dorm—you'd wake up with your throat slit and your money missing."

Katie smirks. "Why are you reading that?"

I lower my voice. "I'm not really reading it. What is it?"

"It's a history of Lewei." She flips the front cover open. "From seventy years ago—before the current government was established." She shuts the book and shakes her head. "Simply owning this book could be grounds for arrest—I'm surprised Venderle leaves it out here."

A trickle of cold runs down my back. I take the book and tuck it into the empty slot on the shelf. Is it a stupid mistake or a signal of the hostel owner's political leanings? What are the odds that Katie would be staying at this particular hostel?

I flick on my audio disrupter and lean close to her ear. "Who told you about this place?"

She pulls back, staring at me. "Nick's handler told him to recommend it. You don't think—"

I hold up both hands. "I think we need to finish the job and get out of here. Come on."

We climb the stairs. The two cardplayers stand beside a door, whispering. They straighten up when they see us.

"You two lost?" Katie jokes softly.

The shorter guy takes a menacing step forward. "Yeah, we lost. We lost our dough to a cheater."

The tall guy grabs his friend's arm and drags him back. "Cut it out, Farnsman." He turns to us. "We didn't want to wake the others. Good night."

"Good night." We leave them and go into the women's dorm.

Two other beds are occupied, and both women appear to be sound sleepers. Katie and I take our shoes off and perch on the edge of my bunk, listening. The hiss of whispering reaches us, but I can't distinguish any of the words. After a few more seconds, a door opens and closes. Then another one, farther down the hall—probably the bathroom.

We wait in silence until the second man returns to the dorm across the way. Katie picks up her shoes and ties them onto her small backpack. I put mine inside my empty bag. We move to the door, pressing our ears against it.

I'm just about to open the door when a loud click sounds. I step away, putting my back to the wall on the hinge side. Katie backs away on the other side. The knob turns slowly, and the door rotates open a few degrees. Light from the hallway nightlight stabs into the dark room like a spotlight. Katie takes another step back.

The door opens farther, and a shadowy figure creeps in. The door eases shut, and the person—I can't tell if it's a man or a woman—tiptoes toward the bunks. They stop by Katie's bunk, and a hand shoots out, patting the empty mattress. A voice swears softly, and the figure turns.

"Looking for someone?" I whisper.

The intruder stiffens, then relaxes. "Let's talk outside, shall we?"

The light falls on her face as she opens the door, illuminating white-blonde hair, teased into a huge, smooth bob with perky, curled up ends. Bright red lips and thick lashes finish the retro look.

Katie stares at her in surprise. "Betzy?"

CHAPTER THIRTY

"WHO'S BETZY?" I whisper fiercely as I follow Katie out of the dorm.

"Nick's handler."

Zark.

The woman leads the way to the end of the hall and opens a door, revealing a closet. A vacu-bot sleeps in its recharger, and various cleaning supplies stand on the shelves. The back is shrouded in darkness. "In we go."

"Are you going to lock us in here?" Katie whimpers.

Betzy shushes her. "I should, but no. Get in."

The three of us cram into the tiny, antiseptic smelling space, and Betzy pulls the door closed. Then she flicks a switch, and a beam of light stabs into my face. "Who are you?"

"This is Triana," Katie says. "Her friends were meeting with Nick when he got nabbed."

The light moves away, shining on a door at the back of the closet. "That goes to the attic. Move."

I cross my arms and lean against the wall with a nonchalance I'm not feeling. "I'm not going anywhere until you tell me who you are."

"Katie told you. I'm Betzy. Let's go." She jerks the light at the door again. Katie's already pulled it open and is creeping up the steep steps. "You can stand here all night if you want—you aren't my responsibility." She pushes past me, snapping the light off.

"Fine," I mutter. If this Betzy is Nick's handler, then she's going to want to get him out of whatever he's landed in. That makes her my best ticket to getting Ty and Vanti free. I scuff forward, hands outstretched so I don't ram into anything in the dark.

My eyes adjust, and the faint moonlight from above guides me up the steps. I pause to close the door behind me, then climb the stairs, coming out in a steep-roofed space with open rafters and a single dormer window looking over the back yard.

The moonlight feels brilliant in comparison to the dark closet. Betzy pulls one side of the window open, and a clean breeze blows away the musty attic smell. "That way."

We climb onto the steep roof, the shingles grating under our shoes. As I exit the building, I flick my holo-ring and send Philpott the signal. A soft buzz intrudes on the quiet night, and the creatures creaking in the yard below go silent.

Betzy freezes, the whites of her eyes flashing in the moonlight as she looks for the source of the sound. "What is that?"

"Special delivery." I hold out my hand, and the drone zeros in on my signal. As it touches down beside me, legs extend from the capsule-shaped body, automatically adjusting for the slant of the roof.

Katie plops down on the shingles. "You've got some pretty cool tech."

I use my ring to unlock the capsule and pull out the items. Five grav belts. A thick packet of Leweian keis. A toolkit—one with more items than the tiny one in my pocket. A box of protein bars—the nasty-tasting ones Vanti likes. Ugh, I should have specified the brand. Doesn't matter—I have no intention of eating them. A backpack with several changes of clothing, and a sleeve of PVD capsules. I flick my comm icon. "Perfect. You're an ace collaborator, Carol."

"Just get to the rendezvous point and call me." The captain sounds grumpy, and she doesn't wait for me to sign off but disconnects with an irritated click.

I bite back a grin and step away as the drone takes off.

Betzy grabs my arm. "Where did that come from? How'd it get here right now?"

"It was scheduled to start looking for my signal about ten minutes ago. Why do you think we were sneaking out of the dorm?" I tap the controls of a grav belt, slaving it to mine, and hand it to her. "Do you know how to use one of these?"

She snatches it from my grasp, snapping it around her waist and adjusting it like a pro.

I set the second one and hand it to Katie. "You don't have to do anything—I've got it tethered to mine. Just put it on, and it will follow me automatically."

Katie takes the belt and wraps it around her waist. While Betzy helps her adjust it, I clasp the other three around the backpack strap, then sling the thing over my shoulders. "Since you seem to know what's going on here, how about you give us a rundown on the LIA station. How difficult will it be to get them out?"

"It won't be difficult at all," Betzy says. "Nick is waiting for my signal."

"You have a plan?"

"We always have a plan in case a meet goes sour. Follow me." She taps her belt, then swears. "Why is this locked?"

"I wasn't sure a Leweian rebel would know how to use one." I flick my controls and adjust the settings, setting her free.

"They wouldn't." She lifts off the roof, and Katie rises with her. "But a Commonwealth agent does."

"Wait. What?" Katie's eyes go wide, and her body stiffens. "You're Commonwealth?"

"Hush—let's get aloft." Betzy adjusts the belt and lifts faster.

I tap my own controls, and we follow.

We fly over the dark city. We're far from the glittering signs and lighted bubble bridges of the core, and it's late in this working-class neighborhood. Below, the occasional window glows behind closed curtains, but the street-lights are all focused downward, so we're virtually invisible.

About ten minutes later, Betzy and Katie land on the purple porn shop's flat roof. I touch down beside them.

"I thought you were LFF?" Katie hisses at Betzy as soon as her feet touch the plasfalt roof.

We crouch in the shadow of the roof-top door. "What's LFF?" I ask.

"Leweian Freedom Federation. Resistance organization." Betzy doesn't bother hiding the sneer on her face. "They're trying to reform the Leweian political structure to allow more freedom but not very successfully. I'm a Commonwealth liaison."

Katie covers her face with her hands. "Why didn't you tell me that? I'm a traitor!"

"Honey, you're no more of a traitor than you were as an LFF member. You're trying to save your nation, not subvert it. We're trying to help." Betzy pats Katie's shoulder, but the dark-haired girl flinches away.

If Betzy is Commonwealth, why did Vanti meet with Nick? "Is this 'Nick' person Commonwealth, too?" I ask.

Katie's hands drop, and she stares at Betzy, as if willing her to answer in the negative.

Betzy's eyes flick from my face to Katie's. She shakes her head slowly. Katie buries her face again with a whimper.

"Why was Nick meeting with Vanti?"

"He was supposed to pass information back to our headquarters. It's standard any time a Commonwealth visitor comes to Lewei. The Commonwealth installs an agent in the team or security detail, and we meet with them. I'm not sure how the meet got flagged." Betzy taps her Ncuff. "I'm going to tell him we're in position."

I grab her hand before she can tap again. "How is he receiving your messages if he's locked up?"

"He's not locked up. He's the arresting officer."

CHAPTER THIRTY-ONE

"WHAT?!" Katie and I both whisper-yell.

"Calm down. Nick is a double agent." Betzy taps her cheek, staring over my head. "Or maybe he's a triple agent—I'm not sure if the LFF counts. It doesn't really matter." Her eyes snap back to mine. "He's a deep plant—been on Lewei for years. Inserted into the system as a teen and trained up through their law enforcement. The LIA planted him into the LFF—but he really works for us."

"Are you sure?" I ask. "How do you know he wasn't subverted if he grew up here?"

"He wasn't really a teen—he just looked like one."

"How old is he?" Katie asks. "He says he's twenty-eight."

"Does it matter?" Betzy taps her Ncuff again. "Do you mind if I do this?"

I nod for her to continue. "If he's the arresting officer, what do we need to do? Why can't he just let them go? Deport them back to Kaku? That's what they did with the rest of us."

"Us?" Betzy looks up, the glow from her Ncuff giving her face a creepy glow.

"My team—the Morgan party. They all got sent back to the ship."

"The rest of your team didn't meet with an LFF operative. I think someone in the LIA was tracking Nick, not realizing he's with them, and blew the meet." She looks at her screen, nods, and shuts it down. "That meeting marks your friends as LFF sympathizers at best. The LIA won't let that go. So, we need to break them out. But still preserve Nick's cover."

"Does the LIA know the man is Annabelle Morgan's fiancé? She's a fairly high-profile figure in the Commonwealth."

"I know who Annabelle Morgan is." Betzy gets to her feet. "Let's move. We have an ambush to stage."

"And the LIA doesn't care that Morgan's fiancé is in their custody? That she'll cause all kinds of trouble if he isn't sent home healthy and in one piece?" I'm not sure how far Mother's influence extends on Lewei, but the government obviously wants us to do business here. Holding the board chair's soon-to-be son-in-law doesn't seem like a good way to promote those interests.

"They may not know. In fact, I'd guess they probably *don't*. I haven't heard any whispers of it. Which means he isn't telling them. Perhaps there's a reason for that?" Betzy gets to her feet and opens the door to the building. Dark stairs drop away, but she doesn't go down. She taps her belt and lifts off, gliding up inside the structure. Her head and shoulders disappear above the door. When she drops again, she hands me a stunner. "Come on. They're transporting *dangerous suspects* to a more secure location, and we're going to stop them." She flies away without offering Katie a weapon.

I trail behind Betzy and Katie as they glide across the dark rooftop. The moon sails behind thick clouds, and darkness closes in as we descend into the street. We fly along, just above the ground, until we're about three blocks from the LIA building. We drop to the ground and huddle in a shadowy doorway.

"Triana, I assume you know how to use a weapon?" Betzy ignores Katie.

My holo-ring buzzes before I can answer. "Sorry, that's the captain." I flick the icon.

"Annabelle, you have to talk to Hy-Mi!" my mother wails over my audio implant.

"Mother? How—"

"He's left me!"

Betzy glares at me, and I turn away, lowering my voice. "Mother, I'm busy. On Lewei, remember?"

"Do you think I'm senile? I sent you there!" The hysteria leaves her voice for those few words but comes back in full force. "You need to talk to Hy-Mi."

"Are you talking to *your mother* during a mission?" Betzy's voice ratchets up a few octaves.

I wave her off. "What did he do?"

"He quit! He walked away—the day you left Kaku. I didn't believe him, but he hasn't come back! Annabelle, I *need* him!"

"Have you talked to him yourself?" I swear, when Mother is off her game, she's worse than a teen. Luckily, it doesn't happen often.

"I certainly did. I demanded he come back. He refused." She says this as if demanding someone do something is the normal way to resolve a difference of opinion. To be fair, it usually works for Dame Morgan.

"Did you ask him why he quit?"

"He said he wouldn't come back unless I let you have your stupid private wedding. So, I need you to tell him—"

"Hy-Mi quit for me?" I told him I'd take care of it. In fact, he'd made it clear he wouldn't get in the middle of this argument. Yet, he'd quit in an effort to force her hand. He left a job he loves, for me. My eyes burn, and I sniff.

"Hy-Mi?" Betzy's eyes narrow, and her lips purse.

Zark. I shouldn't have said that out loud. Cover blown.

"Mother, I need to go. I'm in the middle of an intense negotiation—"

"It's the middle of the night in Lewei City, and you were sent back to the ship. Which reminds me, you can tell Fioravanti she's done. I can't believe she risked my reputation for some stunt. I won't have troublemakers in my employ!"

"It wasn't a stunt, Mother, and we're getting her back to the ship right now. I'll talk to Hy-Mi. Good night." I cut the connection before she can respond, then set my comm system to go to message.

Betzy pins me with a glare. "How, exactly, did you get a call from your *mother* in the middle of a mission? An interstellar call at that. Kind of expensive for a security agent—even one paid by SK'Corp."

"The captain must have relayed it." I'll have something to say to Philpott when I get back to the ship. Although, I suspect Mother didn't give her any options.

"And your mother has an employee named Hy-Mi?" Betzy steps closer, her attitude menacing despite her slight figure.

"Someone is coming!" Katie's whisper freezes Betzy in her tracks. Lights shine from the far end of the street, the glow banishing the darkness as the vehicle approaches.

"Places." The blonde points at Katie.

"I'd be happy to take my place if you'd tell me what the heck I'm supposed to be doing," I grouse.

"If you weren't busy talking to your mama during the mission brief, you'd know." Betzy pushes me into place. "Stand over there, and point your weapon at the auto. *Don't* fire." She moves to the middle of the road and turns to face the approaching vehicle.

The bubble's lights catch her full in the face, but Betzy doesn't flinch. She just fires straight into the angry red script flowing across the top of the windscreen. The bubble stops with a lurch.

The door opens, and a man leans out. He fires a weapon at Betzy, but the beam splashes against an invisible shield, wrapping her in a sphere of blaster fire. The bright light dissipates, leaving Betzy unharmed in the middle of the road. She fires again, this time a non-lethal stunner. Her adversary falls to the ground with a thud.

The door on the other side opens, and the performance is repeated. Betzy holds something over her head, and the bubble's lights go out. "Clear."

Vanti climbs out, but I ignore her, throwing myself at the man following her. A guy I don't recognize catches me by the shoulders. He's taller than O'Neill, with massive shoulders and a smile like a Norse god.

"I think you're looking for someone else."

My heart belongs to Ty O'Neill, but I can't pretend I don't get a little thrill from his deep, rough-velvet voice. I give myself a shake. "Where's Ty?"

"I'm here. Good thing I recognize your voice—that disguise is hideous." Warm hands grab me from behind and swing me into a kiss that lasts the ages. My toes curl, my heart pounds—I think my hair even smokes.

"Either you're Annabelle Morgan, or there's something fishy going on." Betzy's dry voice breaks us apart.

I roll my eyes. "I thought you already figured that out."

"The call from your mother kind of clued me in."

Vanti chokes. "Dame Morgan called you? Here? Now?"

"Yeah, and I think you've been fired." I shrug. "I might be able to help with that."

Vanti waves this offer away. "Probably time for me to move on anyway. Now that my cover is blown."

"Where's Katie?" I peer around the others, but it's too dark to see very far.

"She's with Nick." Ty nods behind me.

When I turn, Nick and Katie are standing about a meter apart. My lips twitch—Katie's hair is mussed, and Nick is straightening his shirt. If I had to guess, I'd say they were doing the same thing as Ty and me.

"Okay, lovebirds." Betzy claps twice. "Time to finish this game. I'm escorting Anna—Triana and her team to the pickup location. Nick, get into position. Katie, you go back to the hostel."

"Maybe we should take her with us to Luna." Vanti put a hand on Katie's arm. "She's been through a lot, and she's a civilian. I don't think sending her home on a shuttle is a good idea."

Since when does Vanti care about Katie? She never met the girl until now.

Before I can ask, Katie pulls away. "But I'm supposed to—"

"Your mission is cancelled." Betzy scowls at Katie. "I'm sending you back to Luna City. Riding with our friends is an excellent idea." She raises an eyebrow at me.

Before I can answer, O'Neill interrupts. "We can't go to Luna City—we were deported."

"You were deported from Lewei." Betzy turns back to me. "Luna City has a strange relationship with Lewei. You've got a meeting there, right?"

I nod.

"Then you'll be expected to keep it. I suggest you leave this one—" she points at Vanti "—and lover-boy on the ship, but the rest of your team will be fine. Katie can show you around if you'll take her home."

"Won't people wonder why Katie is with us?" I glance at the other woman.

Betzy exchanges a look with Nick.

The big man shrugs. "I'll book a flight for Katie on the early shuttle out of Lewei. She'll go with you, but for record-keeping purposes, she'll have been on the shuttle. I don't think making her fly home alone is a good plan."

"Why are you talking about me like I don't exist? I'm right here." Katie stomps her foot. "I'm not a child."

Betzy glances at Katie's foot and raises an eyebrow. "Really?"

Katie's face goes red. Nick steps forward and puts a hand on her arm. She swings around and points a finger at him. "You're just as bad as her."

Nick wraps his hand around her finger and gives a gentle squeeze. "Now that you've rescued your friends, I need you safely off planet. You've done a great job. I'll see you next week, right?"

The anger drains out of her face. "Okay. But we're having a long talk—about who you really work for."

"Deal." He glances at Betzy, then shrugs and pulls Katie in for a fast kiss.

I turn away to give them some privacy, but Betzy and Vanti watch with identical expressions—disgust and a little bit of envy. I slide my arms around O'Neill and snuggle close.

"Enough kissing." Betzy looks like she'd like to stomp her own foot but restrains herself. "Let's get moving. Those other two agents will be coming around soon. Get back in the transport, Nick. I'll hit you with the lowest stun I've got."

Nick leans back but doesn't let go of Katie. "What about the dash cams?"

"My disabler took them out—or should have. Double check when you get in."

Nick releases Katie, touches her cheek with one finger, and moves to the vehicle. "Keep her safe."

Betzy waves dismissively. "Where are those grav belts?"

I unlatch two of them from my backpack and hand them to Vanti and O'Neill. "Next stop, rendezvous."

As we lift off the ground, Katie cries out. "Wait, what about the cat?"

CHAPTER THIRTY-TWO

I TAP my grav belt to change directions. "We have to go back to the hostel and get Apawllo."

Vanti zips over and grabs my arm. "The cat? Didn't he go back to the ship with the team?"

I shake my head. "No. One of your teammates left him with the Protocol Omega Three tag. That's the only reason we were able to call the ship."

Betzy swoops around us, like a dog herding sheep. "We need to move. We've got to get you off planet before daybreak."

"But I can't go back to Kaku without the cat—Elodie will kill me. She loves that thing."

Vanti nods and changes directions. "We need to get the cat."

"Are you kidding me?" Betzy swings after her. "What cat?"

We all try to explain at the same time. Betzy sticks her fingers in her mouth and blows a shrill whistle. We all wince.

"Way to wake up the neighborhood," Katie mutters.

"We can't compromise your escape over a cat!" Betzy keeps trying to herd us the other direction.

I duck around her, lifting higher to fly over the buildings instead of down the streets. "You aren't going to win this one."

"Look, tell me where to find him, and I'll send him to meet you on Luna. I can have an agent travel as Katie."

"You know they won't let an unquarantined animal into Luna City." Katie glares at Betzy. "Nice try."

"How about this?" I turn to face the others, still moving toward the hostel.

"I'll have the ship send the drone to the hostel. You can load Apawllo into the drone, and we'll scoop it up as we leave the planet."

"Do you trust her to do that?" Katie asks.

I look the blonde up and down. "I think she'll do that if she knows what's good for her."

Vanti flies in behind my shoulder. "Yeah, she will."

Betzy flings up both hands. "Fine. I'll put the cat in the drone. If it gets there on time."

"We'll wait for you." I flick my holo-ring. O'Neill tethers my belt to his and pulls me toward the rendezvous point while I explain to the captain. By the time we land in a field on the outskirts, the drone is en route.

Katie calls Betzy on her Ncuff. "I want to see you put him in the drone."

Betzy stares out of the Ncuff screen, spit flying from her lips as she spews a string of vicious sounding words. I assume she's cussing—since my translator was supplied by my mother, I only hear muzak.

I stare at the image on Katie's wrist. "I do believe Betzy might have been planning to skip the cat."

Vanti inspects her fingernails. "I hope she knows that would not be in her best interest. I know the people she works for."

Betzy finally becomes coherent. "What is with you people? It's a cat!"

"He's *our* cat." Vanti points at the image, putting her face close to the screen. "And we want him back."

"Ugh. Give me ten minutes."

Seven minutes later, Betzy sends us a shot of the garden behind the hostel. The drone sits on the dark paving stones beside her. Apawllo lounges nearby, splayed out on the grass, apparently asleep. "I'm getting the cat."

She stalks forward, and her hands reach out to grab. Just as her fingers touch his fur, Apawllo springs to life, snarling, fur standing on end, back arched. He spits. Betzy swears. The cat swipes at her hand, and she yanks it away with a yelp.

The fact that the whole thing happens in whispers makes it even funnier. Even the cat seems to know stealth is important.

"I don't think he likes her." Katie has one hand over her mouth, eyes dancing. She's shaking with silent laughter, and the screen jitters on her wrist.

"Try putting some food in the drone," I suggest. "Do you have any fish?"

"Why would I have fish?" The view swings around, and Betzy's face appears. "Do I look like the kind of person who would carry fish around in my backpack?"

"I thought *terkfiske* was a common snack on Lewei."

If her eyes get any narrower, she won't be able to see. Her jaw clenches, and she speaks very softly. "Maybe Leweians carry that smelly stuff in their pockets, but I do not."

Katie masters her giggles and speaks with barely a tremor in her voice. "Put your Ncuff in the drone. I'll try to call him in."

"I'm not putting my Ncuff in that drone—I need it."

I tap my holo-ring. "I'll have Philpott link a call to the drone's internal speakers." I connect to the ship.

The comm officer answers, and I explain what I need. There's disbelieving silence for a second, then she replies, "Putting your call through now."

"Imagine the stories you can tell when you get home." When the call connects, I turn to the others. "Who wants to try first?"

O'Neill and Vanti try enticing the cat into the drone, but he ignores them.

"At least he isn't running away." I turn to Katie. "You wanna try?"

"It might be funny to watch Betzy chase him," she says.

"I can hear you," Betzy snarls.

Katie ignores her. "Here kitty, kitty. You don't want to be left behind with the mean lady."

Apawllo stops licking his leg and glances up at Betzy. He stares over the cam for a few seconds, obviously locking eyes with the agent. Then he gets to his feet, saunters to the drone, and leaps inside.

Betzy slams the door shut and cuts the connection before we can cheer.

I flick the command to lift the drone, and the icon turns green. "He's on his way."

"I hope she didn't let him back out—she's kind of spiteful," Katie says.

I put an arm around her. "She won't if she knows what's good for her."

"An agent like Betzy knows when to cut her losses." Vanti stares at the sky. "She might be a bit pissy for the next few days, though. Good thing you're coming with us. Did you call the ship, Triana?"

"The drone lift off was their signal to land. They'll be here in—" I check my holo-ring. "Five minutes."

"That's good, because Betzy just sent me a message." Katie's voice shakes but not with laughter this time. "She said the LIA is headed our direction."

CHAPTER THIRTY-THREE

I GRAB O'NEILL'S ARM. "How do they know where we are?"

He looks at Vanti. "Do you think Betzy turned us in? Or are they tracking us in some manner?"

"Zark! I had clothes for you to change into—in case they tagged yours." I unlatch my backpack.

O'Neill puts a hand over mine, stopping me. "Too late now—we'd have to change the rendezvous point. We'll space the clothes once we take off. Katie, ask Betzy what the ETA is."

Katie's brows draw down in confusion.

"Estimated time of arrival," O'Neill says. "How long before the LIA gets here?"

Her face clears. "Oh, you mean the TTA. Time to arrival. I guess acronyms don't translate well." She taps her Ncuff and waits a second. "Betzy says five minutes."

I check my holo-ring. "The ship will land in three."

"Perfect." Vanti looks around the field. "Let's move behind that tractor. It won't fool them for long, but if they don't know our exact location—"

"If they've tagged us, they'll know." O'Neill shrugs out of his jacket and shirt. "Triana, give us those clothes. And divert the ship to the next field."

I message the ship, then pull out the clothing as he and Vanti strip down. Katie turns away to watch the road, and I appreciate her consideration. Vanti doesn't bother. I have to remind myself these two have changed clothes in front of each other hundreds of times, and nothing has ever happened. At least not as far as I know.

159

I also get a chance to appreciate O'Neill's fine physique in the moonlight. A quick glance reveals Vanti is completely focused on her own clothing, so I relax a fraction.

"I see autos!" Katie cries.

"Triana, Katie—go!" O'Neill makes shooing motions at us as he shimmies into the jeans I brought. "We're right behind you."

Vanti slides the leggings up over her butt and fastens a grav belt around her waist. She's wearing a sports bra and has a shirt clenched in her fist as she rises off the ground. "Move!"

We streak across the field just above the long grass, Katie pulled along in my wake. The moon drops behind a cloud, and darkness covers the area again, making the bubbles' lights stand out in bright relief. It also hides us— nature is on our side. Unless they've got night vision devices. Or heat mappers. Or—

"I see the ship!"

I glance back to see Katie pointing at the sky. The captain has turned off the external lights, so a huge black bulk descends toward us. Another look over my shoulder reveals nothing but the approaching vehicles, still on course for the first field.

I activate my near-field coms. "Ty, where are you?"

He doesn't reply—the LIA probably took his holo-ring. I panic, thinking I've just led the LIA right to us again, then remember our comms don't work very far without a network connection. Unless they've brought the holo-rings in the bubbles and have figured out how to turn them on without the original owner, the call did nothing.

My ring flashes, and I cut our speed, dropping to the dirt. "Here."

Vanti rockets out of the darkness, her unbuttoned shirt flapping around her. Just before she plows into me, she swoops upward. My belt digs into my back, and I'm yanked into the sky. Somehow, Vanti managed to tether my belt to hers in motion. I didn't know that was even possible. Katie yelps as she's dragged upward.

As we shoot up, the *Black Panther* plummets like a chocolate strawberry from an overloaded buffet table in high G. I expect to smash into the ship any second.

"Tell them Protocol Theta Seven!" Vanti yells.

I toggle my ship comm and repeat the words, clenching my teeth against the wind as we streak upward. The comm officer acknowledges. Overhead, a metallic gong rings out as a hatch slams open. Light spills out of the ship's airlock. The ship rolls as it descends, giving us a straight shot into the open- ing. Vanti arrows inside, with Katie and me on her heels.

O'Neill hits the airlock seconds later and slams the hatch shut.

Vanti slaps a hand on the comm panel. "Theta Seven complete!"

The ship rolls to level, and we're thrown against the side of the airlock as we blast out of the atmosphere. The artificial gravity kicks in, and we slide to the floor.

"Everybody up!" Vanti has opened the internal hatch. "Grab a seat and strap in. Now!"

I grab Katie's hand and drag her into the hallway. The lounge door opens as I approach, and we dive onto the couch. I show Katie how to strap in, and we all heave a sigh of relief.

Ty runs a hand through his hair, dropping it back into its usual shiny perfection, then turns to me. "Do you think you can give up the PVD now? I like the *Księżna*, but I don't really want to kiss her."

My hand flies to my face—I keep forgetting I don't look like me. I reach into my bra and pull out the capsule, twisting it off. Then I kiss my fiancé.

THE CAPTAIN'S voice interrupts our make-out session. "We'll reach Luna in four hours."

I glance up to find Katie studiously ignoring me and Ty, which is difficult, given we're sitting on the same sofa. Vanti has disappeared.

O'Neill clears his throat. "You can unbuckle now, Katie."

I unlatch my own restraints. "Do you want something to eat? I'm starving."

O'Neill shakes his head. "You're always starving."

Katie fumbles with her buckle, then gets the straps undone. "Is that why they sent food in the drone? I mean, there was enough cash in there to buy a restaurant, so I wondered why we needed the protein bars, too."

"Vanti likes to be prepared." I tap the AutoKich'n control panel and order a pair of milkshakes. "I wouldn't eat those things unless they were the last food on earth. They're nasty."

Vanti stalks into the room. "Catch." She tosses a ring at O'Neill.

He catches it, slides it onto his finger, and activates it with a flick.

I pull the plastek mugs out of the AutoKich'n and turn to Katie. "It will take him a while to get that thing set up. Let's go find Apawllo."

Katie's hand flies to her mouth, and she leaps to her feet. "I can't believe I forgot about him! Where is he?"

"He'll be in the cargo pod." I take her down the hall to a door at the end, slurping on my milkshake as we walk. The door opens in response to my holo-ring, and we climb down a ladder, carefully juggling our mugs.

Sinbad, the cargo chief, stands beside a closed hatch. He's got scratches on his arms, and one of them is bleeding. "What kind of cat is that?"

I pat his shoulder. "Go find the med pod. We'll take care of him." I open the hatch as Sinbad disappears up the ladder.

We climb through the hatch. Large crates line the walls—some of them undoubtedly holding my vast wardrobe. Several of the spaces are empty—probably the equipment left behind on Lewei. The drone sits in its cradle on the far wall, with the hatch open.

Katie peers into the drone. "Apawllo! Here kitty, kitty."

In response to Katie's crooning, the cat sticks his nose out of the drone. He looks around, as if checking for Sinbad, then jumps lightly to the deck to rub against Katie's legs. She sets her milkshake aside to pick him up and snuggle her face into his fur.

"Safe and sound." I reach out to scratch the cat's ears, but his eyes slit open, and he gives me a death glare over Katie's shoulder. I pull my hand back and retreat to the ladder. "You can bring him upstairs if you want."

When I get to the top, Leo stands in the corridor, waiting. "Triana! You're back. Where's the cat?"

"Good to see you, too, Leo." I roll my eyes at him. "He's got a new best friend now. It's a good thing Luna City doesn't allow animals, or you'd be explaining to Elodie why Apawllo didn't come home with you."

"You make it sound like I brought him." He puts his hands on his hips.

"Who else would have done it? It's not like the cat got here on his own."

He shrugs. "He's pretty smart for a cat."

"Even a smart cat can't close himself inside a suitcase."

"Good point. Must have been Vanti."

I burst out laughing. "You think Vanti brought him on the ship? And took him to the surface?"

"We may never know."

I introduce Katie and Leo when Katie finally comes up from the cargo pod. They bond over the cat while I escape to my compartment to shower and change clothes. I need a real meal and a nap.

I've just gotten dressed when I get a call from O'Neill. "Luna City isn't letting us land. They say we're *personae non grata*, and the port is closed to us."

"What? They can't do that!" I yank my soft boots onto my feet and head to the lounge.

"We're in here." O'Neill waves from the conference room on the far side. The others are with him.

I take a seat. "Is this because we got deported? I have a meeting to get to. Or was it cancelled, too?"

"No, the executives at LCL are expecting you this afternoon. But we can't dock at the port." O'Neill shoves his hands through his hair.

Captain Philpot enters from the corridor. "I think it's my fault. They haven't said anything about the deportation. The refusal to let us dock is apparently tied to our 'unorthodox atmospheric maneuver.' I guess they don't trust me to follow the rules."

"How did they even know about that?" I plop into a chair.

"LIA told them? They monitor the planet's air space? They were watching us, specifically?" Vanti ticks the possibilities off on her fingers. "Doesn't really matter—they know, and they don't trust us to dock."

"They should trust us *more* after that amazing flying." I nod at the captain. "Skimming through the atmosphere without damaging anything has got to be a difficult skill."

The captain acknowledges my admiration with a nod. "It takes some practice. But it also displayed supreme disregard for regulations."

"I though Luna City was kind of loosey-goosey when it came to Leweian rules." I turn to look at Katie.

She shakes her head. "Most things are a little looser on Luna. But security at the port is a big deal. All it takes is one rogue captain making a mistake—" She glances apologetically at Philpott. "If we lose air pressure, people die."

The captain raises a hand. "I understand their reasoning. Of course, any captain who risks damaging her ship is facing the same. My ship doesn't hold air if I sheer a corner off."

"What about one of the other cities?" Katie suggests. "Port Royale might let us dock—they might not know about the pick-up."

The captain taps her holo-ring and turns away to check.

"How would we get from there to Luna City?" I ask.

"Trains run several times a day." Katie picks at a loose string on her shirt. "I've been to Port Royale once. It's—"

Philpott interrupts. "No dice. Apparently, the word has been spread."

Vanti pushes her chair back from the table. "I guess we'll just land on the surface. If we knock at the airlock, they'll have to let us in."

"Why are you so anxious to get to Luna City?" I ask.

"I have a meeting, too."

"You scheduled my meeting at LCL to provide cover for your activities? You should cancel. One of your local agents can do whatever it is. Nick. Or Betzy."

"We still have to get Katie home." Vanti's eyes zero in on the girl.

Katie squeezes Apawllo, and the cat squirms. "Sorry," she whispers into the animal's fur. Then she looks up. "Yes, I want to go home. I should have taken the shuttle—"

"But then Vanti wouldn't have an excuse to go to Luna City." O'Neill's eyes bore into Vanti's. "You're the one who suggested we take her home. She could have taken the shuttle. I thought it was odd you were so concerned over her traveling alone."

Vanti stares him down. "I have a mission to complete."

"It would serve you right if we leave you on the ship. That's what Betzy recommended, remember?"

Her lips quirk. "I don't have to look like me. Maybe I should be Sera Morgan."

"Enough." As I stand, I shove my chair back so hard it hits the wall. "It doesn't matter if we can't dock."

"We don't have to." Vanti taps her ring and tosses a schematic onto the table projector. "We'll land here—" A large red X appears near the circle labeled "Luna City." A dashed line runs from the X to the circle. "We'll walk to the airlock, and they'll let us in. Easy."

"Why will they let us in?" I ask.

"Why not? We have a meeting in the city, and we aren't a threat. Luna City is all about commerce—they have that in common with Morgan."

I look at Katie. "Will they let us in?"

Her eyes grow big, and the hand stroking the cat pauses. "How would I know? I sell whoopie cushions for a living."

CHAPTER THIRTY-FOUR

I PUT in a call to our contact at LCL. "This is Annabelle Morgan. I have a meeting scheduled at four this afternoon."

The face on my screen is dark, with bright green eyes and curly green hair. "Yes, I see you on the schedule with Citizen Meteo."

"We have a little problem." I explain that we've been denied access to the port, without giving a reason.

The green eyes don't even blink. "Can you land in the San Teradian crater? That's only a five-minute walk from the Ibarra Dome external airlock. We can have a representative meet you there."

"Excellent. Send me the coordinates. We're orbiting right now, so we can meet in—" I raise my eyebrows at Philpott.

"Ten minutes."

"Ten minutes," I repeat.

"Excellent. By the time you reach the airlock, I'll be there." She signs off.

THE SHIP SETTLES to the dust. Vanti, O'Neill, Cris, Nash, Katie, and I stand in the airlock, dressed in full pressure suits. Vanti and Katie wear PVDs designed to make them look more Leweian. They have dark hair, unremarkable brown eyes, and round, bland faces. Faces designed to blend in instead of standing out.

The external hatch swings open, and we step onto the lunar surface. The lighter gravity hits as I step across the threshold, and I accidentally launch myself high into the air. Well, not air because there isn't any, but basically, I go flying.

O'Neill grabs my foot as I sail past. My momentum pulls him off center, but he's ready for it and yanks me to the ground. I laugh as I land against him, pressing my helmet into his. He grins and rolls his eyes.

"Enough goofing off." Vanti's voice comes through my audio as she sails away from us. "The airlock is this way."

Katie bounds after Vanti, making long, graceful arcs and pushing up little puffs of dust at each landing. I try to follow their lead, shoving away from the ground. The flying part goes well, but when my feet hit the dirt, I skid, and huge clouds of grit boil around me.

O'Neill chuckles. "Like this." He demonstrates a proper lunar bound. Has he been to Luna before? There are very few lunar cities in the Commonwealth. Why bother with an airless rock when there are so many habitable planets?

I copy his movements, getting better with each step. By the time we reach the airlock, I think I've got the technique down.

The hatch opens, and we step into an empty room. It's large enough to hold all six of us with room to spare. Cris closes the hatch, the air cycles, and the inner hatch opens. We move into a larger room, and the green-haired woman from LCL greets us. "Welcome to Luna City! I'm Candy Green."

That seems a bit on the nose. Maybe in Leweian, it means something different?

I hold out my fist to bump my knuckles against hers. "I'm Annabelle Morgan. This is my team." I don't introduce the others—as if they're beneath our notice. "Do we leave our pressure suits here?"

Candy stretches her arms wide, indicating the lockers on either side of the room. "Please. Choose a locker and set it to your handprint. When you're ready, meet me in the next room. Then we'll go to headquarters." She waves a door open into what looks like a comfortable lounge.

"Thanks." I casually angle toward Katie and choose a locker next to hers. I lean close under cover of unlatching my suit. "Stash your suit in that locker. Vanti will get it later. Thanks for your help on the dirt—I hope we'll see you again before we leave."

Shielding my hands with my body, I pass her the roll of Leweian kies that came in the drone.

"I can't take this much." She pushes my hand away.

I shove it at her. "It's worthless on SK2. Give me a couple of bribe-sized notes—in case I need them in the next few hours. The rest is yours. You deserve it."

She peels off five bills and hands them back. "These are for big favors—if it's a little thing, don't bother tipping." She looks up, her eyes shining. She isn't going to cry, is she? "Thanks for this—for everything. I gave Vanti my comm address. I had fun." She turns away to peel off her suit.

Once we've stripped to our indoor attire, Candy leads us up a series of tunnels and into an open area, much like the central concourses on SK2. Here, however, walls rise around us, with balconies and windows overlooking the central area. People sit at tables in front of cafes and restaurants and shop in stores along the various levels. Like a terrestrial city, there are streets between some of the buildings, but bridges arch over the streets, connecting the upper stories. High overhead, a dome arches, and light glows against the blue material, imitating a sun. I check my chrono—it's late afternoon local time.

"This way, please." Candy takes us up an open stairway that curves around a building and along a gallery above a side street. She waves her Ncuff at a door, and it opens. "Welcome to Luna City, Limited. Citizen Meteo is waiting to see you."

The four of us enter—Vanti and Katie peeled off at some point, as we'd planned. Candy's brows draw down as we pass—as if she's counting and has realized someone is missing—but she doesn't say anything.

The meeting with Citizen Meteo goes exactly as expected. We spend some time chitchatting and more time drinking tea—grown here on Luna, and it tastes terrible. After some time, we move into vague discussions of how nice it would be to do business together, and we finish by agreeing to connect our underlings to discuss potential points of interest.

I stand and bump knuckles with Citizen Meteo. Candy leads us out of the room and back to the central concourse. "Do you want to return to your ship immediately, or would you like to visit the other domes in Luna City?"

"I'm not sure when we'll get back here again, so I'd love to see more of the city." I sniff—this place smells of canned air and people. "Is there a restaurant you'd recommend for dinner?" I ignore O'Neill's smothered laugh.

"I'd be happy to take you to Reanta's in Beijing Dome—it's a highly rated restaurant." She takes us to a pair of drop chutes tucked into a hidden alcove in the wall. We drop a couple of levels and step into a low-ceilinged room. The echo of dozens of voices against hard walls assaults our ears, but the room is not exceptionally crowded. "This is the interloop connector—it takes us to the A train. The outer domes are served by the B train." As she speaks, the series of double doors on the far wall open, and people spill into the train.

We step inside. There are doors on both sides—people exit on the far side, which explains why no one seemed to get off. Candy offers me a seat, but I decline. "We've been doing a lot of sitting today."

O'Neill and the other two agents surround me and Candy, creating a buffer in case anyone attempts to get too close.

"I hope your friends didn't get lost." Candy tosses this out as if it's merely a conversational point, but her intent eyes make it clear she wants to know where Vanti and Katie went.

This woman is too observant. We need to get rid of her before we leave, so she doesn't notice Katie isn't with us. "They had some other business to attend to. They'll meet us later."

"Have they been to Luna City before? It can be confusing."

I do my best bored face. "They have a local connection. Tell me about the domes."

She launches into an obviously memorized explanation of how Luna City was built, starting with the central dome, now called The Hub, and adding the two rings later.

Our arrival at the station cuts off her monologue. Here, we move down a level to catch a second train. "Beijing is one of the finest domes in Luna City. Some of our most prominent citizens live here."

To my unfamiliar eyes, Beijing looks very much like the other dome. The same central concourse with buildings reaching toward the blue dome overhead. The lighting is different, but it's later in the day. The brightest lights shine from one side of the dome, and the color has deepened to an orange glow.

The restaurant is on an upper level, overlooking the central area. Candy and I are seated at a table by the railing, and my security team is directed to the next one. Is this to provide better protection or because Candy believes they don't deserve to sit with us?

"How long have you lived in Luna City?" I sip my water—it's room temperature and has been sanitized to the point of tastelessness. It slips down my throat as if it doesn't exist.

"Three years." She nods at the glass. "Make sure you drink plenty of water —they try to keep the dome humidity at thirty-five percent which is a tad low for us planet folk. It takes some adjustment."

"Do you like it here?"

"It was a career move. I plan to go back to Lewei within the next ten months." She winks at me. "Don't tell Citizen Meteo that."

Since I'm unlikely to ever speak with him again, that's a safe bet. "I wouldn't dream of it," I say, as if discussing his assistant's plans is beneath my interest.

A hint of pink washes across her cheeks. "What would you like to see while you're in town?"

"After dinner, I think we'll just wander around. It's safe here, I assume? With such stringent controls on the port..." I trail off. Tight controls mean weapons should be scarce and bad guys can't get in. Of course, coming through the airlock, we could have brought a case of grenades and a cannon with us, so maybe that's a bad assumption.

She waves a negligent hand. "It's completely safe here. Our crime statistics are extremely low."

"Fantastic. What do we need to do to leave? Just show ourselves out the airlock?"

"Oh, no, you'll need an authorized representative to let you into the prep room. That's part of my job. We're a full-service team at LCL."

Zark. How am I going to get rid of her, so she doesn't notice Katie's stayed behind?

The waiter arrives with our meal, and I turn to look over the balcony as he sets the plates in front of us. Below, a figure moves through the plaza, graceful, self-assured. I'd recognize that walk anywhere, even when she's wearing a PVD—Vanti. She pulls out a chair and sits across from another woman.

My eyes snag on her companion. A dark-haired woman whose coloring fits in with the general Leweian characteristics sips something from a tall glass. She turns her head to look across the plaza, and I catch sight of her face.

My water glass slips from my nerveless fingers and crashes to the table, splashing water over our newly delivered food.

CHAPTER THIRTY-FIVE

THE WAITER SWOOPS in to blot the tablecloth. Another hurries forward to whisk away the soaked food. "We'll have fresh meals in an instant."

"I'm so sorry—" I break off when I notice Candy assessing me. This is not how the Ice Dame would react—she'd blame someone. I'm playing a role, and I need to remember that. I harden my tone. "—your glassware is so slippery. You're lucky I didn't cut myself."

"I apologize for the poor design." The waiter reaches out as if to blot my blouse, then stops just before he touches me. "Would you like—"

I snatch the cloth from his hand. "What I would like is a glass that isn't slippery and a dry shirt." I raise my brows at Candy as I speak.

She jumps out of her chair. "Yes, of course. Let me take care of that for you, Lady Morgan." She taps her Ncuff and starts swiping through screens. "I can get something similar delivered in moments."

"You won't find this blouse—it was custom made. But anything not wet will be sufficient." I suppress the crawling under my skin as I blame everyone else for my clumsiness. But I need to get rid of Candy long enough to speak with O'Neill. This woman is watching me too closely to risk a sub-vocal call. "I don't suppose you can find a private place for me to change?"

The hovering waiter clears his throat. "The ladies' room is available. Or the employee's lounge if you'd prefer."

"What about the manager's office?" Candy suggests.

"Go see which one is less… objectionable." I throw the command at Candy without looking up from the napkin in my hand.

"Yes, Lady Morgan." She and the waiter scurry away.

I accept the incoming call from O'Neill.

"What happened?"

I duck my head so my lips won't be visible on any cams pointed my direction and murmur. "You need to see who Vanti is meeting."

He rises and moves toward me. "Where?"

"Lower level, across the dome. Café table at two o'clock."

He moves to stand at my shoulder, leaning over to hand me another napkin. "Can I help, Sera?" As he speaks, his eyes rove over the plaza below. I keep my own eyes on my shirt but feel his stillness when he spots them.

"Is it really her?"

He jerks in response to my words. "Yeah," he says out loud, his tone wondering. "That's my sister."

Before I can respond, Candy returns to lead me away to the "least objectionable" changing space—a nicely appointed office that has been hastily vacated for my use. Steam rises from a full mug on the table, and the chair I sit in is still warm. I take one of the three shirts Candy offers and start unbuttoning my own. The woman glances at my face and hurries to the door. As soon as it clicks shut, I ask O'Neill, "Do you want to go down there?"

"No, I'll talk to Vanti when we get back to the ship. I don't want to interfere with whatever they're doing."

"You trust her that much?"

"I trust Aretha. Or maybe it isn't Aretha—maybe it's a PVD that looks like her. Or maybe Vanti ran into her after her meeting. She's not being very stealthy about it. But drawing attention to them might be a mistake." He doesn't sound like he believes what he's saying.

Ty's older sister Aretha is a lawyer on Grissom. She writes contracts for couples who want to commit to each other. She also helps them break those contracts when a relationship goes wrong. But a few months ago, we discovered records for an Aretha O'Neill working in security at SK'Corp. Once we started digging, those records disappeared. Could Aretha's legal career be a cover for something else—like Vanti's job protecting me?

I slide the new shirt over my head and fasten the single button at my throat. It's snug across the shoulders and around the ribs, but it will have to do. "I'm coming back."

"We need to get rid of Candy when we're done with dinner."

"What do you think I've been trying to do since we left LCL? I don't think it's going to happen." I open the door to find the woman waiting for me.

We return to the table, and waiters deliver two new meals. Between bites, Candy maintains a flow of meaningless small talk and the occasional tourist gem. "Would you like to view the surface? We have an excellent viewing station in the Hills."

"I've been *on* the surface." I shake my head at the waiter offering coffee. "I think we'll just wander. Shall we meet you at the airlock in, say, two hours?"

"I can guide you." Candy pushes back her chair, trying not to look too eager. "I've been detailed to your party for the remainder of the day."

I do my Ice Dame imitation. "I wouldn't dream of troubling you. Surely, you have personal matters to attend to? Working full time makes it so difficult to get those things done. I won't mention it to Citizen Meteo. It will be our little secret." I give the terrifying close-mouthed smile that says, "Don't mess with me."

At least it does when Mother does it. Candy goes a little pale but doubles down. "No, really, I'm supposed to give you everything you need."

"What I need is some alone time with my team. There's no real privacy on the ship." I do a slow look up and down her body. "Although maybe you'd be a welcome addition to the fun."

Her eyes widen, and her jaw drops. She recovers quickly—or at least tries. "Yes, of course. I mean, no, I don't—I can get you a room at the Seasons." The words come out in a rush.

"Excellent. Take us there, then we'll meet you at the airlock in two hours." As I stand, I check on Vanti and Aretha. Their table is empty.

Candy leads us to the A train, which whisks us to the Paris Dome. We ride up the drop chute in silence, and she takes us straight to the concierge at the Seasons Hotel.

I have this theory that every hotel in the galaxy is actually the same hotel but in an alternate universe. They all look the same—at least the high-end ones my mother visits. Plush seating surrounds small coffee tables that hide the latest in projection systems. A faux fireplace crackles gently while a musician plays soft music—in this case, it's a harp. The employees all look like they were cast from the same mold and polished to a high gloss. There's a dark bar in a corner and healthy-looking plants to provide an illusion of privacy.

My detail gathers around my chair while Candy whispers with the woman behind the desk. "Cris, get me a drink," I say without looking at the short security agent.

She opens her mouth to ask something, but O'Neill gives a tiny headshake. I can almost feel them whispering via their comm links, then Cris disappears into the dark bar.

When Candy finishes with the concierge, I hold up an arrogant hand, cutting her off before she can begin. "I need my drink first." We wait in awkward silence until Cris returns with the glass. I peer into it, then take a sip. Bubbly water with a wedge of some kind of citrus. I heave a sigh. "A bit stingy on the liquor, but good enough. Candy, take us to the room."

Candy nods uncertainly. "Do any of you have an Ncuff?"

I wave at O'Neill, as if this is beneath my notice.

"No, we don't. We didn't think we'd need one."

I get up and stalk across the room toward the drop chute. The others scurry after me, discussing access to the room in low voices. I interrupt. "What floor?"

Candy waves a palm-sized circle at the drop chute and gestures for me to step inside. "The key will take you there." She holds it out, but I turn away, leaving one of my minions to take it from her. When we reach the sixteenth floor, we exit, and Candy leads us to the double doors across the hall. "The best suite in the house."

The doors swing wide, revealing a massive room. There's a sitting area on one side, a bar with an Autokich'n near the entrance, and a table that will easily seat ten. Through an open door, I catch a glimpse of an enormous round bed beside floor-to-ceiling windows. Candy hovers in the hall, clearly anxious to depart. I wander around the room, touching things and offering not quite suppressed sneers at random moments. Finally, I turn to the woman. "This will do. We'll meet you at the airlock. Unless you want to stay?"

Her face goes pale, and she swallows convulsively. "No, I have other things I must attend to. I'll meet you in the lobby and escort you to the airlock. Thank you for the time off, Lady Morgan." She backs out, pulling the doors closed behind her with a resounding clang.

Nash puts an ear to the door, then gives us a "clear" signal. Cris holds up a hand, pulling out her testing gear. "Do you want another drink before we, uh, begin, Sera Morgan?"

I clap my hand over my mouth to stop the giggles. "I'll finish this one first," I say in a bored voice that comes out strangled.

For a while, there's nothing but the clinking of ice cubes in my glass as the agents silently scour the room for bugs. Then, Cris sets a small cube on the table and depresses a button on the top. "Clear. That will feed appropriate audio to their surveillance system."

I fall over on the couch, giggling. "I never knew you all found me so physically unattractive. I should be insulted."

O'Neill's lips twitch. "Ogling the boss around me is highly discouraged. That was some impressive acting, Triana. What would you have done if she wanted to stay?"

I sit up and wiggle the fingers on my right hand. "I guess I would have used the tranq pin Vanti gave me."

"When did she give you that?" O'Neill catches my hand and pulls the ring from my finger. "I'm not sure I'm comfortable with this, considering I'm the one you usually put your hands on."

I chuckle as I take it back. "The safety is on. And it requires a bit of force to activate." I slide it back on and rise. "Let's go exploring."

CHAPTER THIRTY-SIX

"Don't you think Candy will be watching the lobby?" Cris gathers up her box and holds it in her palm to continue jamming and spoofing any listening devices.

"That's why you and Nash are going to stay here to run interference. Katie told me about the tunnels under the city. Keep watch while I jimmy the drop chute."

Nash swings the door open, and I sweep past him to the lift. My little toolkit comes through again, and I connect my ring through the adapter. A few easy tweaks, and our card is authorized to take us to the maintenance tunnels. I take a moment to turn on a PVC—the one I named Randy, not the one that makes me look like the *Księżna*.

We send Cris down to the lobby to make another very conspicuous run to the bar. Why would she get drinks there instead of using the AutoKich'n in the room? It doesn't matter—no one is going to question her after my performance.

As soon as she's gone, we drop to the basement. The tunnels under the hotel are cold, gray, and dark. O'Neill consults an app on his holo-ring and turns left. I trail along behind.

A locked door yields to my hacking skills and opens to a wider tunnel. We walk through a narrow alley formed by a bright yellow blanket hung from an overhead conduit and a dingy gray tarp draped over some kind of frame. Makeshift tents line both sides of the tunnel, and a smattering of people travel through. They don't seem to notice us coming out of the nearly hidden doorway.

177

"This is one of the main connections between Beijing dome and the Hub." O'Neill points one direction then the other to indicate which is which, then heads toward the Hub. "The Hub connects to everything else."

"Perfect. What are we looking for?"

"I'm tracking Aretha." O'Neill steps in front of me as a group of older people approach. Once they pass, he falls back in step beside me. "I'm also interested in the general feel of the area. People on Lewei were nervous, always looking over their shoulders. I've heard the iron rule is a bit softer on Luna—I want to see if that's true. If Dame Morgan decides to do business here, she might want to make Luna City our primary point of contact."

"That's why we met with LCL." I loop my arm through his, holding loosely, so he can break free if anyone attacks. It shouldn't be necessary—no one here knows us, and I'm in disguise—but I've been with Ty long enough to know that's important to him. "Let's go find your sister."

We stroll into the Hub, then on to the Hills. I gasp as we step out of the tunnel onto a rolling green field covered by a series of clear domes. The transparent hulls offer a breathtaking view of the stars and Lewei floating above our heads. Nearby, a hidden animal makes a croaking noise. A flock of projected birds chirps, swirling overhead in a realistic display.

Before we left the ship, Katie warned us about the odd acoustical characteristics of these interlocked domes. We keep our conversation superficial—which isn't hard because the view is incredible. I point at Lewei. "It looks so peaceful from here."

O'Neill chuckles. "It is peaceful—our recent experience might have been an anomaly."

"Hey—that's Katie!" I point across the dome to a pair of women sauntering along the crest of a hill. At my soft exclamation, Katie's head turns. Her eyes pass over us, then snap back. Her friend says something, and she shakes her head. The friend yanks her arm, pulling Katie toward us.

"Zark."

O'Neill nudges me toward the exit, but Katie's companion reaches us in three low, long bounds. "Katie's being bashful, but I heard you say her name. I'm Marjatta Lipinski."

We all turn to look, as if surprised. Do we deny it? Pretend she has us mixed up with someone else? O'Neill bows. "Delighted to meet you Lady Lipinski. I'm Ty O'Neill. This is—"

"Call me Randy." I bump fists with her.

"O'Neill. That name sounds familiar—" Lipinski taps her finger against her cheek for a moment, then she smiles. "You're with the Morgan party, aren't you? I see you managed to slip your handler."

A trickle of panic seeps through my veins. How does this woman know O'Neill, and what does Luna City do to people who explore without an official watcher? I attempt a subservient nod. "Sera Morgan gave us some time off. Are we not allowed here without Candy?"

"I'm sure it's fine." Her eyes narrow for a brief second, then her face clears. If I wasn't so used to watching for my mother's moods, I probably wouldn't have noticed. This woman is as controlled—and controlling—as the Ice Dame. What is her relationship with Katie? "They don't want visitors to get lost."

"I have a good mapping app," O'Neill says. "And your city appears to be pretty straightforward. We'd love to stay and chat, but—"

Lipinski cuts him off. "You have to tell me how you met our Katie."

My audio implant pings. O'Neill, of course.

"Annabelle, have you spoken to Hy-Mi yet?"

Zark! Not O'Neill. I tap my ear and turn away. "Mother, this is not a good time."

"Your meeting with LCL should be finished by now. When are you going to call him?"

"I'll call when I get back to the ship, Mother."

"You're still on Luna?" Her tone conveys distaste. "Why?"

I check over my shoulder. Lipinski, Katie, and O'Neill are still chatting, but they're all casting glances at me. I turn away. "I'm meeting Lady Lipinski. I'll have to call Hy-Mi later."

"Oh, excellent idea, Annabelle. I'm impressed. Meeting with the local mob boss is a fabulous idea."

"What?!" Another look over my shoulder reveals the others have stopped pretending to not listen in. "I have to go, Mother. I'll call him from the ship. Goodbye."

I flick the audio off, take a deep breath, and let my embarrassment show in my expression as I turn. "Sorry. Mothers. I shouldn't have left her alone on the ship. She's gotten bored."

"I knew things were different in the Commonwealth, but why would you bring your mother on a corporate trip?" Lipinski's eyebrow goes up, and her eyes bore into me.

Zark. How to answer that? I can't admit my mother is calling from SK2—only the ultra-wealthy can afford that. But why would a low-level security agent bring their mother on a mission? I stare at Lipinski, my brain spinning in circles.

"Sera Moore, senior, is one of our pilots," O'Neill says. "We're a family business—lots of multi-generational employees."

At the name Moore, Lipinski's eyes dart to me then back to O'Neill.

"Moore?" She titters in that fake way people use to tell you they know something. "It seems I've heard that name in reference to the Morgan heir. That she uses it when she wants to go incognito."

I wrinkle my nose and put some disgust into my voice. "She pretends to be me when she's 'slumming.' So flattering. I guess she couldn't come up with her own pseudonym."

Lipinski looks me over again, then dismisses me. "It's a pity she isn't here. I'd like to meet her."

"She's at the Seasons, but they're getting ready to leave." I tap my ear again and turn away. "Roger that." I cast a meaningful look at O'Neill. "In fact, that was Cris. We need to get back to the hotel. Runner is ready to move."

O'Neill does the bowing thing again. "Duty calls, Lady Lipinski. Perhaps we can arrange a meeting between you and Sera Morgan for a later date?" He bows at Katie. "Nice to see you again, Katie."

We take two steps back, ignoring Lipinski's murder eyes, then turn and hurry over the hill.

"This way—don't talk," O'Neill says through my audio implant. He angles across the backside of the hill, toward a tunnel marked with tall blue letters. At the entrance, he turns to check our six, then motions me into the passage. "Aretha's headed to Boston dome."

Like the other one, this tunnel is lined with makeshift shelters. "Who lives here?" I whisper.

"Anyone who can't afford the rent, I'd guess." He nods at an elderly man sitting under a black tarp with a cup in front of his legs.

"I guess it's better than deporting them, like they do on SK2." I swallow hard. Like *we* do on SK2. When I lived on Level 2, we were constantly hoping we'd make enough credits to pay the rent because failure would mean being sent back to the planet. Which doesn't sound so bad, except it would mean losing our jobs. Now that I was becoming Morgan, I'd be the one sending people back to the dirt. One of the many ugly truths I'd run away to hide from. Was there a way to fix it? Were tent cities in the corridors any better?

We take a drop chute up and emerge in Boston Dome. It's built on the same basic plan as Beijing and Paris—tall buildings with narrow "streets" between them and a central plaza. But everything here looks older and less well-kept.

"Didn't Katie say she lives in Boston?" I follow O'Neill into the plaza.

"Yeah, she did, but her friend certainly doesn't live here." He leads me across the dome, pointing at things as if this is a tourist Mecca. We dutifully examine the arched colonnades along the lower level of the buildings and an unremarkable statue in the center of the plaza.

"What's the deal with her—how'd you know to call her 'Lady'? And how is Katie friends with a mob boss? I thought she was an average Luna City resident. You don't think she was playing us, do you?"

"Mob boss? The Lipinskis are one of the most prominent families in Luna City, maybe the whole moon. I don't know how Katie knows her—and how does someone who claims to be a Commonwealth agent end up working with Lipinski's best friend?"

"Mother said her family is the head of the local mob. She thought meeting with her was a great idea." I breathe deep to quiet the churning in my stomach. I've dealt with the Poelish Mafia—I don't want to get involved with another one.

"You are not meeting with the local mob. I put my foot down there." O'Neill points at something random, and I pause to ooh and ah. Warmth washes through me in response to his protective nature but also a streak of obstinance. Which is stupid—I really don't want to meet with the mob.

"Luckily, they're Vanti's problem, not ours. But the sooner we get out of here, the better." He turns slowly and waves a hand through the air as he says something aloud about the windows.

A woman bumps into me, dropping a shopping bag. As several pieces of fruit roll out, she murmurs, "What are you doing in Luna City, little brother?"

CHAPTER THIRTY-SEVEN

O'NEILL and I drop to our knees to help Aretha gather up the produce. "Just showing my friend Randy around," he says. "What are you doing here?"

Aretha scoops the brightly colored globes back into her bag. Her brown eyes meet mine and dismiss me. "Trying to leave. I've been made. Can you get me out?"

O'Neill flicks his ring as he gets to his feet, glancing at his chrono. "Ibarra airlock in thirty minutes." With a curt nod, he takes my arm and steers me toward the drop chute, leaving Aretha staring at the stone of Sir Isiack Nooten, one of the founders of Luna City.

We drop to the tunnel level, not speaking as we return to the Hub. "Can you get us back in that door we came out of?"

"No problem. Aretha didn't seem surprised to see you."

"I'm sure Vanti told her I was here." His voice is grim through the audio. He doesn't want to talk about this. I think about pushing, but it will be safer to wait until we're on the ship and can hear Aretha's side of the story.

We return to the hotel room. My security detail lounges on the couches, playing some kind of game on their holo-rings.

"Dude!" Cris exclaims, breaking off in surprise when we enter.

Nash jumps up. "You're back earlier than I expected."

"Change of plans. We need to get out. Now." O'Neill grabs the little white box on the table. "What do we do with this thing?"

"There's a five-minute ending sequence." Nash takes the box. "Or we can just cut it, if you don't care what the spooks hear."

O'Neill glances at me. "Start the ending sequence."

I put a hand on his arm. "Aretha seemed to be in a hurry. Maybe we should just go. We don't even know if anyone is listening to us."

He shakes his head. "She's here on her own. If she can't elude them for five more minutes... I won't put you at risk. Even for her."

I start to protest, but he holds up a hand. "We've already risked enough, sneaking out today. Turn off your PVD, and get ready to go."

I pull out the capsule and twist it off. A quick look in the bathroom mirror reveals I'm back to my usual appearance: crazy red curls, blue eyes, white blouse that's slightly too tight. "What does that box do, anyway?"

Red washes over O'Neill's face.

Nash takes pity on him, speaking in a deadpan voice. "It sends an AI-generated audio to the listeners. Giving them exactly what they'd expect to hear from a top-lev having 'private time' with her team."

"So... discussions of marketing strategies and return on investment?" I bite back a snicker.

"Exactly." Nash lifts the box. "We're clear in three, two..."

"I'm going back to the ship," I say in my best top-lev voice. "Cris, do whatever you have to do."

Cris makes a confused face at me. I gesture toward the door. She nods. "I'll check the corridor."

The rest of us nod and follow her out the door.

In the lobby, Candy stands waiting by the drop chute. She knew we were on our way. I raise my brows at O'Neill.

"Amateur move—now we know they were listening," he says through the audio as he moves in behind me. "That's why we have the tech."

"Thank you for arranging this, Candy." I pull a couple of Leweian kies out of my pocket and pass them to her as she falls into step beside me. "You've been extremely helpful."

She palms the money and slides it into her own pocket, not even glancing at our hands. "My pleasure, Lady Morgan."

"Now, we'd like to return to the ship. O'Neill will settle the bill."

"No. Luna City, Limited is happy to host you, Lady. This little respite is our pleasure. It's done." She gestures to the door. "This way, please."

We return to the Ibarra Dome by train and make our way through the tunnels to the airlock. "Is the rest of your party meeting you here?" Candy asks.

"If they expect a ride home—and a job when they get back." I don't bother explaining where they went—I have no idea what I'd say—and she doesn't ask. I'm sure Luna City agents attempted to follow Vanti and Katie, and I have no doubt Vanti was able to lose them easily.

When we reach the locker room, two women with dark hair and brown eyes are already pulling on their suits. They're the PVDs Vanti and Katie wore when we got here, and I recognize Vanti by her slender build. The other one must be Aretha. There's no way anyone will know it's her.

Candy waits until I've donned my suit, then steps forward and bows deeply. "Thank you for visiting with us on Luna City, Lady Morgan. It has been my deep pleasure to assist you."

"The meeting was productive, and you have been an effective guide. I hope to see you next time I come to Luna. Or Lewei. I'll have my staff mention your good work in our next communication with Citizen Meteo." I turn away without waiting for a reply and stride toward the airlock.

Behind me, O'Neill claps. "Move out, team. Citizen Green, thank you for your assistance."

Vanti opens the airlock, and we troop inside. I move to the exit without looking back, even though I feel like I have a target painted between my shoulder blades. It's not like Candy has a weapon. Or any reason to use one.

O'Neill's voice comes through the audio. "Suit check."

Everyone pairs up to inspect suit connections. O'Neill looks mine over. "Morgan, check."

I turn and do the same for him. "O'Neill, check."

The others chime in. "Cris, check."

"Nash, check."

"Vanti, check," Aretha reports.

"O'Neill, check," Vanti says with a snicker.

"Closing the airlock."

O'Neill presses his hand against the control panel, and the big circular hatch begins to roll into the portal. Behind Candy, the internal door slides open, and a team wearing Leweian uniforms bursts into the room. "Halt!" The hatch stops, mid roll.

Vanti dives on me, pulling me to the floor. Nash and Cris jump in front of us, and Aretha hurriedly joins them.

O'Neill raises a hand. "What seems to be the problem?"

I choke back nervous snickers at this *Ancient TeVe*-style answer.

"We believe you have a terrorist among your security team." The voice issues from one of the helmeted officers, but it's impossible to tell which one. At a guess, I'd say it's the guy with three fat gray stripes on his arm. Two of the others hustle Candy out of the room.

"Nonsense." O'Neill glances back at us. "This is my team. I vetted all of them myself. They're doing their job—protecting Sera Morgan." His tone implies they're the ones I need protection from.

Vanti stands and gives me a hand up. I push through my protective detail and stop at the threshold of the airlock. "What is the meaning of this? Are you implying I would harbor a fugitive? This team has been with me for ages."

"Can you name them?" Three Stripes asks.

Should I? "This is Tiberius O'Neill y Mendoza bin Tariq e Reynolds, my chief of security. The others are none of your business. Agent O'Neill, I want to leave." I turn my back on the Leweians and make a scared face at Vanti.

"Keep calm." Vanti's flat tone comes through my audio. "They can't keep us here."

"They can if they don't let us close the airlock," I whisper.

"Then why don't you make sure they can't do that?"

While O'Neill continues to argue with Three Stripes, I move to the back of the airlock. My team closes in behind me, hiding me from the Leweians. I pull off my gloves and start up my holo-ring. I flick through screens at high speed, trying to find a wireless connection to the dome. I could probably plug my adapter into a port somewhere, but that would be obvious to Three Stripes and his marauders.

"Leweian security police have no jurisdiction on Luna," O'Neill says.

Three Stripes laughs. "That's what these Lunatics would like you to think. Believe me, we own this whole system."

I find a connection. There's a security wall, but most of it is easy to defeat. The trickier bits take a few seconds, and I'm in. I access the Ibarra sub-system and find the airlock controls. "Ready."

"When I say now," O'Neill says through the audio. Then he speaks aloud. "Sera Morgan."

I turn my head with a heavy sigh. "What? I want to leave."

"These men want us to come with them. Now."

I flick the control. The door begins moving again. "I don't want to go with them. Tell them I'm bored, and I'm going back to my ship."

"Who's closing that hatch?" Three Stripes points at the heavy door moving into place. "Stop it."

One of the others slaps his hand against the inner access panel, but nothing happens. "It's not responding, sir!"

"Stop it!" He points at two of his underlings. They dash forward, pushing their shoulders against the huge disk as it slowly rolls into the opening.

"That's going to kill them!" O'Neill points at the narrowing opening, yelling at the officer. "That door is going to crush your men."

The two guys visibly waver, but Three Stripes growls at them. The door fills most of the opening now. "Drag them out. Get the woman—they won't leave without her!"

The heads of the two men pushing fruitlessly against the door snap around to stare at their boss as the door continues to close. "You heard him—this thing will crush us! I'm not—"

"Get out! Zhin, arrest Doring! Get out of the way. I'll get them!" Three Stripes shoves the two men away and dives through the narrow opening.

"Don't let him in!" I hiss. "He's not wearing a suit. We can't open the outer hatch if he's in here."

"Yes, we can." Vanti's voice is hard.

"Killing a Lewian security police sergeant is not going to make SK'Corp popular in this system."

O'Neill puts his hands on the man's shoulders, shoving him backward. Nash tries to help, but there's no room. The two men struggle in the narrow crescent of space between the thick hatch and its home.

"Get out of the way," Aretha mutters. She yanks something from her pocket and yells, "Ty, clear!"

O'Neill steps back, and Three Stripes falls halfway through the opening. I scrabble at the controls, halting the door just before it squeezes him in two. Aretha points her device and fires. Three Stripes goes limp, sagging across the hatch opening.

We all—Leweians included—stare at Aretha.

"Open the door ten centimeters, Triana," she orders me.

I flick a command, and the door rolls open a handspan.

Aretha shoves the limp officer by his helmet, and he falls into the locker room. "Close it." Her voice carries the terrifying cold of deep space.

Ignoring the Leweians as they surge forward to check on their boss, I do that, too.

CHAPTER THIRTY-EIGHT

WHEN WE GET the outer portal open, Aretha wedges a rock into the circular aperture. "That should stop them from opening the inner hatch."

"They probably have an auxiliary access nearby." Vanti gives me a push toward the ship. "No time to waste."

We bound across the airless expanse, ignoring the beauty of the stars and planet spread out above us. The *Black Panther*'s outer hatch slides open as we approach, and we pile in. The door shuts, and before the airlock can cycle, we're thrown against the bulkhead in liftoff.

Vanti pulls off her helmet. "Team meeting in five minutes. Conference room."

We shuck our gear and make our way to the lounge. Vanti doesn't need me at her meeting. I grab O'Neill's arm when he heads for the conference room. "Let her do it. You need to talk to your sister."

Aretha flicks off her PVD and sags into the plush furniture while I order food and non-alcoholic beverages from the AutoKich'n. The dark circles under her eyes stand out against her pasty skin. Her eyelids droop.

O'Neill stares at her. "You look awful. What were you doing on Luna?"

Aretha taps her fingers against the arm of the chair, then nods to herself. She pulls a little white box from her pocket and sets it on the coffee table. "I was visiting a friend. I'm going to take a nap." She gets up and opens and closes the door to the bedroom, then presses the button atop the box.

The AutoKich'n pings, and I pull out the food, setting it next to Aretha's device. "This is our ship—you don't need that kind of security here."

"I don't take chances. Ever. That's the only way I've survived this long." She takes one of the small plates and returns to her seat.

"What do you mean?" O'Neill demands. "You're a family practice lawyer. What do you need to survive?"

"I'm also a Commonwealth agent." She throws out the statement, then takes a bite of her meat pie.

O'Neill stares at her, his mouth open. She keeps eating, and finally, he regains his voice. "I saw your name on an SK'Corp list of agents."

"I did some work there years ago—legal consulting for the security branch. I should never have been added to a roster, but sometimes you don't manage to catch all the little details."

"But you're actually a Commonwealth agent? Like Vanti?" O'Neill's eyes are bleak, as if he's been betrayed. In a way, he has. These two women, whom he trusted implicitly, have secret lives he knew nothing about.

Kind of like when he met me. I try to hide a wince.

Aretha sips her drink. "I do occasional jobs for the Commonwealth when my skills are required."

"What skills are those?"

She shakes her head. "You don't have a need to know. If you hadn't just rescued me from a lifetime vacation in Xinjianestan, I wouldn't be telling you any of this, of course."

"What were you doing in the Lewei system?"

"I'm not going to tell you that, either. I appreciate the rescue, of course, but I can't give you any further information."

O'Neill jumps up from his chair, pacing around the room like a caged animal. "What if we hadn't been there to rescue you?"

She shrugs. "I would have figured out something. Probably something that would have put me in debt to the mob. Speaking of which, I heard you met Lady Lipinski."

"We aren't talking about me—we're talking about you." O'Neill crosses his arms over his chest.

"No, we're not. I've told you everything you're going to learn. And now, I need a nap." She grabs a pillow and sticks it at one end of the couch.

"Take the bed." I grasp her arm and pull her upright. "Right through here."

When I return to the lounge, O'Neill is still pacing. "What am I supposed to do now?"

I put a hand on his arm. "What difference does it make? It's not like she's a member of the Luna mob or a rival corporation. The mystery has been solved. She's a good guy."

He slides his arms around me, pressing his face against my neck. "I know.

190

It's just going to take some getting used to."

We stand there for a few minutes, then he rouses himself. "I'm going to talk to Vanti. You need anything?"

"I'm good." I kiss him, hard, to remind him of the important things in life.

When he leaves, I initiate a call to Hy-Mi. Interstellar calls take time to set up, so I wander up to the bridge.

"Any problems?" I ask the comm officer.

"They keep hailing us. I've started an auto-responder that tells them we're out-system bound and too busy to chat. They don't seem to like it very much." She grins and flicks a control.

A tell-tale goes red, and a gruff voice yells at us in Leweian. The comm officer flicks a few more controls, and the translator kicks in. "—return to Lewei, immediately! The fugitive on board your ship is dangerous!"

I flick the mute button. "Have they given you any identifying information for this alleged fugitive? Is it one of us or someone else?"

She shakes her head. "Nope, no picture, no name, nothing. They keep repeating that we have someone on board who is wanted by Leweian security police."

I chuckle. "That could be almost any of us. This doesn't bode well for future commerce in the Leweian system."

"You might be surprised." Captain Philpott swivels her chair around to look at me. "They're surprisingly practical when it comes to money."

"I thought you'd never been here before."

"I haven't, but I've studied them. Extensively. That's why I was chosen for this run."

Two hours later, my audio implant pings. I hadn't realized it would take *this* long to set up an interstellar call, and my mind is boggled by the idea that my mother did it. Twice. Waiting is not her strong suit. Maybe she has a secret urgency override.

I drop onto the couch in the lounge and connect. "Hi, Hy-Mi."

"This isn't Hy-Mi, this is your mother. Haven't you spoken to him yet?" Her image appears in the table projection.

"I placed the call request as soon as I got back to the ship, but it hasn't come through yet."

She frowns and looks around the room. "Are you alone?"

"The others are sleeping. We've had a busy week, and they were tired." I'm tired, too, but I don't want to be asleep when Hy-Mi's call comes through.

"How did your meeting with the Lipinski woman go?"

"We didn't have a meeting. We ran into her in the park. She didn't know who I was."

"How could she not know who you are?"

"I was wearing a disguise, Mother. We snuck away from the LCL handler." I'm too tired to be diplomatic.

"You did what? Don't you realize you represent Morgan? Our reputation—"

I do something few dare: I interrupt the Ice Dame. "I'm fully aware of my responsibilities, Mother. That's why I was in disguise. We wanted to get a feel for the real situation, not what they were feeding us."

She stares for a moment, then her mouth snaps shut with an audible click.

"And I will talk to Hy-Mi." I hold up a hand to forestall her. "If you agree to my terms."

Her eyes narrow. "What terms?"

"The same terms I've been offering since I got engaged. I get to plan my wedding and invite the guests I want. You can include twenty people from your list—no more. You can host a reception the next day with whomever you care to invite, with whatever catering, music, etcetera. Your party."

She's still for so long, I think the feed has frozen. Finally, she nods. "Deal. You get Hy-Mi back, and I agree."

"I didn't say I'd get him back. I said I'd talk to him. No promises." I cross my arms and slouch back into the sofa.

"I pay for results, not talk."

"You aren't paying for this. You're asking me for a favor, and I'm offering one in exchange. This isn't a corporate negotiation. People are different, you know."

She droops in her chair and waves a languid hand. "Fine. I accept. Talk to him, please. He needs to come back."

"What if he doesn't want to come back?" I ask softly.

Her eyes go wide, and her jaw drops. It takes a second for her to recover. Finally, she nods regally. "I will do whatever it takes to get him back—please tell him. I need him."

I disconnect and wander through the lounge, restless. I've never seen my mother so distressed. Even when R'ger—her current boyfriend and my father —was kidnapped by the TLO, she didn't look so defeated. She and Hy-Mi have worked together for decades. He's always been like a father to me and apparently more than just an employee to Mother.

This is a major shift in my world. I've never talked my mother into anything she didn't want. Part of me thinks this is a trick—that she'll renege on the deal or come up with some kind of loophole. But my mother's word is good. If she says she'll do something, she does. Releasing control of this wedding is exactly what I wanted, but it's left me in a spiral of confusion.

When my holo-ring vibrates, I nearly jump out of my skin. I check the display this time: Hy-Mi.

"Sera Morgan, how nice to see you." Hy-Mi bows like he always does. His face is relaxed, and he's wearing casual clothing. He appears to be in a comfortable living room, with a view of the sea. Not fancy enough to be Sierra Hotel—probably his son's home on Kaku.

I go straight to the heart of the matter. "Mother says you quit. Because she wouldn't let me have the wedding I wanted." When he nods, I go on. "I told you I'd take care of it."

He smiles, the bigger, more genuine smile I remember from childhood, not the carefully measured response to a top-lev. "I know you did. And I'm proud of you for taking responsibility. But I've been thinking about retiring for some time. This seemed like a good battle on which to use my ultimate weapon."

"You think she'll cave?"

"I don't know. I'm okay with not going back. I had hoped it might give you some leverage..."

"*She's* not okay with you not coming back. I've never seen so much emotion from her. She said she needs you."

Hy-Mi looks shocked. "She said that?"

"She did. And I promised to talk to you. In exchange for the wedding." I let a small smile slide across my face.

His lips curve up, then the smile fades. "She agreed to a private wedding in exchange for my return?"

"No. I said I'd talk to you. No results guaranteed. This is huge." I let that hang there while we both consider what it means. The Ice Dame needs Hy-Mi so badly she ceded control over one of the biggest Morgan events in recent history, in hopes he might *consider* returning.

After a moment, Hy-Mi chuckles. "It's not really as big as you think, Sera. She knows me well. It was a calculated risk, but that's what she's known for."

"You'll go back to her? Just like that?" I snap my fingers.

He shrugs. "I was getting kind of bored already. Plus, you got what we wanted. And now she knows I'm not afraid to walk, which should give me some leverage in the future."

We chat for a few more minutes, then sign off. I drop onto the couch, exhausted and confused. Did I win? Or did she?

Maybe we both did.

CHAPTER THIRTY-NINE

Two weeks later, I wake at dawn, my head swirling with thoughts of my wedding day. Tomorrow.

I've been to a wedding before. Once.

In this part of the galaxy, most people don't get married. Kara signed a ten-year procreational domestic contract with her significant other, Erco. But a wedding, with all that "death do us part" language? That's a forever contract with no escape clause. And around here, we're all about contracts.

Things are different on Grissom, where Ty grew up. His parents have been together for forty years. The single wedding I attended was his sister Lili's. And we blew up the cake. Not really—actually someone threw someone else *into* the cake, but frosting exploded everywhere, so pretty much the same thing. And a carriage blew up for real.

There will be no exploding carriages at my wedding—my mother would disown me forever.

Despite my early wake up, I feel really good about this. Sure, it's way too early in the morning, and I've been awake for hours, but I'm sure that's normal.

I step out on the balcony outside my bedroom at Sierra Hotel and take a deep breath of the salty sea air. A faint whiff of *terkfiske* drying next door hits my nose like a stink bomb. Ser Zhang and Cas are back, staying with Zhang's brother and his son Tarkhan, who were ejected from Lewei a few weeks before we visited. I make a mental note to ask them to take the fish off the line for the big day.

The sun peeks above the cliffs at the end of the bay, illuminating the domed roofs of the buildings on the top of Paradise Alley. Most of the high-end tourist town is still in shadow, and a light fog drifts through the streets. The whole effect is somewhat eerie.

I go back inside and get some coffee from the AutoKich'n. Leo probably has better stuff brewing, but I'm not ready to see anyone yet. The last two weeks have been a whirl of dress fittings, cake tastings, vendor displays, and pre-wedding parties, and I'm ready to be done with all of it.

Someone knocks on the door. I swipe up my security dashboard and flick on the hallway cam. A short, plump blonde woman with dark skin and a sleeping baby in one arm stands outside my door. It takes me a second to recognize my best friend.

"Kara!" I yank open the door and pull her inside.

"Shh. I just got her to sleep." Freya snuggles against her mother's chest, a sleepy smirk on her face. This one will be a handful, but nothing Kara can't handle.

"You just got her to sleep? How long have you been up?" I push her toward the couch and head back to the AutoKich'n.

Kara waves me off. "Don't bother—Leo's on his way with a tray. I need more than caffeine this morning, even if you don't." She slides the baby onto the center of the big bed and positions pillows to keep her on her side.

"Did you sleep at all?" I sip my coffee and stare at the tiny bundle. She looks so cute and peaceful right now, but last night, she was a screaming demon.

"Oh, sure. A few minutes here and there. But enough about me—how are you feeling?"

"Surprisingly good." I sip my coffee again. "Of course, that might be the shot of whiskey talking."

Kara yanks the mug away from me and sniffs it. With an eye roll, she hands it back. "I knew you were kidding."

"Sure, you did."

The door pings, and I pull it open, drawing in cinnamon, butter, Sarvorian coffee and— "Chocolate?"

Leo puts a huge tray on the table by the window. It holds eggs, potatoes, bacon, croissants, coffee, and more. "Is there any doubt? Dav got up early to bake."

"He shouldn't have done that, but I'm glad he did." I take one of the still-warm pastries and bite into the heavenly layers of crisp, buttery confection.

"He said he'd be up anyway—he's on his own time zone."

"That's what happens when you're the Ice Dame's pastry chef." I take another bite. "He's worth his weight in senidium."

"I'm taking some of this." Kara scoops a mound of food onto a plate and sits. "Making milk takes calories!"

"There's plenty. Of food, not milk. I have no idea how much milk you have." Leo flushes and lays a plate and flatware out for me. "Hang on, one more thing." He steps into the hall and returns with another tray. This one holds tall-stemmed glasses filled with bubbly orange liquid.

"Mimosas! My favorite!" I take one and hand the second to Kara. "Where's yours?" I ask Leo.

He grins. "I was hoping you'd offer." He disappears for a moment, then reappears with another glass. "Didn't want to presume, though."

"You're family." Kara raises her glass. "Welcome, whether we want you or not."

"Kara!"

Leo laughs. "I get it. Speaking of family, Elodie said she'd be here by ten."

Kara puts down her glass and starts eating. "We've got a lot to do before then, Triana, so dig in."

BY TEN O'CLOCK, I've been primped to death. My hair and skin look fantastic, of course, but I'm ready to be done with the ehoods, creams, lotions, and powders. And this was just the trial run. The actual ceremony isn't until tomorrow. "I need a break. Let's go sit by the pool."

"You need a break? You haven't done anything but lie around all morning!"

"I held the baby—that's stressful!"

Kara sits on the couch, feeding her daughter. "No, it isn't. It's peaceful and relaxing."

"For you, maybe. I keep thinking I'll drop her. Or launch her into zero gravity like that baby on SK2."

"If you launch her here, she'll hit the ground, so I'd appreciate if you don't. Why don't you walk down and see how the setup is going?"

"You don't mind?" I pull on a pair of sandals, being careful to avoid the polish on my toes. It's a special lacquer that doesn't require drying, but if anyone can mess it up, it's me.

"Just watch out for the groom—I've heard he's not supposed to see you before the wedding. If he does, we're in for six more weeks of winter."

"That's not how it goes." I take the tray of dirty breakfast dishes and hurry past my mother's door, hoping she won't pop out to demand something. I don't think she's here, but the instinct is strong.

I make it to the empty family room. Leo and Dav are working from the professional kitchen on the third floor, so ours is silent and dark. I stick the dishes in the AutoKich'n, set it to "clean," and cross to the full-length windows.

The view from here is the same as from my room. Teakalike decking stretches from the house to wrap around the huge pool. Dozens of white-topped tables stand on the shining boards, and a force generator creates an invisible dance floor over the pool. Flower wreaths with candles float in the water below—when they're lit, it will be mesmerizing.

A bandstand perches on the far corner of the deck. A woman dressed in ragged jeans and a threadbare shirt plays with a tablet—probably a band roadie testing the audio interface.

The lawn beyond the pool holds rows of chairs, with a small platform at the cliff's edge. A pair of white-clad employees sets up an arch over the dais—strands of delicate gold woven together with tiny built-in vases tucked between.

Overhead, the protective force shield sparkles in the morning sunlight—it's set to "decorative shimmer." I hope they still have the sunscreen dialed up, or everyone will be sunburned before noon.

A flash of copper catches my attention. Vanti steps out of the carefully manicured stand of trees, pausing in the shadows. I'd guess she's been checking the perimeter. Ty and I agreed to keep her true employment situation a secret until after the wedding—we didn't have time to vet and hire a new chief of security since O'Neill will be otherwise engaged.

I hurry down the stairs and across the deck. The temporary employees setting up the tables on the deck ignore me, but Hy-Mi calls out. I wave him off. "Back in a second!" By the time I reach the tree line, Vanti has disappeared again.

I shuffle back to the deck. "What's Vanti doing?"

"Security, I'm sure." Hy-Mi is impeccable in his customary collarless tunic and slim pants. He gestures to the set-up. "Are you happy with this arrangement?"

I sigh. "It's exactly what I wanted. Thanks to you."

"You're the one who made it happen," Hy-Mi says. "I was merely the catalyst."

I trail a finger along the edge of a table set off to one side. There are place cards at each seat. Kara, Erco, Elodie, Leo. Sera O'Neill. That's odd.

I hold the card out to Hy-Mi. "I thought Ty's parents were sitting over there with Mother and R'ger."

"That's your place card," Hy-Mi says. "Technically, they should say Ser and Sera Morgan, but I thought we'd go with tradition."

I stare at the card, and my breath catches in my throat. Sera O'Neill. Lifetime commitment. 'Til death do us part. My chest tightens, and my vision goes dark. I drop into the chair.

"Sera Annabelle, are you okay?" Hy-Mi leans over me, his voice distant, as if he's speaking through a funnel.

"Yeah, I'm good." I straighten my back. "Just a little overwhelmed. Maybe I'll go upstairs and lie down."

I turn toward the house, and another place card catches my eye. "Hy-Mi, will you *please* tell me who Ser Smith is, and why he is still coming to my wedding?"

Ser Smith is the pseudonym for someone with a higher security rating than Mother. But all of the high-asset guests were cut from the list. Those valuable business contacts will attend the private reception Mother has scheduled the day after. This is supposed to be family and friends only.

"You know I can't tell you that," Hy-Mi says, as if having a mystery guest at one's wedding is completely normal.

"I'm going to find out tomorrow."

"Yes, you will."

CHAPTER FORTY

A SHOUT ECHOES down the stairs as I return to the house. Several shouts, in fact, but since they sound happy and Vanti isn't hustling me into a safe room, they must be vetted guests. I bypass the door to the family quarters and take the steps two at a time to the public level.

"Tree!" A pair of nearly identical voices assaults my ears, and arms wrap around me. Ro and Yuri, O'Neill's younger, twin brothers squeeze me in a group hug. "We made it!"

I kiss their cheeks and pull back. "Did you think you wouldn't?"

Ro shrugs. "You never know with interstellar travel."

"Sometimes shuttles blow up," Yuri—I can tell by the faint scar running through his eyebrow—says.

"Only when Triana is on them." Ro grins, his eyes ranging past me down the stairs.

"Or Bill." Yuri punches his brother's shoulder. "Where's Vanti? Ro has a hankering to see her."

"A hankering? Are you a rube from Armstrong?" I grab their arms and pull them down to the guest lounge. "She's here somewhere—give her a call." I flick the comm codes for the house to their holo-rings. "Where's Angie?"

"She's chatting up some kids—I think they're from next door." Ro drops his bag on the couch and flicks his holo-ring.

"Pick any room you like—if the door opens, it's available." I push Yuri toward the hall, then sprint up the stairs.

When I reach the front entrance, Serena and Brad, Ty's parents, cross the driveway to meet me. Angie Mendoza, Ty's great-grandmother, is deep in conversation with Cas and Tarkhan.

"Triana!" Serena pulls me into a long hug. "It's been so long since we've seen you!"

"You saw her on a call two nights ago." Brad takes his turn squeezing the air out of me. He leans back to kiss both cheeks. "But in person is better. This is quite the place your mother has."

"Grandmother," Serena calls. "Triana is here!"

"Oh, goody." Angie loops her arm through Cas's and drags him toward me. Tarkhan trails behind. "These nice boys have been telling me about the adventures I missed." She stretches up to ruffle Cas's hair, then releases his arm to hug me.

"That was ages ago. Did he tell you how they got over here?" I glare at Cas over Angie's shoulder. "Vanti said she closed all your sneak holes."

Cas grins. "I'll never tell."

"He followed the carriage through the front gate." Angie releases me and heads toward the front steps. She moves quickly for a ninety-something-year-old woman with no rejuv treatments.

I hurry after her. "You coming inside, Cas?"

"Nah, we'll catch up with Angie later." He waves, and the boys angle across the front lawn.

"That's not the way to the front gate," I call.

Cas waves again without looking, and they disappear into the jungle-like foliage surrounding the neatly trimmed yard.

I flick my holo-ring and pull up Vanti's comm link. Busy. Probably talking to Ro. I leave a message. "Cas and Tark are on their way home—if you hurry, you can follow them and find out how they're getting in."

Serena, Angie and Brad follow me into the house. They ooh and ahh over the massive formal rooms on the top floor and the stunning view.

I take them down to the next level. "There are guest rooms on this floor— ten on each hall. Take your pick. There's an AutoKich'n in each room and a real kitchen back here." I wave at a door beside the stairway. "If you have a strange desire to cook something. I'm not sure what kind of food you'll find in there. Normally, you can message Leo if you can't find what you want, but he and Dav are pretty busy with the wedding stuff."

"This is amazing." Serena turns slowly in the center of the room, taking in the floor-to-ceiling windows of the parlor, the beautiful carved wood tables and plush upholstered chairs, walls of bookshelves with old-style paper books, and thick carpets beneath it all.

"The twins were here a few minutes ago." I peer down the dark hall, but no one is in sight. "They've probably chosen rooms. If you register your hand-print on the access panel by the door, your luggage will be delivered when it arrives."

Serena pauses her tour of the room by the tall windows. "Ooh, the wedding venue looks lovely. Do these open?"

I show her how to operate the windows, and we cross the balcony. The house is terraced so that the balconies below aren't shadowed by those above. The lower levels can be obscured by high-tech shields. "The screens are for security—and privacy. They'll also prevent Yuri and Ro from dropping things on peoples' heads."

Angie cackles. "You've got those boys pegged!"

"Speaking of boys, there's Yuri." Brad points to the left. His son waves from a balcony far along the wing, then he blurs.

"I see they figured out how to use the screens." I point down. "The family quarters are on the next floor. I've given you access to that as well. Just wave your ring at the door panel, and it will open."

I turn and point toward the wings. "There are float tubes at the end, so you don't have to use the stairs."

"Are you looking at me?" Angie asks. "I've got no problem with steps. You've seen where we live." Angie's room is on the third floor of the O'Neills' Grissom home, and they don't have a float tube.

"Not for you. But if the twins get anyone too drunk to walk, you don't want to carry them." I grin, remembering my first night at the O'Neills' house, when the twins spiked my drink. Repeatedly. "There's BuzzKill in the bathrooms, of course. I'll leave you to get settled. Just holler if you need anything. There's a float tube to the beach if you want to go—but I recommend you *not* do it at four o'clock."

"Why is that?" Brad lifts the bag he dropped on the sofa and gestures for Serena to precede him down the hall—the opposite end from Yuri.

"It rains at four."

"Always? Precisely at four?"

"Close enough. Weather here is very predictable—one of the many reasons Mother picked this location. Dinner is at eight. Cocktails at seven in the family room on the second floor." I point down. "Call me if you need anything before that."

Angie wanders past me. "Don't suppose you've got any whiskey?"

"Grandma!" Serena's face flushes.

"I ordered some just for you. It will be delivered to your room when you get settled." I give her another hug. "See you downstairs."

AT SIX, we meet to do a run-through of the wedding. I think Hy-Mi has been watching documentaries on traditional weddings—he runs the rehearsal like a drill sergeant.

We practice walking down the aisle between the chairs to the stage. After the fourth try, I call a halt. "Why does it matter how fast we walk or what order we go in?"

"Tradition dictates—" Hy-Mi begins.

I appeal to Serena and Brad. "It doesn't matter, does it?"

Brad and Serena exchange a glance and burst out laughing. "We had this same argument at our rehearsal," Serena says between giggles. "Brad's family wanted it to be perfect. My family just wanted to party." She jerks her chin at Angie, who's sitting on the far side of the pool, drinking with Cas.

I turn to Leo. "You might want to make sure Angie isn't getting your brother drunk."

Leo starts. "He's only twelve." He points a commanding finger at the boy and crooks it. Cas heaves a sigh and trots around the pool.

O'Neill steps up onto the low dais. "How about this. We'll walk through it one more time, start to finish. No stops. If someone messes up, we'll just press on. Pretend it didn't happen. We aren't a precision drill team. As long as no one falls over the cliff, we'll be fine."

"Even if they do, you'll be fine." Cas veers away from Leo and sprints toward the edge. He uses the dais like a springboard, pushing off with his left foot. His right foot arcs up, then stops when it lands on the low, invisible wall. He pushes off again and flips forward, feet swinging up over his head.

Someone screams. People surge forward.

Cas's feet thud into the invisible barrier, landing in a crouch. He leaps up and thrusts his hands over his head, spinning to face us. "Tah da!"

While Vanti and O'Neill calm the crowd, I stalk forward. "Don't ever do that again! Don't you know these things can fail? What would I tell your father if you fell off my cliff? Not to mention, you could have scared someone to death. Angie's not young."

Cas flushes. "I told her it was safe. Plus, I'm wearing this." He pulls back his jacket to reveal a grav belt.

Loki, Cas's bodyguard, thunders up to us. "Master Caspian! What—"

Cas cuts him off. "Just trying to get everyone to relax."

"That was incredible!" Yuri pushes past the giant Loki. "How'd you do it?"

I grimace at Loki. "Keep these two out of trouble, will you?"

He points at Yuri. "This one is not my responsibility."

"He appears to be bent on corrupting a minor, so you might as well—" I wave my arms vaguely in their direction.

"I can take Master Caspian home." Loki reaches over Yuri's shoulder and grabs Cas's collar. "He should have stayed there with Master Tarkhan."

Cas shakes to dislodge Loki's hand but has no effect. "Tark's a baby! I'm an adult!"

"Then behave like one." I pry Loki's fingers off Cas's jacket. "I promised he could hang out here. Just stay with them and make sure they don't plot any more pranks."

Loki heaves a heavy sigh and pushes the two young men away from the cliff edge.

O'Neill steps onto the low stage again and raises his voice. "One more time. From the top. No stopping. If you mess up, acknowledge it and move on. Go!"

I climb back up the steep, grass-covered hill to the deck. The end of the pool is a transparent aluminum wall, between the two hillsides, which allows swimmers to see and be seen. In preparation for the wedding, Hy-Mi had steps installed in each hill, allowing guests to move easily between the different levels. We gather on the pool deck, ready to file down the steps and to the dais in front of the cliff.

Music plays over the speakers and through our audio implants. Hy-Mi walks down the steps and along the runner, with one of the temporary staff playing the role of the Ice Dame. She tips her head back so her nose is as high as it can go and waves languidly to the non-existent crowd as they walk. Someone snickers.

When they reach the front row, Hy-Mi seats the girl and says something. Her face goes red, then pale. She bites her lip. Clearly, she's been reprimanded for her portrayal. Even if it was spot-on.

Hy-Mi moves to the middle of the dais and waves the next pair forward. "Ser O'Neill, senior, Sera O'Neill, your turn."

Brad and Aretha march up the aisle. Halfway there, Brad pushes Aretha back and launches himself into a cartwheel. He knocks over two chairs and lands on his backside. Aretha helps her father up.

"Brad!" Serena, standing beside Ty on the pool deck, covers her face. "The boys have been a bad influence."

Brad turns slowly, holding his lower back. "I'm fine. But I won't do that tomorrow."

Ro and Vanti go next. I hold my breath, but nothing happens. Maybe dating Vanti has helped Ro mature?

Kara, with the baby in one arm, steps to the end of the aisle. "Where's Yuri?"

"Here!" Yuri vaults over a folding chair and lands beside Kara. He pokes a gentle finger into the swaddled folds of blanket. "Is she coming with us?"

"Not tomorrow." She shifts the baby to the other side and takes Yuri's arm. "I have a baby minder lined up for the whole evening." They walk to the end and take their places across the aisle from Vanti and Ro.

"Now Ser O'Neill," Hy-Mi calls.

Serena and Ty walk down the left side of the pool and through the sea of chairs, stopping at the low stage. He kisses his mother on the cheek and hands her off to his father in the front row. Then he turns to watch me. The music changes.

"Go time." I grip R'ger's arm. It isn't the real R'ger, of course. He's still on SK2 with Mother.

"Your fingers are cold." Leo pats my hand as we start down the right side of the pool. "Are you nervous?"

"No." The word comes out higher than I expected. I try again. "Don't be silly."

Leo chuckles and nods. "You don't sound nervous at all."

"Shut up." I take a deep breath and let Leo steer me behind the chairs to the white runner. The late sun sparkles on the wall of water to our left.

When we reach the end, we stop.

"Kiss, kiss," Leo says, making smoochy faces at me. Then he takes my hand and pulls me toward O'Neill. "Here ya go."

"What am I, a football?" O'Neill and I say together, quoting an *Ancient TeVe* vid. We chuckle while everyone else looks bemused.

"Then the minister will begin the ceremony," Hy-Mi says. "Just repeat what he tells you to say, and it's done."

"Where is the minister?" Serena looks around, as if he's hiding somewhere.

"He was unable to attend tonight." Hy-Mi offers this as if it's perfectly normal. In the world of the Ice Dame, it is.

"I've never been to a wedding rehearsal where the minister was a no-show." Angie has moved to a chair at the end of the second row, with a bev-bot beside her. Cas perches nearby, a glass in his hand. Loki stands behind the bev-bot, glowering.

"He had other duties." Hy-Mi's voice is even, but the words almost feel like a reprimand. "He knows what he's doing. If Sera Annabelle and Ser O'Neill simply follow his instructions, all will be well."

O'Neill points at me. "I can follow directions, but I'm not sure about this one."

I know he's teasing me, but the words hurt. "I can follow directions. When I want to." I lift my chin and take his arm.

"I know. I love that about you." He leans in to kiss my cheek.

I think about pulling away, but I don't. "Good thing. It's not going to change any time soon."

"Then we'll go back, opposite the way we came in. The new couple first." Hy-Mi makes shooing motions, so Ty and I turn and wade through the sea of empty chairs. Angie and Cas applaud, so I wave. We turn past the swimming pool and climb the steps to the deck.

"This might be more difficult in a wedding dress." I mime lifting my skirts in front.

"Maybe I should carry you up." He grabs my waist and flings me over his shoulder.

I shriek, but he doesn't put me down. He runs up the steps and takes me into the house for dinner.

CHAPTER FORTY-ONE

THE NEXT MORNING, I wake to darkness again, but the clock says five-fifteen. After grabbing a cup of hot chocolate from the AutoKich'n, I sit on the balcony outside my room to watch the color wash across the sky.

I haven't slept much, but all the ancient vids assure me this is normal for a bride. Kara's magic will erase any ill effect from my face, so I just have to drink enough caffeine to power through.

Brilliant reds streak the sky, followed by pink and purple, yellow, and a hint of green. Birds start chirping. A platoon of frogs discuss plans to take over the universe. The faint waft of *terkfiske* dissipates almost before I register it, replaced by an almost overwhelming wave of sweet and spicy as the florists arrive.

As the last of the pink turns to gold, a soft knock echoes out of my room. I check the holo—it's O'Neill. I pad across the room and let him in.

"You aren't supposed to be here. It's our wedding day."

"I know." He kisses me, and I forget what I was saying.

Cocoa sloshes in the cup, splashing on the leg of my *Sachmos* pajamas. "Yikes!" I jump back, spilling more cocoa.

"Let's put that away." Ty takes the cup and sets it on a side table, then pulls me toward him.

After a few more delirious minutes, I step back to look at him. "Did you sleep well?"

"Like a baby. Although I'm not sure why they say that—Kara and Erco are next door to me, and Freya woke me at least twice."

"I know that kid has a loud voice, but the sound-proofing in Sierra Hotel is the best known to mankind." I yawn and rub my eyes.

"We both had windows open, I think. You should go back to sleep."

"I need to change these pants first." I hurry into the huge bathroom and pull on a new pair. "What are you doing today?"

As I return to the bedroom, he takes my hand and pulls me to the couch by the windows. He wraps an afghan around me and settles me against his chest. "I'm going to sit here with you until you go to sleep. Then my dad said he has something lined up."

I lean against him, his warm body relaxing mine. My eyes grow heavy as he murmurs a long story about an O'Neill family pre-wedding tradition called "golf."

THE NEXT TIME I WAKE, it's mid-morning, and I'm alone in my big bed. Ty must have moved me after I fell asleep. Either that, or I dreamed the whole thing.

I sit up. The cocoa mug is gone, but that doesn't mean anything—the cleaning bots are quiet, and I'm used to them. With a shrug, I get out of bed and take a long shower.

When I emerge, Kara and Vanti are waiting for me. The three of us spend the morning drinking weak mimosas and fussing with hair and makeup.

Serena and Angie join us after a late lunch. They're accompanied by a tall woman who bears a striking resemblance to Serena, despite the startling difference in height.

Angie pulls the woman forward. "Triana, this is my daughter Evaline. Serena's mother. I don't think you got a chance to meet her on Grissom."

Evaline holds out a fist. "My flight from the Academy was delayed that day, so I barely made the wedding. Then there was that whole evacuation and cake explosion."

I bump fists with her and try not to feel guilty. "It got pretty crazy. How long are you on Kaku?"

"Dad and I are here for the wedding, then we have to return to the Academy."

"Dad?" I glance at Angie. "Didn't you tell me he died in a freak rainstorm?" She also told me he was alive and well.

"Mother," Evaline says mildly. "Again?"

Angie grins, unrepentant. "When you're a hundred and two, you gotta take your joy where you can get it."

"You're only ninety-three." Evaline turns to me. "Dad does some consulting work at the Academy. We are investigating a previously undiscovered senidium deposit on Sarvo Six. The mineral doesn't usually present—"

"Blah, blah, blah," Angie breaks in. "Triana doesn't care about minerals. Although that one *is* a pretty color. Do you have a piece she could carry as her 'something blue'?"

"It's worth more credits per gram than platinum, so no, I don't happen to have any on me." Evaline's lips turn down.

How is this serious woman Angie's daughter?

I bring the conversation back around to Angie's mysterious husband. "I'll get to meet Safwan today?"

"Of course, dear. He's right upstairs. Shall I bring him down?" Angie jumps out of her chair.

Kara glances at her chrono. "We have a pretty tight schedule."

I grimace. If it were up to me, I'd just throw on a sundress, and O'Neill and I would sign the papers. But the wedding is important to his family, and now that I've wrested control of the ceremony from my mother, I want to do it properly. "I'll meet him at the reception."

Evaline ushers her mother and daughter out of the room, somehow cowing both of them without a word. Angie gives us a wink over her shoulder as the door slides shut. "See you in a few!"

"I guess humor skips a generation." Kara pulls a white slip dress out of a closet and hands it to me. "This goes under the gown."

I shudder. "I hope that doesn't mean O'Neill will be like her when he gets older."

"Don't be ridiculous. He has an excellent sense of humor. Your children may be a problem. Or maybe she got scared by a clown as a child. Let's get you dressed."

I SQUISH the sides of my massive, white wedding gown and cram myself through the door into the bedroom room.

"Don't squash the lace!" Kara calls.

"I can't believe the designer sent this monstrosity. It's not what I picked." I thought I'd escaped my mother's influence, but this dress was waiting in the closet with a note from her.

"The latest in wedding fashion?" Vanti suggests.

The bell-shaped skirt swings around me as I move, creating its own gravity well. A small side table gets sucked into the vortex as I sail across the room.

"It *is* traditional!" Kara sits on the couch, baby snuggled to her chest. She covers Freya with kisses, then hands her off to the babysitter who's still gaping at me as she leaves.

Vanti smooths down her slinky green dress with a grin. "Plus, it provides cover for an entire army of security personnel in case of emergency."

"You are not hiding under my skirt."

"Hopefully, there won't be an emergency." She pins a glare on me. "There won't be, will there?"

"How would I know? I don't go looking for emergencies. They come to me." I turn and stare at the mirror. "Nope. Not gonna work." I sail back to the bathroom.

"What's the Ice Dame going to say?" Kara calls.

"Don't care! Besides, she'll probably make me wear it for the corporate reception tomorrow. Vanti, will you help me out of this monstrosity?"

Snickering, Vanti follows me. "Do you have another option?"

"Of course. I'm going to wear the dress *I* picked out." I wait impatiently while she unfastens the nine million buttons, then I slide my arms out of the sleeves and drop down inside the enormous, hooped skirt.

Vanti lifts the dress so I can escape. She examines the nano-tube structure, flexing the lightweight hoops. "Add a little titanium plating, and this could be a portable shield."

"If I need a portable shield in my own back yard on my wedding day, I should fire my security detail." I pull a pink bag with a designer logo from the closet.

"I've already put in my resignation, so don't sweep me up in your purge." She pushes the dome of lace and satin into a corner and takes the new dress from me to hang it on a hook. With a flourish, she unzips the bag. "Is this a Garabana?"

I laugh. "No. Gary did not come anywhere near my wedding gown." I pull out the silky, white fabric.

"Do you need help?"

"Nope, that's the best part about this one." I drop the dress into a puddle at my feet and pull it up over my hips. "One fastener at the neck, and one at the waist." The fitted top has a slightly scooped neck in front and an open back. The full skirt swishes around my calves, light and comfortable.

"What do you think?" I twirl in front of the mirror, and the skirt flares around me, showing off layers of petticoats in a pale rainbow of colors.

Vanti doesn't say anything.

"You don't like it?" I don't know why I care what Vanti thinks, but I do. I guess we've become friends over the years.

"No, it's perfect." She grins. "Excellent for running in, poufy enough to hide a weapon. This is what I'll get if I ever..."

I break in. "Are you and Ro talking about getting married?"

"Don't be ridiculous," she snaps. "There's nothing between us. We just hang out together on the rare occasions when we're on the same planet."

"Nothing? Does he know that? He hasn't spent any time with Yuri since he arrived, and you know how close they are."

"They spend their entire lives together." She waves this off. "Besides, where do you think they are now? Together."

She stalks out of the room.

"I wanna see!" Kara calls.

I slide on my strappy sandals—flats that are excellent for running in, as Vanti would say—and follow her out of the room.

CHAPTER FORTY-TWO

THE MUSIC INTENSIFIES, and the chatter dies. R'ger and I stand in the family room, staring down at the yard. People mill around, filing into the rows of chairs lined up in front of the dais.

R'ger squeezes my hand. "This is exciting!"

"Have you been to one of these before?" My heart is beating fast and light, as if it wants to fly out of my chest. I suck in a deep breath, trying to settle my nerves.

"Back in the day. They aren't as common on Armstrong as on Grissom, but I had a few friends get married. And my sister, of course. She's here, you know." He swipes from his holo-ring, and the scene before us magnifies on the floor-to-ceiling windows.

The view zooms in on a beautiful redhead in the third row. She's not young—if she's had rejuv, it's minimal. Her wavy hair swirls around her head in a gravity-defying updo. She turns to look back at the house, and I can see her bright green eyes and pert nose. Her lips curve into R'ger's smile as she speaks to a neighbor, and the dark man next to her smiles back.

"She looked just like you that day." He flicks his ring, and a picture of a woman in a monstrous white dress appears.

"I looked like that a couple of hours ago. In fact, I think it was that exact dress." I flick an image onto the window.

He chuckles as he compares the two pictures. "Probably not the same dress, but close."

Is that why Mother sent me the dress? Because she knew R'ger would recognize it? Is she trying to tell him something?

The music changes again and fades as Hy-Mi's soft voice issues through our audio implants. "Time to come down, Sera Annabelle."

R'ger takes my cold fingers and places them on his arm. "Ready?"

I nod shakily. "As I'll ever be."

At the door to the pool deck, R'ger hands me something. It fits easily in my palm, smooth and cool. In the dim light, I can't see it, but I recognize it by touch. "Is this one of your Vistula River rocks?"

I can hear the smile in his voice. "Of course."

R'ger gave me one of these the first week we met—before I knew he was my father. The thin rock had been carved and painted with a pastoral scene, including cows in a meadow and a castle on the hill. It was intended to be a bribe to the *Księżna*, but I didn't need it. I still have it in my compartment on SK2.

"What's on this one?" I ask.

"You'll have to wait and see. Do you want me to hold it during the ceremony?"

"No, I have pockets." I slide the stone into the pouch hidden in the skirt seam and seal it shut.

"Speaking of Vistula River rocks, I saw a woman today who looks like she might be the *Księżna*'s daughter."

I bite back a smirk. "That's Sonia. There might be some connection." The favor I'd promised Sonia in exchange for the PVD had been called in—she wanted an invite to the wedding. I'd suggested adding her to the corporate reception list, but she'd pointed out the favor was personal, not corporate. All that stress over the deal, and she just wanted to come to the party.

"Now," Hy-Mi says.

R'ger opens the door, and the music swells. We pace slowly down the teakalike deck. I focus on the floating candles encircled by flower wreaths in the pool, letting their flickering, drifting beauty soothe my nerves.

We pause at the top of the steps. My eyes fly to O'Neill, but the crowd stands, and I can't see him. My throat tightens.

R'ger squeezes my fingers, then leads me down the steps.

A cloud of colorful wings flutter into the sky, swirling around us as we pass the end of the swimming pool. The hologram is realistic and spectacular. Apawllo leaps out from under a table, lunging at the brilliant creatures. They flutter away, unharmed. Apawllo looks disgusted, then slinks into the woods.

We stop at the end of the long white carpet running toward the sea. Brilliant streaks of color spread across the sky as the sun sets beyond. A tall, muscular man, robed in red, steps in front of the spectacular display. His longish platinum hair flows back from his face in the slight breeze.

I do a double take. "Is that Scott Calvin? The minister is Scott Calvin?"

"Call him Ser Smith," Hy-Mi confirms through my audio-implant. We met Scott on SK2 last Christmas. Kara swears he's Santa Claus. I'm not sure, but there's definitely something magical about him.

The music changes one last time. We make our way down the aisle. Faces pop out of the crowd: Farq and Rash from the Ops Center on SK2. Joan Lesley and the crew from the *CSS Morningstar*—even the interns Ambar and TC. Ty's cousins, aunts, and uncles. My half-siblings. Angie waves and points to a distinguished old gentleman beside her—he must be her husband Safwan.

I invited all these people, of course, but the fact that they took the time to come to my wedding catches me off guard. Tears sting my eyes.

Then O'Neill takes his place next to Scott, and every other thought flies from my brain.

My heart thumps hard, once, then settles into a content, even pattern. My chest goes warm, and when he smiles, his face is all I can see. My nervous energy evaporates like the holographic flutterbies. I smile, and his love wraps around me like a warm hug.

The rest of the ceremony passes in a haze of contentment. Scott talks for a few minutes, but it washes over me like the warm sea splashing on the beach below us. Ty O'Neill consumes all my attention. His hand warm on my cold fingers. His smile answering mine. His deep voice ringing through my soul like a perfectly tuned bell.

I repeat words Scott tells me to repeat, and when I say, "Till death do us part," every cell in my body agrees.

"I now pronounce you husband and wife." Scott beams at us, and even in my bemused state, I can't ignore his magnetic twinkle. "Go ahead, Triana, kiss him."

Ty's lips meet mine, and an electric frisson courses down my spine. After a lifetime, we break apart to loud applause. Scott gives us a little push, and we turn to grin at our friends.

As we start down the aisle, I toss my bouquet into the air. The flowers land in Ro's hands. With a giggle, I wink at Vanti and leave the two of them staring at each other.

THE PARTY PASSES IN A BLUR. As the sun sets, torches are lit, and twinkling lights sparkle in the trees on either side of the huge lawn.

The temporary staff, dressed in elegant black and white, pass glasses and food, constantly rotating through the crowd. Toasts are made and people dance.

At one point, the Ice Dame approaches us, holding hands with R'ger. "I'm so happy for you, dear," she whispers as she gives me an air kiss.

Behind her, the invisible dance floor suddenly dissolves. Twenty guests scream and splash into the pool. A huge wave crashes over us, but miraculously, the four of us remain dry.

I squeeze O'Neill's arm. "How?"

The Ice Dame smiles smugly. "I'm always prepared." She turns and steers R'ger through the sopping guests. Her personal protective shield shimmers in the torch light.

Hy-Mi appears with towels and sends the wet guests to change into clothing provided by the estate.

I grab his arm. "Were you expecting this?"

Hy-Mi bows. "It is my job to expect the unexpected. With those trouble-makers in the house..." He gazes across the pool.

Cas and Yuri dart away into the tree line. Beside me, O'Neill tenses.

I squeeze his hand. "Don't bother. We know where to find them. And they know we know."

"I don't blame Cas—that stunt would be impossible for a twelve-year-old to resist. But you'd think my brother could act his age."

"Let's call it an opportunity for the guests to change costumes. I'm sure whatever Hy-Mi provided is at least as amazing as anything they wore here." Since none of Mother's top-lev contacts were dancing, this is undoubtedly true.

After a while, I sneak away from the crowd. Kara finds me near the door to the Starfire estate. "Where are you going?"

"I just need to—" I wave my hands.

She grins. "I get it." She reaches for the old-fashioned key, but the hook is empty.

"You looking for this?" Vanti steps out of the shadows, the key hanging from her index finger.

"How do you know me so well?" I ask.

"We've been through a lot together," O'Neill says from behind me.

I smile and take his hand.

Vanti opens the door, and the four of us slip out of the brilliant party and onto the moonlit strip of grass between the wall and the trees of the Starfire estate. We make our way to the top of the steps that lead to the beach. As we settle onto the carved stone steps that overlook the sea, I lean against O'Neill, his heat warding off the chill as night falls.

Something hard presses against my hip. "Oh, I almost forgot." I open my concealed pocket and pull out the rock. "R'ger gave this to me."

O'Neill flicks his holo-ring and shines the light on my palm. The rock is painted in exquisite detail: a replica of Sierra Hotel as it would appear if one hovered over the bay. The water below the cliff almost seems to splash against the beach. A tiny bride and groom stand at the edge of the cliff.

"It's perfect." I lean my head against Ty's shoulder. "Everything is perfect."

"Yes, it is."

ACKNOWLEDGMENTS

I wrote this book for my Gooey Galactic Center Kickstarter Backers. Here's a list of everyone who pledged to the campaign at Level 10 and above—thank you from the bottom of my heart!

Angelica Quiggle
AnnaMarie Enerson
Anne K.
Annie Jenkins
Anonymous Reader
Barb Collishaw
Brent Held
Bridget Horn
CAP
Charles Rich
Chris Patterson
Chrissy Chronert
Damian Mullins
Don Bartenstein
Donivan Patwell
Donna Meraz
Duane
Edward C Smith
Emma Allen-Goss
Eva Holmquist
F.A. Hakimian
Gary Olsen
Grace Ela Miah Jack Sarah
Ian Bannon
James Vink
Jane
Jane Bond

Jen L
Jennifer Vayhinger
Jim Gotaas
John Jutoy
John Lagerquist
John Prigent
Jon Buller
Just Jeff
Kari Kilgore
Kathy
Kelli King
Krystal Bohannan
Lawrence M. Schoen
Liliana Espinoza
Lucas D.
Lydia T.
Marc Sangalli
Meredith Selvoski
Mike Hall
Moe Naguib
None
Norm Coots
Paul Godtland
Paul Parker
Paul Winfield
Paul Wright
Regina D.
rlparker
Rob Crosby
Rosheen
Ross Bernheim
S Busby
Sam B.
Sandy Anderson
Sarah Heile
Sheryl Knowles
Stephen Ballentine
Steven Bolbot
Steven Whysong
Sue Laing

Ted Klosowski
Ted M. Young
Thomas Cook
Tim Greenshields
Your old pal, Marcus

Thanks to those who pledged at lower levels, too, but I don't have permission to share their names, so I won't. But your support was crucial to reaching our goal.

AUTHOR'S NOTE

January 2022

Hi Reader,

Thanks for reading! If you liked *Waxing the Moon of Lewei*—and if you're still reading, I'm guessing you did—please consider leaving a review on your retailer, Bookbub, or Goodreads. Reviews help other readers find stories they'll like. They also tell me what you like, so I can write more.

This story completes the first Tales of a *Former Space Janitor* trilogy, but I'm sure Triana and the gang will be back. If you sign up here, I'll let you know when I start working on the next one. You can also download free prequels and find out about sales. I promise not to SPAM you.

I'm currently working on a romantic comedy series that I will publish under a new pen name. The name won't be secret—it's mainly to keep my science fiction separate from the hearts and flowers. If you like romantic comedy, then you might enjoy these stories, too. I'll post the news in my newsletter, social media, and website when it's ready to publish.

After that, I'll be back to my *Colonial Explorer Corps* series to start a new trilogy about Siti, Joss, Peter, and the crew. Then, something new in the *Space Janitor* realm.

As always, I need to thank a few people. Thanks to my sprint team: A.M. Scott, Paula Lester, Kate Pickford, Hillary Avis, Tony James Slater, and *Your Old Pal, Marcus* Alexander Hart. They keep me working when I really don't want to.

Paula at Polaris Editing polished my manuscript to perfection, for which I thank her profusely. Any mistakes you find, I undoubtedly added after she was done! My deepest appreciation goes to my alpha reader and sister, Anne Marie, and my beta readers: Anne Kavcic, Barb Collishaw, and Jenny Avery.

My grateful thanks go to my faithful readers who keep asking for more Space Janitor.

Thanks to my husband, David, who manages my business, and to Les at GermanCreative for the beautiful cover.

And of course, thanks to the Big Guy for making all things possible.

FOR MORE INFORMATION

Use this QR code to stay up-to-date on all my publishing:

ALSO BY JULIA HUNI

Colonial Explorer Corps Series:
The Earth Concurrence
The Grissom Contention
The Saha Declination
Colonial Explorer Corps (books 1-3)

Recycled World Series:
Recycled World
Reduced World

Space Janitor Series:
The Vacuum of Space
The Dust of Kaku
The Trouble with Tinsel
Orbital Operations
Glitter in the Stars
Sweeping S'Ride
Triana Moore, Space Janitor (the complete series)

Tales of a Former Space Janitor
The Rings of Grissom
Planetary Spin Cycle
Waxing the Moon of Lewei

The Phoenix and Katie Li
Luna City Limited
Krimson Empire (with Craig Martelle):
Krimson Run
Krimson Spark
Krimson Surge
Krimson Flare

Krimson Empire (the complete series)

Milton Keynes UK
Ingram Content Group UK Ltd.
UKHW031307020924
1463UKWH00044B/701

9 798201 979652